I0565714

FEAR OF FEAR

FEAR OF FEAR

Florence Ryerson
and
Colin Clements

COACHWHIP PUBLICATIONS
Greenville, Ohio

FOR OUR FRIEND
WILLARD HUNTINGTON WRIGHT
AND
HIS FRIEND S. S. VAN DINE

Fear of Fear, by Florence Ryerson and Colin Clements
© 2023 Coachwhip Publications edition
Introduction © Curtis Evans
Cover: Vishnu, Los Angeles County Museum of Art

First published 1931
Florence Ryerson, 1892-1965
Colin Clements, 1894-1948
CoachwhipBooks.com

ISBN 1-61646-566-2
ISBN-13 978-1-61646-566-7

Ryerson and Clements Do Murder
Curtis Evans

As the decade of the Thirties dawned in the United States the author of the bestselling Philo Vance mysteries, S. S. Van Dine (pen name of critic and author Willard Huntington Wright), strode over the mystery fiction landscape like a monocled colossus, his five detective novels, the most recent of which was *The Scarab Murder Case* (1930), having sold over ten million copies and been translated into twenty-two languages. To be sure, the hard-boiled boys of American pulp fiction, such as Dashiell Hammett, who had recently hit it big with *The Maltese Falcon* (1930), had Philo and his creator in their pitiless gunsights and would soon enough shoot them down, so to speak. Yet for now that posh, g-dropping, cosmopolitan aesthete and gentleman amateur sleuth, Philo Vance, was still Big Man on the murder campus. When the cousins Frederic Dannay and Manfred Lee began successfully publishing mysteries as Ellery Queen in 1929, they used Van Dine's books as their model. There were other, lesser known Van Dine imitators as well who published their first detective novels in 1930, just a year behind Ellery Queen, including two collaborative teams: Roger Scarlett, pen name of partners Dorothy Blair and Evelyn Page, and Florence Marie Ryerson (1892-1965) and Colin Campbell Clements (1894-1948), a prolific spousal writing team who co-authored novels, plays and film scripts. Like Roger Scarlett, Clements and Ryerson only ever published five detective novels and their mysteries were soon mostly forgotten; yet their mysteries, like Scarlett's, are now being revived for modern-day readers charmed, like an earlier Depression-era generation, by the baroque splendors of the Van Dine school of Golden Age detective fiction.

As stated Florence Ryerson and Colin Clements published only five mystery novels, these being *Seven Suspects* (1930), *Fear of Fear* (1931), *Blind Man's Buff* (1933), *Shadows* (1934) and *The Borgia Blade* (1937), the first four of which, the Jimmy Lane series, bear the greatest impress of Van Dine. (*The Borgia Blade* is a standalone.) For Ryerson and Clements, mysteries were just the proverbial drop in the writers bucket. The couple wed in 1927, not long after Clements, Director of the Little Theater in Memphis, Tennessee, met Ryerson, a scenario writer for MGM Studios, while out in California. After their marriage Clements settled with Ryerson in Hollywood, where he also wrote for the film business, though playwriting remained his first (and most lucrative) love. Ryerson had the more notable screenwriting career, working on scripts for the mystery thriller films *The Canary Murder Case* (1928) (based on the Van Dine bestseller), *The Mysterious Dr. Fu Manchu* (1929) and *The Return of Dr. Fu Manchu* (1930), (with Charlie Chan portrayer Warner Oland as the nefarious Asian mastermind), *The Crime of the Century* (1933), *The Casino Murder Case* (1935) (Van Dine again, albeit adulterated) and the operatic mystery *Moonlight Murder* (1936). She is best known, however, for being one of the credited scriptwriters (there were many who stuck a finger in the pie) of *The Wizard of Oz* (1939).

Working on *The Canary Murder Case* led to Ryerson meeting S. S. Van Dine himself, and the two became friends after Ryerson, in Van Dine's eyes, rescued his book from the clumsy handling of what he bluntly termed "Hollywood morons." Observes Van Dine's biographer John Loughery of Ryerson: "She wasn't the usual studio hack," even having actually read the book on which the film was based. Ryerson worked with Van Dine to iron out the unsightly wrinkles in the script, deleting "sentimental love scenes," a "gratuitous car chase" and a "stock villain." She "was happy to do battle with the studio bosses for her new friend and saw to it that a workable script was ready by the summer [of 1928]. In September the movie went into production with a screenplay more appealing to everyone."

A few years later in 1931, Van Dine, accompanied by his second wife, came out to California to work with Ryerson on the script of the mystery film *The Blue Moon Murder Case*, which, unfortunately, was scrapped, later emerging in 1933 as the much altered film *Girl Missing*. "Ryerson gave a dinner in honor of the Van Dines and treated them to a lavish weekend at Palm Springs," notes Loughery. Sadly Ryerson and Van Dine later had a falling out over the script of *The Casino Murder Case*, filmed at a time in the mid-thirties when Van Dine's stock as a film property was falling, the hottest thing in mystery films now being not celibate gentleman sleuths like Philo Vance but rather wisecracking couples like Nick and Nora Charles, introduced by Dashiell Hammett in his popular detective novel *The Thin Man* (1934).

Both Philo Vance and Nick Charles in fact were played by William Powell, symbolizing Van Dine's diminution of status relative to Hammett. Ryerson and her scripting partner Edgar Allan Woolf first hit upon the idea of "Hammettizing" Van Dine by introducing Myrna Loy, who played Nick's wife Nora, into the Philo Vance series as the love interest of Vance, who would still be played by William Powell. Thus the pair managed to outrage Van Dine, who loathed the character Nick Charles, deeming him plebeian and vulgar. In any event Powell opted out of the project, letting it be known he had tired of playing Vance. "I know Bill is glad the [S. S. Van Dine murder mysteries are out of his life]," Hollywood gossip columnist Louella Parsons confided to her readers. Ultimately Hungarian-born Paul Lukas was cast as Vance (a rather bizarre choice as Vance is decidedly an Anglo-American type), with a young Rosalind Russell playing his wisecracking love interest. Van Dine washed his hands of the whole affair, just making sure he collected his check.

While Ryerson ultimately may have bastardized Van Dine's work, the Jimmy Lane mysteries that she wrote with Colin Clements were very much modeled after the Philo Vance tales. The four books are narrated by Jimmy Lane's self-effacing attorney and old college chum Philip Carter, recalling the narration of the Philo Vance mysteries by Philo's self-effacing attorney and old college chum Van Dine. All four books, like many of the Van Dine mysteries, are infused with outré atmospheric elements, particularly *Fear of Fear* and *Blind Man's Buff*, the two novels in the series reprinted by Coachwhip. *Fear of Fear* involves spiritualism and eastern mysticism, while *Blind Man's Buff* takes place at a mansion on a storm-isolated island, complete with a creepy family tomb, wherein lies interred (or so they say) the family's deceased eccentric patriarch. Both have involved plots, including house plans, artist illustrations, family trees and tabulations. Assuming Van Dine ever read either book, he should have been pleased to see his own influences in them.

* * * * *

Fear of Fear, which carries a dedication *"For our friend WILLARD HUNTINGTON WRIGHT and his friend S. S. VAN DINE,"* might well have been titled, had Van Dine written it, *The Spirit Murder Case*, or perhaps *The Jasmine Murder Case*. It opens with Jimmy Lane's literary chronicler Philip Carter explaining why now "the time has come to tell the truth about the murders on Russian Hill." The events in the tale take place primarily at three adjacent Victorian row houses in the San Francisco neighborhood of Russian Hill, wherein reside an interconnected group of people: Harlan Grant, a famed spiritualistic medium; his brother Colonel Grant, late of India; Chanda Steeb, the colonel's beautiful daughter; Otto Steeb, her scientist husband; Singh and Lalah, Indian servants to Harlan Grant; and Dr. Waverly, a physician friend of the Grants.

Somewhat reminiscent of Earl Derr Biggers' Charlie Chan novel *The Black Camel* (1929), an actress, Norah Fallon, comes to Jimmy Lane, Hollywood scenarist, playwright, ex-journalist and recent solver of a Hollywood murder mystery (see *Seven Suspects*), complaining that she is being blackmailed by Harland Grant. Soon she and her boyfriend, scientist Richard Stoddard, are implicated in Grant's locked room murder at his home on Russian Hill and Jimmy is called upon to get the couple off the hook. That he does, though not until he has confronted more murders and considerable bamboozlement and hoodoo. (Speaking of the latter, readers are reminded that Ryerson and Clements' portrayal of Jimmy Lane's unsubtly nicknamed man, Friday, while regrettable, is of its time.) The *Sacramento Bee* was impressed, declaring "it will be a wise solver of mystery detective puzzles who will guess the right answer."

Blind Man's Buff takes Jimmy and Philip to New York, where they receive a telegram from novelist Lucia Conroy, with whom Jimmy is collaborating on a play, imploring them to come to her ancestral mansion (complete with mausoleum) on Sycamore Island, where the Conroy clan has made its annual gathering. Upon their arrival at

Sycamore Island the pair is plunged, along with the Conroy clan, into a nightmarish series of slaughters reminiscent of S. S. Van Dine's *The Greene Murder Case* (1928), as a storm cuts them off from outside aid. The cast of characters is a large one indeed, with no fewer than nine Conroy connections, a housekeeper and a caretaker, giving ample scope for both a ruthless murderer and puzzle-solving readers.

Buff is an atmospheric and creepy tale indeed, owing a not insignificant debt to another "Edgar Allan" besides Ryerson's screenwriting partner Edgar Allan Woolf, a man by the name of Poe. "This is one great yarn," proclaimed the Camden, New Jersey *Morning Post*. Reflecting on the escalating body count in their detective novels, Florence Ryerson recalled humorously: "[W]e had to top ourselves each time in gore. The first story only killed one person. The second killed three. And then it got to be a kind of slaughter house."

Ryerson composed the first drafts of all the mystery novels, dictating them into a Dictaphone, from which written transcriptions were made. Colin Clements then would read them, making revisions. "We have found that it to pays to dictate," observed Clements, his eye as ever on the saleable market. "It somehow seems to move faster—and if there's anything a modern-day detective story has to have, it's speed."

* * * * *

Speed of production characterized the career of the two authors. Among other thing the couple wrote over one hundred one-act plays, which, although not staged on Broadway, proved quite lucrative during the Depressions years. "Fact is," boasted Clements, "I understand that 365 nights a year somewhere in the world, at least one of our plays is being produced." One of their many plays, *Through the Night*, was a three-act inverted mystery dramady that was tried out in Hollywood in 1939 and produced in both London and Glasgow to great success, with debonair English actor Esmond Knight taking a well-praised sinister turn as the play's treacherous killer. (Nearly a half-century later he would appear in British television's 1987 adaptation of Agatha Christie's final published Miss Marple mystery, *Sleeping Murder*, starring Joan Hickson.) "The appeal of the piece lies in the unravelling of the crime by the characters," pronounced a delighted Scottish reviewer. "There is bright and sparkling dialogue filled with true American wisecracks." Declared a similarly impressed American reviewer: "Chuckles, chills, and a whirlwind finish. When the Ryerson-Clements team twists a plot it stays twisted up until 10:29 P.M., and then unravels so fast you are amazed to find not a single loose end."

The husband and wife also enjoyed a pair of non-criminous successes on Broadway. *Harriet*, a drama about *Uncle Tom's Cabin* author and abolitionist Harriet Beecher Stowe starring Helen Hayes in the title role and staged by future famed film director Elia Kazan, ran for over a year and 377 performances at Henry Miller's Theater in 1943-44. Catching a wave of patriotic fervor, *Harriet* became the authors' biggest hit and was even praised by First Lady Eleanor Roosevelt. Another play, the romantic comedy *Strange Bedfellows*, ran for six months and 229 performances in 1948, surviving Clements, who was stricken with a heart attack during an out-of-town tryout in Philadelphia and never lived to see the play make it to Broadway.

Florence Ryerson survived her partner of over two decades by seventeen years, passing in 1965 at the age of seventy-two. During their heyday as a power writing couple in the late Thirties and Forties, the spouses resided and wrote in the San Fernando Valley at their domicile

Florence Ryerson

the Shadow Ranch, a historic structure still standing today. Petite, sloe-eyed and crowned between the wars with a bob of black hair, Ryerson certainly had not needed a man to achieve success, though Campbell clearly made a congenial writing partner for her. The daughter of Charles Dwight Willard, a progressive Los Angeles journalist and booster and secretary of the Municipal League, and Mary MacGregor, she graduated from Pasadena High School and for three years attended Radcliffe College, where she was deemed a "brilliant young writer." However, in 1914 she unexpectedly married Harold Ryerson, youthful president of Ryerson Manufacturing Company and her late father's assistant in the Municipal League, immediately after the wedding sailing away with him for a honeymoon on his recently purchased yacht. The yacht notwithstanding, however, love turned. The couple had one son, Hal, in 1915 before Harold left Florence for another woman in the early 1920s. Florence began publishing short stories the year of her son's birth and in 1926, a year before she wed Colin Clements, she was hired by MGM as a script-writer, where she quickly made the grade.

Tall, fair and handsome, Colin Clements was born in Omaha, Nebraska, the son of William Clements, a native Cornish cattle driver, and Ada Swanback, an adventurous nurse of German and Dutch derivation. (After she and William divorced, Ada later practiced her profession in the frozen wilds of Alaska.) A 1917 graduate of the University of Washington, Clements, or "Clemmy" as he was nick-named, also attended the Carnegie Institute for Technology and George Pierce Baker's playwriting class at Harvard and worked as a play-reader, actor and stage manager for Stuart Walker's Portmanteau Theater, a traveling repertory company which performed plays in the homes of patrons using an ingeniously designed portable stage. ("The Theater That Comes to You" was its motto.) Described as

Colin Clements

a "he-man" in spite of his artistic temperament, Clements soon proved a restless globetrotter, serving as a lieutenant in the U. S. Army after American entry into World War One in 1918, plunging into humanitarian relief efforts in Armenia upon the conflict's cessation, and even, before his eventual return to the States in 1922, spending a stint with the Rumanian National Theater in Rumania, where he staged plays for Queen Marie. Between 1922 and his marriage to Florence Ryerson five years later, he directed little theater companies in Gloucester, Massachusetts, Santa Barbara, California and Memphis, Tennessee.

A frequent collaborative writing team of varied and prodigious talent, Florence Ryerson and Colin Clements affably proclaimed to the English press, at the time of the debut of their play *Through the Night* in 1940, that they "have had no professional jealousies in twelve years of happily married life." This equable and able entertaining couple deserves to be better remembered than they are today. Perhaps the reprinting of a pair of their Thirties Van Dinean detective novels by Coachwhip will help accomplish this.

Those Concerned in the Murders

Philip Carter, *who tells the story*

Jimmy Lane, *a writer*

Norah Fallon, *an actress*

Richard Stoddard, *a scientist*

Harlan Grant, *a medium*

Colonel Grant, *his brother*

Chanda Steeb, *Colonel Grant's daughter*

Otto Steeb, *her husband*

Singh, *Harlan Grant's servant*

Lalah, *his wife*

Dr. Waverly, *a physician*

Mrs. Elfrieda Jane Chapman, *a Spiritualist*

Captain Hemming, *Chief of the Detective Bureau*

Sergeant McCarthy, *his assistant*

Corrigan, *a reporter*

Wilson, *a detective*

Kellogg, *a detective*

Friday, *Lane's man*

Ruggles, *a wire-haired terrier*

Mowgli, *a pet monkey*

CHAPTER 1
"STARS AND SPIRITS"

I believe that the time has come to tell the truth about the murders on Russian Hill. Although the last of them occurred almost two years ago, the recent heroic death of Chanda Steeb in that mission-school fire in India has roused the San Francisco newspapers to a new frenzy of interest, and reporters are once more on my trail. They can scarcely be blamed. The Press is, after all, but a projection of the public mind, and the shadow of the supernatural which hung over the Grant murders, combined with the fact that the affair spread out over a space of time and lent itself, like a well-planned serial, to recapitulation in the dailies, gave it a strong grip on the popular imagination.

Now that Chanda Steeb is dead, Captain Hemming retired, and the Singhs have disappeared into the vastness of India, there is no one who can be harmed by the truth. Therefore, with no expectation of producing a piece of literature, but with a faint hope of saving myself endless verbal repetition, I give the facts here.

This writing should really be done by Jimmy Lane, whose business it is to put words on paper. But Jimmy has betaken himself to the Caribbean Islands where he is poking around among voodoos and taboos, leaving me to face the predaceous reporters unaided.

Failing Jimmy Lane, Corrigan should be the *raconteur*. He is what is known as a journalistic "ace", and much better equipped for writing than a dry-as-dust lawyer such as I. But Corrigan is sulking. Although he went through the Grant affair from beginning to end, the fact that the murders occurred at night put him at a distinct disadvantage. Corrigan is the bright and shining light of a morning paper and all the deaths were discovered, or at least the news was given out, just in time for the evening journals to skim the cream. I believe his City Editor indicated that Corrigan might have managed things better if he had set his mind to it, and the wigging hurt his professional pride to such an extent that he threatened me with an ink-well when I suggested his chronicling the case. Mrs. Elfrieda Jane Chapman is, unfortunately, confined in an institution upstate. She is very sweet and happy, I understand, and quite rational on her good days, but scarcely in a condition for writing; while Wilson and McCarthy are also out of the question. Wilson left the service immediately after the case was closed, and McCarthy can't even talk about it without swearing; but once, when he thought I was looking the other way, I distinctly saw him cross himself.

It began, so far as I am concerned, when Jimmy Lane ordered me up to dinner one November evening. I stand *in loco parentis* to Jimmy; also in the position of banker, creditor and, occasionally, jailer. Since there is a difference of just two years between us, that needs explanation. Jimmy and I were in the same college and the same fraternity house for four tempestuous years. That is, during the four years I was there Jimmy checked in and out more or less intermittently, his presence or absence depending upon whether the incumbent governing board did or did not happen to have a sense of humor.

We roomed together as freshmen, and since then there has always been between us what might be termed an exasperated friendship. During college my chief value to Jimmy lay in my ability to deliver alibis for him when he'd done something particularly brilliant and outrageous. Jimmy was perfectly capable of thinking up his own alibis but his delivery lacked the sober conviction of mine.

During the years that followed college, when he was struggling with journalism and I was starving my way into the law, the same relationship continued. When I wasn't explaining to enraged editors that Jimmy didn't know the story could be considered libelous, I was bailing or bribing him out of places where he had no good reason for being.

Now Jimmy Lane is, of course, James Lane: author of *The Priceless Girl, Naughty Nan* . . . and others. If you're not fond of that kind of play you may not have seen them but there's no use pretending you haven't heard them talked about, and the same goes for his novels and pictures—which are equally low-brow and profitable.

Someone once said that if all his readers were placed end to end with all the people who saw his plays they would reach the moon, and Jimmy himself remarked it would be a perfect place for them. That shows you what he thinks of his own stuff.

All of which will explain why Jimmy's affairs have gradually assumed a proportion which overbalances the rest of my legal business and why, when I returned from court and found a note on the desk from my secretary (*"Mr. Lane called up and said he needed you to-night, for dinner at seven. He says you are to bring pistols for two"*), I hurried out to his house at once.

Of course I knew that "pistols for two" was Jimmy's literary license, but it was a relief to find him stretched out quite calmly in front of the fire in his study. Jimmy never stands up when he can sit down, nor sits down when there is six feet of floor space vacant. He's not exactly fat, but his outlines have noticeably blurred and softened since we left college which, combined with his pink cheeks and round blue eyes, gives him something the look of a plump and rosy cherub.

He waited until I had settled into a chair by the fire before he offered any explanation of his summons, then:

"Hope I haven't upset any dinner plans of Diana's," he said. Diana is my wife, and Jimmy, having been more or less responsible for our meeting at his Lodge during the ghastly week of the Lopez murders, has always retained a fatherly interest in our affairs.

"Diana's away," I told him. "She had a touch of bronchitis, and I've sent her to the hot springs."

"All the better. You can move over here and dig in with me for a while."

I sighed. "That means you've got yourself into some sort of a mess, and you want me to pull you out."

"It's not me this time. I want you to help Norah Fallon."

"You *don't* mean the musical comedy star?"

"The same. Take your time—you'll get used to the idea."

There was nothing unusual about the situation in itself. Jimmy was always knight-erranting and I'd been called in before to assist damsels in distress, but never anyone like Norah Fallon. In the first place, I knew of no one who seemed less likely to need assistance. For coolness and cleverness, if rumor was correct, she hadn't her equal. Financially she must be far beyond worry; no one can play musical comedy leads in New York for six seasons without accumulating a small fortune, especially if one is as shrewd and thrifty as Norah was reputed to be. Then, too, there was her motion-picture contract; ten (or was it twelve?) thousand a week for lisping her famous baby talk and displaying her equally famous curves on the visible-audible screen. The thought gave me pause.

"So that's where you met her . . . in Hollywood?"

"No." Jimmy shook his head. "After six months in Hollywood I had to wait until I got up here. It was Ruggles introduced us."

"Ruggles?"

"Yes. You know that handkerchief trick of his?"

Of course I knew it. Ruggles of Red Gap is Jimmy's wire-haired terrier, so named because his mouth is generally open in a cheerful grin. Jimmy is nauseatingly proud of Ruggles's four tricks. They are, in reverse order of their importance: 1. Sitting up. 2. Playing dead. 3. Playing hide and seek. 4. The handkerchief trick.

In the last, which Jimmy considers his masterpiece, some woman in the room is ordered to break down and sob, the more convulsively the better. At the first breath, Ruggles pricks up his ears; at the second, he bounds to the woman and noses her eagerly; at the third, he is back at Jimmy's side, jumping and barking. This racket he keeps up until Jimmy bends over and permits him to snatch the folded handkerchief out of his breast pocket. A moment later Ruggles is back to the sobbing woman, pawing her, and offering her the handkerchief. I admit that he looks very bright and attractive when he does this, but not that it shows the amount of intellect which I Jimmy attributes to him.

"Yes," Jimmy repeated, "the handkerchief trick did it. The pup and I were walking in the park this morning. We were passing some shrubbery and all of a sudden he was off like a shot. A moment later he came dashing back, jumped up, nipped my 'kerchief and was off again. Of course I followed. On the other side of the bushes I found a girl crying her head off, and, at the same time, trying to get away from the pup."

"You could hardly expect her to know it was a trick."

"Well, I explained, and she thought it was great. Made him do it three times. After that she sort of cheered up. We got to talking, and you know how I am . . ."

"To my sorrow I do." When Jimmy meets a woman they invariably get to talking. At least, *she* gets to talking and he to listening and making little clucking noises in his throat indicative of interest and sympathy. And he is interested, hang him. To Jimmy the whole world is a gorgeous story-book and everyone he meets is another page. That's why I'm always having to haul him out of difficulties with ladies whose husbands don't realize that he isn't interested in their wives, only in their wives' emotions.

"We got to talking," Jimmy continued blithely, "and she told me all about it."

"About what?"

"Oh, about Dick Stoddard . . . and Harlan Grant."

Now wouldn't that floor anyone? Hoover and Al Jolson, Henry Ford and Queen Marie—almost any other combination would have been less surprising.

Of course I knew Dick Stoddard. If he hadn't belonged to the Stoddards (who sailed into San Francisco Bay so early that they consider the Forty-niners mere upstarts and parvenues) he would still have been known as the All American half-back for his college year. And now, five years later, he was slipping into print again for some discoveries he'd made of a scientific nature. Just what they are I've never quite understood any more than I understand the Einstein Theory, but I know they have something to do with light and, indirectly, with astronomy.

Now Harlan Grant had dealings with the stars as well, but his line was astrology—a particularly pernicious and well-paying variety, which would, I knew, infuriate a man like Stoddard.

One heard that Grant told the most amazing, the most unbelievable things. At his house on Russian Hill he advised about business deals, drew up horoscopes and arranged love-affairs in a manner satisfactory to both parties. He was also something of a medium. In fact, of late, his work had been largely done in the form of séances, and the spiritualists had already sent investigators, who solemnly looked, listened and reported, via the Press, that there was no explanation except the supernatural for what they had seen take place under their very eyes. Slowly but surely he was building up something very like a cult.

All this was whirling through my brain as Jimmy bracketed the names Dick Stoddard and Harlan Grant in his casual fashion, and, before I could ask for an explanation, Jimmy's man Friday threw open the door.

Friday is not his name, of course, but he is very large and very black, with the head of a perfect savage and a savage's naiveté. By a natural association of ideas, Jimmy dubbed him Friday at sight and since then he has never been called anything else.

"Miss Norah Fallon to see you, Mist' Lane."

Probably you've seen Norah on the stage, or on the screen. Certainly there have been enough pictures, in color, of her red hair and green eyes upon magazine covers to imprint her indelibly upon the public mind. But nothing indited by her most exuberant Press agent could give you any idea of Norah at close range. Having said that about the Press agent, I won't attempt it myself; I'll merely state that Friday's eyes were rolling in his head, and Friday, after five years in Jimmy Lane's service, is used to pretty women.

I'm bound to admit that Jimmy didn't seem particularly impressed either by her beauty or her fame. It's true, he half sat up and moved Ruggles from his chest to his lap, but his only greeting was a wave of the hand and a casual "Hello, there!"

Norah didn't seem piqued. "Hello, yourself!" she said. "And how's my blessed pup?" She flopped down on the other end of the hearth-rug, tossed her bag and hat on to a chair, and was putting Ruggles through his tricks when Jimmy introduced me.

"This is Phil Carter."

Instantly Norah Fallon turned and bestowed upon me one of her dazzling smiles.

"Mr. Lane's told me about you, Mr. Carter. If half he says is true, I wonder that Heaven has spared you so long."

"There's no use wasting time on old Phil," Jimmy admonished. "He's a married man with a wife almost as good-looking as you are. If you want him to pull you out of this hole, you'd better get right down to brass tacks and tell him your troubles."

For a moment she regarded me a trifle nervously, as though I were, in some way, the arbiter of her destiny. "I wonder," she asked abruptly, "how much you know about me?"

"Oh, just what the papers and magazines say."

"That stuff!" Her tone was scornful. "That's all non-sense, of course, publicity blurbs. You've got to know the truth if you're going to help."

"Fire ahead," said Jimmy.

She hesitated, looking into the fire, then: "I was born in the slums," she told us. "And when I say 'slums' I mean just that. The whole family in one room, and the baby in a basket on the fire escape. The earliest thing I remember is the cops taking my mother to jail for getting drunk and beating up another woman with a whisky bottle." She shuddered. "Well, I won't go into that. I just want to give you an idea of why I was willing to do anything . . . *anything* to get away."

Jimmy didn't interrupt, but he leaned forward and slipped a couple of pillows back of her as she went on.

"At first I was a funny scrawny kid with carroty hair, but by the time I was fifteen I began to fill out and . . . you know the sort of men that are always hanging around, looking for girls of that kind. I managed to fight off most of 'em, but there was one who offered to get me a job in a factory, modelling. I let him do it, then turned him down for the man who owned the factory. I left the man who owned the factory for a salesman who could get me in a cheap burlesque show. A Ziegfeld scout saw me, got me into the *Follies,* and the rest you know. . . ."

It is impossible to give any idea of the quiet casualness of this recital. From the intonation of her voice, she might have been recounting a walk up Market Street: but at her last words Ruggles gave a little yelp, and I saw that her hand on his collar had tightened until it hurt.

"I'm telling you all this as baldly as possible for a reason," she went on. "I want you to know just how damning it can be made to sound. Now I'll go back and tell a little more. The man who got me the job in the factory did it in hopes of a payment which he never received. Before he could collect I was already out of his reach. The man who ran the factory was sixty and one of the finest men I have ever known. He was the one who taught me how to walk and how to talk, and who made me learn what colors I should wear with my hair. When I left him he cried, not because he was in love with me, but because he felt I was his work of art."

"Pygmalion," murmured Jimmy; "and Galatea."

"Yes, but the next man was different. He wanted to marry me, but I found him making love to another girl and I broke our engagement." She paused and looked up at me. "I don't know whether or not you get what I'm driving at," she said, "but I told all this in that crude way at first because I wanted you to see how awful things can be made to sound when they are told maliciously, and why I'm so afraid of Harlan Grant."

"Harlan Grant?" Sheer astonishment raised my voice. "What on earth has Harlan Grant to do with it?"

She stared at me, equally astonished, and Jimmy from his place on the hearth-rug smiled lazily. "I waited until you got here to tell him," he informed Norah. And to me: "That's the mess she's in. She's being blackmailed by Grant."

I suppose after what I'd heard about Grant nothing should have surprised me, but somehow this did.

"Blackmailed," I murmured idiotically, "Are you sure?"

"Of course she's sure," Jimmy snapped. "Grant's trying to separate her from Dick Stoddard."

This was news with a vengeance! Stoddard and Grant were a weird enough combination, but Stoddard and Norah Fallon. . . . She saw my bewilderment and smiled a little twisted smile.

"It *is* sort of a knock-out, isn't it?" she asked. "But he's fallen for me, really has. And I," she paused to light a cigarette with elaborate casualness, "I've rather fallen for him."

"You're crazy in love with him," Jimmy growled. "Why not be frank about it? It's the crux of the whole thing."

"Well, I suppose it is," she admitted. "I don't mind telling you I'd be willing to be boiled in oil if it would give Dick any particular pleasure." She broke off and turned to me. "Do you happen to know him?"

"Not intimately. He was after my time at college."

"You'd have to really know him to appreciate what he's like. He's the funniest, most adorable combination of a small boy, Sir Galahad, and—" She snapped her fingers toward Jimmy. "Who was that crazy Spaniard who used to go around butting into windmills?"

"Don Quixote."

"Yes; Don Quixote. How on earth he's ever grown up such an innocent, I don't know. I guess it's because he's had so much money, that life hasn't ever really touched him." She paused and smiled at the fire, then: "The minute I met him," she said softly, "I knew he was the only man I'd ever be willing to look at the rest of my life. I didn't even know who he was, but I found out, and after that he didn't have a chance. I'd have made him fall for me if he'd been the King of Siam."

Her words sound flippant as I write them, but there was nothing flippant about her tone.

"Well, anyway," she ended, "we're engaged. At least . . . he's never actually proposed, bless him! He just got a lovely bright pink and told me he was having the family pearls taken out of the safe and re-strung. You know about the Stoddard pearls?"

I did. Everybody does, of course. They are always presented to Stoddard brides the night before the wedding.

"But where does Grant come into all this?" I asked.

"I hate to admit it," she said, "but I've been going to him for a long time. I suppose it's in my blood. All the Irish are idiots about spells and things; and I can't help feeling, even now, that there's something in it."

"Not with Grant," growled Jimmy.

"I don't know." A little puzzled line showed between her brows. "There are things I've seen in that room of his that I simply can't explain. And the things he's told me about myself are absolutely uncanny. Fallon isn't my real name, of course, nor Norah either. My mother and father have been dead for years and I thought I'd entirely blotted out the past, but he knows about it all. The slums, the clothing factory, and the burlesque show . . . even about the man I was engaged to."

"A detective could have done as much."

"Well, perhaps." Her voice didn't sound convinced. "But a lot of people in Hollywood swear by him. Some of 'em won't even sign a contract that he hasn't o-kayed."

"I wonder he doesn't move to Hollywood."

"I've wondered myself. I guess it's because everyone comes to him and he doesn't need to. Then, too, he likes to stay with his brother, the Colonel, and *he* won't leave the place because a lot of his old friends from India live here."

"Is Grant from India?"

"Yes; he rarely talks about himself but he's got an Indian servant who takes care of the house. Singh is his name."

She gave a little shudder. "He's awfully dark and wears queer costumes. There's something about him that always got on my nerves."

"Then why did you keep on going?"

"Because Grant has really given me good advice. Besides, he knows so many things about me that I can't explain. I thought he must have . . . some sort of power. It's only lately that he's begun to act like a beast."

This was a new twist and one that I hadn't expected. "He's gone nutty about her," Jimmy explained. "Wants all sorts of things. That's what complicates matters."

"Just what is he threatening?" I asked Norah.

"He's threatening to take all that awful stuff I told you about my past life to Dick. Of course, he'd make it sound a lot worse than it is . . . the way I told it to you at first."

"But good Lord, what if he does? Stoddard would only kick him downstairs."

"That's just it." she said despairingly. "He'd not only kick him downstairs but he'd probably take a pot-shot at him as well. Dick's got all those lovely romantic notions of chivalry and knight-errantry you read about. He thinks," she flushed, "well, he thinks I'm sort of a cross between Joan of Arc and the Angel Gabriel—and if Grant should dare go to him with anything against me I'm afraid to think what might happen. I was with Dick once when he caught a teamster beating a horse, and I helped bandage the man when he got through." She paused, then added, a trifle unevenly: "He bought the horse."

I don't know whether you'll understand or not but that one little sentence had a lot to do with my being mixed up with the case. I'd never really known Dick Stoddard. With his millions and his social position he'd always seemed more or less of a legend. But that: "He bought the horse" seemed to round him out somehow, to make him human and likeable.

Norah had risen from the hearth-rug and was curled up among the cushions on the davenport. She seemed to have calmly accepted Jimmy's assurance as to my ability in handling the situation and the fact worried me.

"You'll have to tell me a bit more," I said. "You think it's jealousy that's started Grant on this rampage?"

"I think so. Although *he* says it's because the stars are against my marriage to Dick. He declares the spirits will bring some terrible curse on us if I marry him."

"Stars and spirits," murmured Jimmy. "My word, the fellow does mix things, doesn't he?"

"Yes; and lately he's seemed sort of confused, almost as though something were wrong with him."

"You mean you think he's crazy?"

"No," she seemed to have difficulty in expressing her thoughts, "not exactly that. It's more as though he were worried about something. I've noticed it particularly when I've been alone with him. The other day he got up right in the middle of a conversation, walked across to some curtains at the farther end of his study and jerked them back quickly as though he were expecting to catch someone, although he must have known there was nobody there."

"Well . . ." Jimmy considered. "That sounds jumpy, but there's probably a simple explanation for it."

"I suppose so." She was plainly making some mental reservation. "But that wasn't the thing I really meant. I only mention it because of what happened later. You see, he was advising me about a contract and it was lying open on his desk. After he'd looked behind the curtains he went on talking, and while he talked he was fiddling with a pencil. You know how some people are about a pencil, they simply can't help writing with it? Well, Grant is like that. He's always writing letters and words on everything." She paused and leaned forward, her eyes growing large. "Do you know, when I got home and I looked over my contract, I found three words scrawled all over it."

"And they were . . . ?"

"'Fear of fear.'"

"*What?*"

"Just what I said, 'fear of fear'. Sometimes it was in capital letters and sometimes it was written small, but always the same words."

"'Fear of fear'," Jimmy mused. "Now that's what I call good copy. If I were let alone I could make something out of that. It's short, succinct, and suggests a lot of things. It suggests—"

We never learned what it suggested because Friday opened the door at that moment. His black face was inscrutable, but his eyes were rolling slightly, a sure sign of emotion.

"Dinner's ready, Mist' Lane."

We all rose with the pleased anticipation of people whose last meal was some six hours past. I remember I was even essaying some feeble joke when Friday's next words fell like a bombshell.

"Yo' maid been telephonin' you, Miss Fallon, but I tol' her yo' wasn't to be disturbed so she give me the message. She says as how a gen'leman name of Grant has been foun' dead."

"Dead!" Norah grasped my arm. "Dead!"

"Yes, ma'am. Dead."

"Did . . . did she tell you who . . . I mean, what killed him?"

"She said they didn't rightly know, but he was foun' in his séance room, an' she said it looked like he'd been plumb scared to death."

Chapter 2
Murder is Suspected

There was no dinner eaten that night. Jimmy and I tried to persuade Norah to take something, but it was useless. From the moment Friday made his announcement, she seemed to be consumed by some inner excitement. Her first quick movement was toward the telephone. Getting her maid on the wire, she asked a few questions which elicited no new information, then hung up the receiver and turned to Jimmy.

"I hate to ruin your dinner-party," she said, "but I couldn't possibly eat a bite after this. I'm too upset."

"I should think it would relieve your mind," I told her. "If Grant's dead, he can't do any more harm."

"*He* can't," she agreed, "but how do I know those awful things he dug up about me won't fall into the hands of someone else?"

"Did he commit them to paper?"

"Yes; there was a long envelope full of typewritten notes. He kept it in a file near his desk and anyone could get hold of it."

There was a moment of silence while we pondered the situation, then Jimmy spoke slowly. "I think I might be able to get the stuff back for you. I'm on rather good terms with the police just now."

"Oh!" Norah gave a little cry of horror. "You don't think his death is anything the police will be brought into?"

"I don't know . . . yet. You'd better lie low until we find out." He paused a minute, then asked: "When did you last see Grant?"

"About nine o'clock last night. He had a séance, but he talked with me for a few minutes before the people came."

"What did he say?"

"Nothing new. Just kept insisting that I break off my engagement with Dick."

"And you refused?"

"Not exactly. You see, Dick's been out of town and I didn't think Grant would do anything until he came back. I figured once we were married, he'd give up his crazy ideas, so I tried to play for time. I've had to handle a lot of men in my life, but never anyone like Harlan Grant. Most of the time he was like a great block of granite, apparently without any feeling, but when he let loose it was like a volcano erupting. He insisted that I was the only woman he'd ever loved, and he was really getting pretty wild when the people began arriving for the séance."

"What did you do next?"

"I managed to get away, but I was so nervous I didn't want to go back to the hotel. It was after nine and I slipped into a theatre to see the last half of a picture. Then I got a cup of chocolate at a sweetshop and went home to bed about eleven-thirty. Even then I couldn't sleep, so I got up early this morning and rode out to the park where I met you and Ruggles."

Jimmy nodded. "O.K.," he said, "I know the rest." He was moving over toward the door and Norah looked up eagerly.

"Where are you going?"

"To find out what's happened. I want you to stay here and eat dinner while we're gone."

"Oh, I couldn't," she protested, but something in his expression seemed to warn her, and she dropped back. "Oh, all right, I'll try."

"Good girl! We may have some news when we get back and I'd rather find you were here." He paused and instructed Friday to serve a tray in the study, then returned to the door. "By the way, you said that young man of yours was out of town, didn't you?"

She swung about, and I saw that her eyes had narrowed a trifle as though she were suddenly on guard. "Dick? Oh, yes, he's been out of town for several days. A lot of scientists are meeting down at Mt. Wilson and he's springing some new theory on 'em."

"You're dead sure he wasn't in the city last night?"

For a fraction of a second she hesitated, then: "I can assure you I haven't seen him for three days. Why do you ask?"

"Oh, nothing," said Jimmy lightly. "Behave yourself and don't worry while we're gone."

In the car he explained his plans a bit more in detail. "We may find it's nothing but a wild goose chase so far as Grant's death is concerned. But that girl's quite right. Those lies about her oughtn't to be left around loose."

"What are you going to do?"

"I'm going to locate Corrigan. He'll know the inside dope if anyone does."

Corrigan is a friendly enemy of Jimmy Lane's; the two were on rival papers some years before and, even now, when there is no possibility of their running counter to each other, they enjoy tilting—in memory of the old days. When anything "breaks" in the Press, Jimmy is pretty sure to seek out Corrigan, who has a bloodhound's nose for news and a bulldog's tenacity for hanging on to leads.

For almost the only time during those hectic days, we played into luck. Corrigan was just leaving the office as we turned in. He was looking sour, and Jimmy's questions did nothing to lighten his gloom.

Yes, he informed us, Grant was dead, beautifully dead, and stiff when found. Too late to do anything for him, therefore the finding might just as well have been delayed a few hours until past the time when the evening sheets could scoop the news. But, of course, they had to discover the body just right for the P.M.s. . . .

There was so much of this keening that it required real firmness on Jimmy's part to get at the facts. Corrigan's answer to the first question raised a load from my mind.

"Sure it was natural death. What made you think it wasn't?"

"Nothing," Jimmy said hastily. "What did he die of?"

"Cerebral hemorrhage. The doctor says he's been in bad shape for some time and had been warned to go slow."

"When did he die?"

"Last night . . . probably around twelve. He'd been having a séance in the evening, and after everyone went he stayed in his study. He didn't show up this morning but nothing was thought of it because he frequently skipped breakfast. Along about noon his brother got worried. He and the servant went up and pounded on his door. When he didn't answer they broke in and found he'd died during the night."

"Not much of a story," said Jimmy shrewdly. "I don't see why you're so cut up about its breaking in the evening papers."

"Well, there's things about it that make it interesting," Corrigan explained. "In the first place, he was a kind of a mysterious guy and a lot of big bugs were mixed up with him. The boss thought I might be able to get a story, so I'm going out to take a look-see."

Jimmy brought out his cigarette case and selected a smoke with some care. "That's all?" he inquired casually.

Corrigan nodded. "Yes; except one thing that the papers have played up big. Everyone who saw Grant after he was found made the same remark. They say his face was all twisted up and his eyes were wide open. He looked exactly as though he'd seen something horrible, and it had scared him to death."

"Fear of fear," murmured Jimmy, and Corrigan stared. "What's that?"

"Nothing. Nothing at all."

"I'll bet it is," said the reporter suspiciously. "I never knew you to ask questions unless there was something in the wind. Are you going to let me in on it?"

Jimmy considered for a moment. "You say you're going up to the Grant house?"

"Yeah, the boss thought I might get something out of the family about the Who's Whoers that went to Grant's séances."

"Who's in the family?"

"Well, there's his brother, the Colonel. They say he's a regular old Shylock . . . would skin his grandmother for a nickel. Then there's the Colonel's daughter and her husband, a chemist named Steeb. The whole lot's on the queerish side."

"See here," said Jimmy, "will you take us along?"

"No can do. I don't work in battalion formation."

"In that case," Jimmy sighed, "I suppose I'll just have to go it on my own."

For a moment the two surveyed each other, and I saw that Corrigan was wavering. "Now what have you got up the little old sleeve?" he asked. "My well-known intuition tells me there's more to this than meets the eye."

Jimmy grinned at him impishly and signaled me to step back into the machine which was waiting at the curb.

"Mebbe," he agreed, "but whatever I find out—remember you refused our help and it belongs to me!"

We drove off, leaving Corrigan still standing on the curb, and Jimmy chuckled. "I'm glad he turned us down," he said. "I've just had a whale of an idea."

"What is it?" I asked suspiciously, but he only yawned.

"I hate to repeat myself. Just listen and you'll find out." He reached back on the seat and brought forth a newspaper. "We'd better look this over. It's got the latest dope."

For a moment we studied the story. It told us nothing beyond what we already knew; but there was a picture of Grant—taken, I surmised, some years before. He was a square-shouldered, heavy-set man with a long, saturnine face, pale eyes and a full sensuous mouth.

"Not bad for a newspaper cut," Jimmy observed. "You can see that he had a sort of rugged good looks. That's probably why two-thirds of his clients were fool females."

The car was already climbing the steep slope of Russian Hill and above us the houses rose tier on tier, like serried battlements. The night was bitter cold and the wind, sweeping in from the bay, blew little flecks of salt moisture against the window-panes. Near the crest the chauffeur drew to the curb and stopped the car.

"You'll have to walk the rest, sir. It's not a driving street." We stepped from the tonneau, and he pointed up a cobble-stoned way that would have taxed a Rocky Mountain goat. "I think it's that house on the corner, third down from the top. The one with the big window that's got a light in it."

Jimmy ordered him to wait and we climbed the terraced pavement that led up the steep incline. There was a group of three houses which had, apparently, been built upon the same plan. They were alike externally, except that each rose a story above the other; their gardens, or the little plot of grass and shrubbery which passed as gardens, ran together, and their roofs topped each other with geometrical precision.

The first of these was plainly the house we were seeking. It stood on the corner where the ground sloped away so rapidly that it seemed to rear to a height almost terrifying. There was shrubbery against its lower walls, cypress and a pine or so, twisted out of shape by the wind from the sea. Ivy was growing up the walls, and hung festooned from the eaves. This was swaying now in the night wind, and the shadows cast by a single street lamp made it look as though a myriad of giant spiders were crawling across the face of the house.

I half-expected to find Corrigan somewhere about, but we had evidently been too quick for him. There was no one on the porch of the house, only some shadowy animal which sprang away as we approached. Probably a cat, I thought; but there was something about the place and the eerie rustling of the leaves which made crinkles run up my spine, and affected my eyesight as well, for it seemed to me that the little creature had not run along the side of the house but that it had sprung up the wall and disappeared among the shadowy spiders created by the street lamp. Without waiting for Jimmy, I put out my hand to ring the bell; but it came in contact with something soft and clinging that hung on the door. A crêpe bow on a funeral wreath. Suddenly I remembered that a man had died in that house less than twenty-four hours before and that he was supposed to have been in close contact with the spirit world. At the same moment I discovered a great distaste for the business in hand.

"Hang it all," I snapped at Jimmy, "this is your expedition. Why don't you do something?"

"I *am* doing something." His voice came back from the darkness, and I found that he was not beside me but at the other end of the porch, glancing up at a lighted window overhead. "I'm wondering what's going on up there."

"It's hardly the time to be spying," I said tartly. "You'd better find the bell before you get shot for a burglar."

He turned back and twisted the old-fashioned handle; an instant later we heard the dim echoes of a bell somewhere within the house. For a long moment nothing happened. We listened intently but the only sound was the faint drip, drip of moisture from the ivy. Jimmy rang again, this time more loudly.

"I'm sure there's somebody in the house," he said, "I saw a shadow cross that window-shade up there when we first came."

He was pointing to a window above us—the only lighted spot in the house—and, as I glanced up, I could have sworn that a hand raised the shade a trifle, then lowered it again. Jimmy applied himself to the bell, and rang so continuously that the sound reverberated through the house. After a time, I when it seemed that my nerves were stretched to the breaking point, I heard footsteps coming from above; they were evidently descending a stair for they became more and more distinct until they were just behind the door—then they seemed to recede, to die away completely.

All this sounds simple as I tell it. Nothing to startle nor alarm. But standing in the dark shadow of the porch with its overhanging veil of rustling ivy and facing the funeral wreath on the door, it was strangely eerie and unpleasant. I said as much to Jimmy. "There's no use your clanging that confounded bell. No one's going to answer."

"Does it get on your nerves?"

"It's giving me the jitters!"

"Then it'll get on the nerves of the fellow in there twice as badly, and he'll open the door if only to shut us up."

With that he went at the bell again until I wondered that the mysterious inmate of the house didn't take a shot at him from the window. I even planned to slip behind a pillar of the porch if I heard the door opening. But when one door did open it was behind us, in the next house. It was thrown open with great violence and a man stamped out on to the porch.

The drop of the land was so sudden that the place where he stood was some ten or twelve feet above us. This fact, combined with his unusual height and the trick played by the light, which came from behind, made of him a giant specter . . . and the specter was that of the dead man, Grant.

I think even Jimmy was startled for he stepped back quickly and I heard him catch his breath. But it was only an instant, for the specter burst into speech and, at his first words, we knew he was no ghost. For the space of a full minute he leaned over the edge of the porch and cursed us. I have heard mule drivers in the Sierras that were accomplished cursers; I have even met a mate on a battleship who won a medal for swearing, but I have never heard anything that remotely approached the horrible fluency of this man. There couldn't have been anything personal in his hatred. From where he stood we were only shadows in the surrounding blackness, and yet there was a reptilian malignancy, a cold diabolical passion in his tone that made it worse than physical violence.

The very sight of him was infinitely shocking; as he talked his face grew, not red, but blue and white, as though the blood had drained from his body into his words; his hands, which were grasping a gnarled cane, grew tense and claw-like. His whole body became, for the moment, inhuman and terrible. For a moment his voice continued beating upon us in a frenzy of sound, then Jimmy stepped forward where, the light from the street lamp fell upon him. He made no attempt to answer. Instead, he removed his hat and stood looking up in an attitude which I can only describe as meek. It was not until the other man stopped for breath that he spoke.

"I'm sorry if my ringing disturbed you," he said. "I came to see Mr. Grant, and I was sure there must be someone in the house because there's a light."

There was a moment of silence, and I saw that the other was gathering himself together, endeavoring to regain his control. When he spoke his voice was still harsh but it was lower in tone.

"Didn't you know that Mr. Grant died last night?"

"Died?" Jimmy's face was so full of astonishment that he almost deceived me. "Oh, I'm sorry. Fearfully sorry. Do you suppose I've disturbed anyone in the house?"

"There's no one over there, but you've disturbed *us* abominably."

"What a shame!" Jimmy's voice was contrite, but I saw that the wretch was gradually edging his way toward the steps of the house next door. "I wonder if you could tell me where I can find Mr. Grant's family."

"They live here," the man said ungraciously. "I'm Colonel Grant, his brother."

Instantly Jimmy was up the steps, holding out his hand. "I'm awfully glad to meet you, Colonel," he said. "I'm James Lane." I saw that the Colonel was impressed, by the way he took the outstretched hand and the change in his face. There was no chance for him to speak because Jimmy was hurrying on. "I wonder if you could give me a moment? I've something important to say."

The Colonel glanced around, a trifle helplessly. Jimmy was smiling at him and glancing suggestively toward the door, and the man was practically forced to capitulate.

"Oh, all right. Only you'll have to be quick about it. We're pretty much upset . . ."

"I understand. My friend and I will only take a moment of your time." He nodded to me and I strode across the grass and followed them inside.

The house was a somber place, furnished with heavy Victorian furniture in mahogany and carved walnut, with tufted upholstery that looked as though it had been cast in iron. The entrance hall was narrow and dark, compressed between a stairway and a square, ugly room which resembled a New England parlor. Through hanging curtains of plum-colored velvet I could see a painted brick fireplace surrounded by a half-circle of exactly-placed, hostile-looking chairs. There was nothing gracious about the room, nothing inviting, and I was thankful when the Colonel passed it by and led us to the end of the hall where a sort of square cubby-hole had been turned into a study. Here there was a flat-topped desk, a revolving chair and a window-seat covered with monks cloth.

He dropped into the chair by the desk and motioned us to the window-seat, then scowled interrogatively at Jimmy Lane. It was apparent that he already regretted admitting us, and I could scarcely blame him. What, I wondered, was Jimmy's game, and how could he possibly explain his intrusion upon a house of mourning at such an hour? As usual, I had underestimated his fertile brain. We were no sooner seated than he plunged glibly into speech.

"I've come from the *Occult Review*," he informed the Colonel. "They have been very much impressed by your brother's work and want a series of articles about him."

Now that was technically a lie, of course, but it was the sort of lie that Jimmy could easily turn into the truth. The *Occult Review,* or any other magazine, for that matter, would be only too glad to get Jimmy's name attached to an article on any subject.

"The editor asked me to write an account of his researches," Jimmy went on. "Of course, at that time your

brother was alive, but now, if you can possibly bring yourself to help, I think the articles might be a sort of memo-
rial."

"I don't know . . ." The Colonel hesitated. "My brother
and I never agreed about his work."

"Oh," Jimmy's voice was shocked. "I'm sorry to hear
that! But perhaps he left notes? I could look over those."

The Colonel stiffened. Evidently the idea of turning
Jimmy loose with his brother's papers did not appeal to
him. Jimmy caught the expression, too, and his voice became as dulcet and guileless as that of a cooing dove.

"Under your guidance, I mean, of course. We would
write in collaboration—and I think you'd find it paid very
well."

Instantly I saw that he had struck something. The
Colonel's eyes narrowed and he pursed his lips.

"H'm," he said, "it would pay, would it? About how
much?"

"That's hard to say. I usually get pretty fair money for
my stuff, and we'd split fifty-fifty. That is, if you were really able to help, although from what you say—"

"Forget all that," said the Colonel crisply. "It's true, I
never had anything to do with his séances, but my brother
used to talk to me pretty freely, and, of course, there's his
notes. . . ." He seemed to go into a brown study, and when
he roused himself it was not to make any definite answer.
"I think we'd better let this all go over until to-morrow.
My brother's death was very sudden, and, naturally, we're
still upset by it. If you'll leave your telephone number, I'll
give you a ring in the morning."

He rose as he spoke, with an indication that the interview was at an end, and Jimmy was forced to take the
hint. As we moved toward the hall we came face to face
with someone who was descending the stairs. If you've

read the newspapers lately, you must have seen a picture of Chanda Steeb. Because of her relationship to Grant, the Press made a good deal of her heroism in that mission-school fire. But no newspaper picture could do her justice. I seem to remember saying something of that sort about Norah Fallon, but the two girls were as different as day and night. Where Norah was all light and sparkle, Chanda was a study in shadows. Her hair, which was very dark, was drawn away from her brow and coiled in a low knot at the back; her eyes were large and blue-grey, with a quaint upward slant at the corners; her nose was long and slender and her mouth mobile, but with a rich sweetness in the curve of the lips. She was in the early twenties, I found later, but already there were tiny lines etched between her brows, and her dark hair showed a silver thread here and there at the temples.

She was dressed in a soft woolen fabric which was neither blue nor grey. The skirt was much longer than the style of the moment, and it was high at the neck, banded with a strip of sheer white which gave her something the look of a deaconess. As she stood at the turn of the stair, regarding us with her faint, sweet smile, it suddenly struck me that she looked like one of those strangely beautiful girls in a Benda drawing, or one of the carved figures of the Virgin that one sees so often in Italy.

For an instant she hesitated, then the Colonel moved forward. "This is my daughter, Mrs. Steeb," he said.

And to the girl: "Chanda, this is Mr. Lane, Mr. James Lane. He wishes to write some articles about your Uncle Harlan for the *Occult Review.*"

She came down the few remaining steps and held out her hand to Jimmy. When she spoke, her voice was low and held a certain husky sweetness.

"I'm afraid you've come at a bad time, Mr. Lane. We're still stunned by what's happened."

"Of course," Jimmy was contrite, "but I hope you'll persuade your father to let me go on with the articles. I'm sure I can do them if he'll give his permission."

She looked at him with an expression that I thought vaguely troubled. "I think," she said, "I think it would be better just to let everyone forget his . . . work."

"Then you didn't believe in his spirits?" Jimmy asked, and she stepped back, flushing.

"No . . . no; I couldn't believe. It is quite contrary to my religion."

"My daughter was raised in a mission-school in India," the Colonel explained. "Naturally she has firm ideas on the subject." He turned to her with a touch of roughness in his voice: "Is there anything you want?"

"No." It seemed to me that she shrank away from him imperceptibly, "I came down to fetch some broth for Otto. He's not so well this evening."

"Then don't let us keep you," said the Colonel brusquely. "These gentlemen are just leaving." With a little smile at us she passed on down the hall, and the Colonel ushered us toward the door. "You will hear from me to-morrow," he promised. "After I've had time to think over your proposition." He paused, then coughed. "I believe you said fifty-fifty?"

"Fifty-fifty," Jimmy agreed, and a moment later the door closed behind us.

Instead of walking toward the street, Jimmy crossed the lawn and stood for a moment looking up at the house next door. The window above was still lighted although no shadow showed against the shade.

"Now I wonder—" he was beginning, then broke off as Corrigan appeared from the street. The reporter was coming on the dead run, and almost barged into us in his excitement.

"That you?" he gasped. And, without waiting for a reply: "Did you learn anything?"

"Lots," said Jimmy. "But I'm not sharing it."

"Oh, yes you are!" Corrigan's voice was shrill with excitement. "You'll be glad to swap it for the news I've got."

Jimmy capitulated. "All right, spill yours first."

"O.K. It's this: after you left I dropped back to the office for my coat, and found hell a-popping. The boss had just got a straight tip from Headquarters about this case. They say this guy Grant didn't die a natural death . . . he was murdered."

I felt Jimmy's hand clutch my arm, but his voice came out of the darkness with assumed calmness. "That all you heard?"

"You bet your sweet life it isn't! The police are already hot on the trail of a suspect. Grant's servant let somebody in to see him late last night and one of the nuts from the séance hung around and heard 'em quarreling like mad. Believe it or not, they both swear it was Dick Stoddard!"

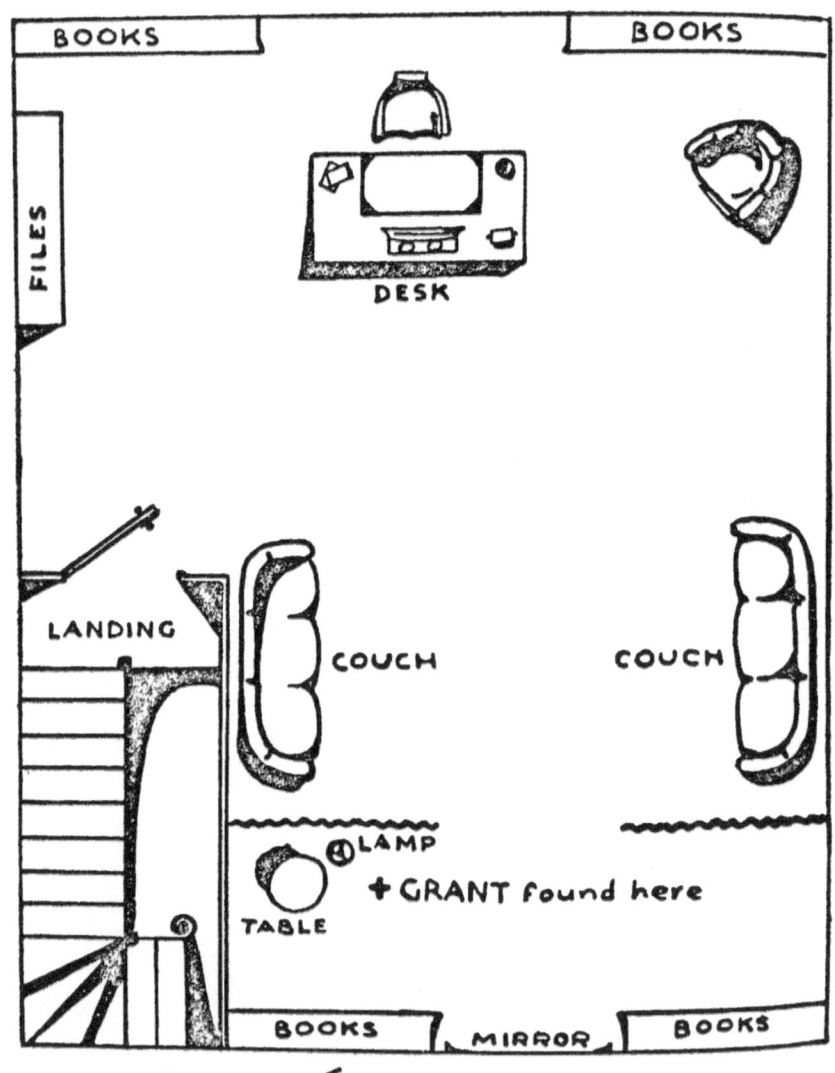

BOOKS   BOOKS

FILES

DESK

LANDING   COUCH   COUCH

LAMP
+ GRANT found here
TABLE

BOOKS   MIRROR   BOOKS

THE SÉANCE ROOM
(Grant's Study)

CHAPTER 3
IN THE SÉANCE ROOM

The trip from Russian Hill to Jimmy Lane's house was made in almost total silence. Both of us were thinking of the girl we had left in the study, and trying to find some ray of light in the situation to offer her. But the outlook was about as bad as it could be.

"It isn't as though Stoddard were a regular follower of Grant's," Jimmy pointed out. "In that case, he might have some excuse for being with him at that hour. But, from Norah's account, I gather he'd never met the fellow before."

"Why do you think he went?"

"Heaven knows. I only wish we'd run across Norah sooner, then we might have been able to prevent . . . whatever happened."

"But you don't think Stoddard—"

"How can I think anything until I know more about it? You'd better stand by in case there's trouble when we break it to the poor kid . . . hysterics, I mean, or fainting."

But Jimmy had forgotten Norah's nationality. When he told her, she neither fainted nor became hysterical; instead, her cheeks flushed and her fists clenched in as pretty a display of temper as I have seen.

"You mean to say they intend to drag Dick's name into the thing?" she cried. "Why, it's outrageous!"

Jimmy was watching her closely. "If you're talking about the police," he said, "you're a little hard on them. You think your young man is guilty yourself, you know."

That brought her up with a round turn.

"What makes you say that?" she demanded. And, without waiting for a reply: "I suppose you mean the silly things I told you about those letters."

"No; that isn't what I mean. I'm basing my theory on the fact that you lied about where Stoddard was last night. You said he was at Mt. Wilson while, all the time, you knew he was here."

For a moment I thought she was going to turn her wrath against him, then, suddenly, she nodded meekly. "Yes; I might as well admit that I did. But you see—"

"You needn't explain. After telling us about the mess you were in, and your fear that Stoddard would do something desperate if Grant went to him, it was pretty much of a sock in the jaw for you to learn that Grant had died suddenly, especially when you knew your fiancé had been in the city. By the way, how did you know it?"

"I found a message waiting when I got home last night. You remember I told you that I'd been to a picture after I left Grant? When I got back to the apartment I found Dick had called twice during the evening. The message said he'd flown up on some business and had to go back about midnight so he wouldn't be able to see me if I didn't get home before eleven. It was eleven-thirty when I got in, so we didn't make connections."

"Does he often fly back and forth?"

"Yes; often. Only, usually, I'm down in Hollywood and he flies down to see me."

There was silence for a moment, then she leaned forward and touched Jimmy's arm. "Please, please don't let what I said influence you. I feel as though I'd betrayed him."

Jimmy patted her hand. "It's the best thing you ever did," he declared. "Don't get worked up over things. Corrigan's information may be all wet, and anyway, he didn't say they were going to arrest Stoddard . . . just that he was heard talking with Grant around eleven-thirty. It'll take more than that to make them accuse a man of his standing." He rose to his feet and drew her with him toward the door. "The best thing you can do, my dear, is to let me send you home to catch up on your sleep. You can leave all the worry to us."

"You mean you and Mr. Carter are still willing to help?"

"You couldn't keep us out of it! I don't know exactly what we can do, but we'll begin by getting those papers."

"Papers!" She stared at him. "You don't suppose I'm thinking about my miserable little reputation when Dick's in danger!"

"It's not a matter of your reputation," Jimmy told her gravely. "Don't you see? If the police find those notes they may regard them as a motive for Stoddard's killing Grant."

From where I stood I could see the horror in her eyes.

"Of course! They're like a sword hanging over Dick's head!" Jimmy was helping her on with her coat, and she looked up at him like a trustful little girl. "Oh, you will get them back for us, won't you?"

He nodded comfortingly and patted her shoulder. "Don't worry, they're as good as in your hands right now."

But, after seeing her to the car, he returned to the study with a corrugated brow. "Now, how," he demanded, "am I going to make good on that damn fool promise?"

"I don't know," I told him dryly. "It's just possible the police may have something to say about those papers."

"Not if I find 'em first."

"I suppose you're thinking about the Colonel. Do you really expect him to swallow all that stuff you spilled about doing a series of articles on Grant?"

"That old skinflint would swallow anything that was buttered with gold. Didn't you see his eye light up when I talked about fifty per cent. of the proceeds?"

"Surely you don't intend to really write them?"

"I don't know," he was staring at the fire thoughtfully, "I've always gone on hunches, Phil, and there's something about this case that interests me. That phrase Norah gave us is responsible. You know, the words Grant scribbled over her contract: 'fear of fear'. It's such a darn good phrase that I feel it's got to fit in somewhere."

"Then you're really going to take the thing up seriously?"

"Dead seriously. I've always yearned to poke around among spooks and specters. Now's my chance."

"Very well," I sighed. "I suppose I'll have to stand by, but I don't like the look of it."

"Neither do I," said Jimmy gravely, "I don't like the look of it at all."

When Friday called me at eight the next morning, Jimmy was already gone, from which I gathered he had affairs in hand that he preferred to transact without me. I went on down to my office and attended to routine business until two o'clock. My mind was naturally on the case, so I was a trifle puzzled to find that the newspapers had nothing to say about Grant's death beyond a brief announcement of the funeral which was to take place the next day. I had sent out for all the evening issues and was poring over them when Jimmy arrived. He saw them spread out on my desk and jumped immediately into an explanation.

"The police aren't sure yet," he said. "They post-mortemed last night, but the department doctors have disagreed and they're sending for experts."

"I suppose you've been to Headquarters?"

"Yes; I had breakfast with the Chief."

There was nothing surprising about that. Jimmy has been an intimate of the police and detective departments since his cub reporter days and frequently wanders in and out of the offices. Since his rather remarkable work on the Lopez case, he has been consulted more than once by Captain Hemming, the chief of detectives.

"The old boy's by way of being upset," Jimmy continued. "Seemed to want to tell his woes to someone."

"I suppose you confided in him in return?"

"I did not. My role was strictly that of listener. He's up against a problem: the District Attorney's tied up just now at a conference in Washington, and his assistant is sick. There's more or less rivalry between the police and the detectives, and the Chief's determined if there's any gravy in this case, he's going to get it. Same time, he doesn't want to rush in and make a fool of himself by yelling 'murder' if it's natural death, so he's sitting tight and keeping the papers quiet until he gets a full report from the doctors."

"Just what started the talk of murder?"

"The undertaker. He let out the information that the death looked phony. It got to Headquarters and they investigated, on general principles. Dr. Waverly, Grant's own physician, reported that he died from hemorrhage all right, but he called it 'cerebral' when he should have said 'subdural'."

"What difference does that make?"

"A lot. 'Cerebral hemorrhage' is apoplexy; 'subdural' means that it was caused by a blow on the head. Dr. Waverly forgot to mention that there's a bad fracture at the base of Grant's skull."

"But why should he keep quiet about it?"

"He says it was because he believed the fracture was caused by Grant's fall *after* the stroke. It seems he was looking for trouble of some sort and had already warned

Grant he was due for a blow up. So, when he found him lying dead, he just did a sort of nice, professional 'I told you so' and reported natural death. The Chief thinks he's perfectly sincere, but they've called in a couple of experts, just the same. While he's waiting for their report, you and I are to go out and see the Colonel."

"You don't mean you're going to bother him now!"

"I do. The Chief's in a tight place. He doesn't want to make a move until the doctors decide whether or not it's murder, but he's tickled to death to have me take a look around, *ex-officio*. I've made him understand my interest in the case is purely scientific. I've been impressed by the yarns I've heard about Grant's pet spooks and I want to look into the matter from that angle."

"Just where do I come in?"

"You're my assistant. You'll have to ask the Colonel lots and lots of intelligent questions about his brother, and put all his answers down neatly in a notebook. That ought to keep him busy while I go through the papers."

"You actually expect to see the Colonel?"

"I certainly do. He phoned this morning that he'd be glad to do the articles. He thought they would be a touching testimonial . . . so long as it was strictly fifty-fifty."

The Colonel was waiting when we reached the top of the hill, not in his own house, but in Grant's. From the calmness of his mien, I gathered that no hint of the suspicions at Headquarters had reached him as yet.

"I'll take you up to the séance room," he said. "All my brother's things are there and we're not so likely to be disturbed."

We passed through the second floor, which evidently contained only bedrooms, and mounted a stairway leading to the third. At the top there was a small railed landing before a closed door. Lay it to nerves if you like, there was something about that stairway and door which sent a cold

chill down my spine. Perhaps it was the fact that I knew
it led to the room where a man had died, perhaps it was
a faint premonition of what was to happen later. In any
event, I hated the place; and hated Jimmy Lane for dragging me there.

As we reached the landing, the Colonel put out his
hand to the door, but before he could touch it, the thing
swung open of itself. For an instant even Jimmy looked
startled. Then we saw that a figure was standing inside, a
fantastic figure, like something from the *Arabian Nights*.
It was a brown-black man, preternaturally tall and thin,
with a high turban and long garments that just escaped
his feet. He was standing absolutely immovable, his hands
in his sleeves; only his eyes darted over us, as though they
were alive and eager—inside of a carven image.

The Colonel gave a quick, angry exclamation, then:
"This is Singh," he explained. "He helped my brother with
his séances. Later he may be able to give you some information." He turned on the fellow and spoke gruffly. "You
don't need to go on wearing that heathenish outfit. There
won't be any more séances."

Singh bowed. His cultured voice, singularly free from
accent except in the case of a few long vowels, was startling, somehow, coming from his black face.

"Yes, sar. It is just as you say."

"It had better be as I say, you black ape!" the Colonel
growled. "What are you doing up here anyway?"

"Miss Chanda told me to put the room in order."

"You tell Miss Chanda that I'll give any orders that
are necessary about this room, and, after this, keep out of
it. D'you understand? If I catch you up here again except
when I call, I'll kick you downstairs."

The Colonel's face was growing pale again and the
veins were showing blue on his forehead; his hands were
tightening about the handle of his cane, and I thought for

a moment he would lose control over himself. But Singh was evidently used to his tempers for he bowed composedly, with no change of expression, and turned toward the door. A moment later he was gone. He didn't exactly go up in a puff of smoke like a genie, in a fairy-tale, but his departure was so quick and so silent that he might have vanished into thin air. The Colonel turned back to us a trifle apologetically.

"Rummy chap," he said. "Always gets on my nerves."

"Was he with your brother long?" Jimmy inquired.

"Over twenty years. He was all right in India, but this country has ruined him. He's been getting above himself, and I don't intend to put up with it. He dismissed the subject with a quick motion of his hand. "Suppose we get down to business. All the stuff of Harlan's that could help us is in this room. He used to spend practically all his time here." There was a certain callousness in his voice, and he spoke with no trace of emotion; evidently there had been no close affection between himself and his brother.

We had been standing by the door, now the Colonel crossed the floor and drew open the heavy curtains which were hanging over a window at the far side. Before, the place had been too dark for us to see clearly, but with the drawing of the curtains, the afternoon light came in from the cloudy sky above and threw part of the room into gloomy relief.

It was not a particularly large room, but so cleverly handled with curtains and tricks of perspective that it seemed like a shadowy cavern stretching away into depths beyond depths. To the north a great window, nine or ten feet high, looked out over a panorama of city and bay; at the opposite end a wall mirror caught the opalescent light and threw it against the great curtains of royal blue velvet which hung from the high raftered ceiling to the floor. To left and right the room was lined with deep bookcases, and here and there, scattered about, were divans and couches, all of them low and soft-cushioned.

Not at all the background one would select for spirits, at first glance, and yet, after a moment, there was something troubling about the place, something vaguely uncanny. Perhaps it was the strange effect of the window and mirror, perhaps it was the height of the raftered ceiling, or, more likely, it was the absolute stillness. Even when one moved across the floor the carpet was so thick that the footsteps were lost, swallowed, as the tide is swallowed by thirsty sand. No sound came from the street below, and even our voices seemed to be deadened by the shrouding velvet curtains. High, detached and silent, with a sort of ominous quietude, the room gave one an odd feeling of being in the fourth dimension, as though the common laws of sound were inoperative there.

"Is this where your brother's séances were held?" Jimmy asked.

"Yes; originally Harlan used a room on the ground floor, but it was so noisy he moved up here."

"I don't see any table," Jimmy remarked. "I thought all mediums used tables . . . for rappings and that sort of thing."

The Colonel smiled. "I don't believe my brother considered himself a medium. He was more a scientific investigator. He never went in for slate writing, table rappings, or trances . . . claimed they were cheap tricks."

"Just what did he do?"

"Mainly he produced exactly the right conditions so that spirits could return to earth. As I told you, I didn't exactly approve of his work. Always felt if there was such a thing it was better left alone. But, I'm bound to admit, he got amazing results. I've had chaps come down from here swearing they'd seen and talked with men and women who'd been dead for years."

"You don't say!" Jimmy was all ears. "Do you know where to find any of the people who had these experiences?"

"Yes; there's a list of my brother's clients in his files."

Jimmy's eyes strayed longingly toward the filing cases in the corner, and I knew he was itching to get at them; but he managed to dissemble his impatience and coolly lighted a cigarette.

"If we're going to work together, we'd better get things down to some sort of a system," he said. "Suppose you sit at the desk with Carter and give him a rough outline of your brother's life. Where he was born and educated, as well as any little details you think might have a bearing on his occult interests. In the meantime, I'll have a look at the files . . . that is, if you have no objections."

"Not the slightest," said the Colonel. "I've already gone through them and removed all his personal papers."

If he had struck Jimmy in the face the blow could not have been greater. For an instant his eyes sought mine, and I read a rueful disappointment in their depths, but he recovered himself and nodded.

"All right! Let's go." He turned to the files and I sat down at the desk by the Colonel, who began to give me the particulars of his late brother's life in a dry, utterly emotionless voice. Since the facts were of the greatest importance later on, I think I shall give them as I wrote them up for Jimmy's benefit that night.

CHAPTER 4
HARLAN MELVILLE GRANT

Harlan Melville Grant was born in Wales on 29th April, 1876. His mother was Welsh, his father an American sea-captain who went down with his ship, leaving two sons, one six years older than Harlan.

The shock of her husband's death seems to have affected Mrs. Grant's mind. After his passing, she began to see spirits and to claim that she was in touch with the other world. She became so successful as a medium that the Society of Psychical Research was about to send a committee to report her séances when she died suddenly in the middle of the night. According to the doctor, her death was caused by a stroke of apoplexy, but the more superstitious in the community claimed that she was murdered by the spirits she invoked.

At the time of her death the eldest of her sons was twenty-two and already embarked upon a military career, while Harlan, the younger, was sixteen. He had been reared in his grandfather's gloomy old house where séances and ghost raisings were an almost nightly occurrence. As a consequence, he was a nervous, sensitive boy who suffered from frequent nightmares. He was, unfortunately, the one to discover his mother's body after she had been dead a number of hours, and the horror of the experience threw him into a brain fever.

When he recovered, his brother had just received his commission and was leaving for India. The doctors felt that a long ocean voyage would be good for Harlan, so he was taken along. The original plan was for the younger boy to return by the next boat to England and enter school, but India seems to have had a strange fascination for him. He refused to leave, and when his brother tried to force him, he ran away and was gone for almost two years.

When he reappeared he had learned two or three Indian dialects and brought such valuable information about the hill tribes, with whom he had been living, that the Government took him into its employ. In some manner, never clearly defined, he was connected with the Indian Intelligence Service for over twenty years.

From here on the Colonel's information about his brother became extremely sketchy. There seems to have been some sort of estrangement, or it may be that the Colonel's marriage and his wife's death, which left him with a baby girl, occupied his attention.

All that the Colonel was able to tell me was that Harlan Grant spent a good deal of his time studying Hindu philosophy and metaphysics. He was, even then, groping through darkness for some ray of light on the subject of the soul after death. The two brothers seem to have made up their quarrel, or come together again about 1920. Harlan had been ill and was ordered to leave India; the Colonel had just resigned his commission and was anxious to take his daughter away from the mission-school where she had been reared. They joined forces and started for California, intending to stay there until Grant's health improved. Something about San Francisco appealed to them; after six months they agreed that they had no real ties binding them to England, and they would make the city their home.

Two years later Chanda met and married a German chemist named Otto Steeb. The family being too large for one house, the brothers bought adjoining residences on Russian Hill. Later, Dr. Herbert Waverly, an old friend from India, came for a visit and ended by purchasing the third house on the hill.

Here my notes on Harlan Grant came to an abrupt end. You will remember I was making them at the desk in Grant's study while Jimmy Lane went through the filing cabinet. My effort, at first, was to keep the Colonel occupied, but as he went on, unfolding the story of his brother's life in India, I forgot my purpose. A little of the sketchy short-hand which I had used for college notes and still employ in moments of stress, came back to me and the even flow of his narrative was unbroken. He enjoyed, I think, remi-niscing about old times and the strange mad life his broth-er had led in the Orient.

"I'm not saying he was cracked, mind you. There may have been a lot in what he found out over there. I've seen things I couldn't explain, myself. Ropes thrown into the air—and boys shinning up 'em like monkeys; flower-pots that blossomed in front of your eyes, and snakes that danced to music. 'Tricks', I always said. But I don't know . . . I don't know. . . ."

He broke off and glanced over his shoulder, almost fearfully. We had been talking so long that the afternoon light had faded, and the distant parts of the room were shrouded in shadow; only the great mirror still reflected a bit of blood-red sky.

"I've never held with my brother's ghost raising," he said. "Just the same, there have been times in this room when I've felt . . . well, hanged if I haven't felt *something* that put my back up."

"You mean," Jimmy spoke softly, and I realized he had left his files and come over to the desk, "you mean you've felt the 'fear of fear'?"

It was only a random shot, but it struck its mark. The Colonel swung about with an expletive. "What made you ask that?" he demanded.

"Oh," Jimmy shrugged with slightly exaggerated casualness, "something I found in the files. . . . The words struck me as a good description of your feelings."

For a moment the Colonel was silent; his hands were clasped on the head of his stick and, in the fading light from the window, his knuckles showed white. When he spoke it was with obvious effort.

"That was an expression of my brother's. I've never heard anyone else use it. Coming from you it was a bit of a shock."

"Do you know what he meant by it?"

"No; at least, not exactly. One day last week I was up in this room talking to Harlan about some business . . . I handled all his affairs, you know. After a moment I realized he was not listening to me at all. He was sitting with his head tilted back, looking into the air above my head. I tried to call his attention to the matter in hand, but instead of listening, he asked me a question."

"What was it?"

"He asked me if I had ever felt a fear of fear."

"Is that all?" Jimmy inquired eagerly.

"No; it isn't. Before I could answer he grabbed my arm and cried out, 'That's what killed mother.'"

"And then?"

"That was all." (For the life of me I couldn't tell whether the Colonel was lying or not.) "He suddenly seemed to come to himself and went back to the business in hand."

"Have you any idea what he meant about your mother?"

"Not the slightest—unless it was the fact that her face, after death, was twisted into an expression of horror. I understand that frequently happens in apoplexy, and my brother was, unfortunately, the one to find her. A boy is naturally impressed by an experience of the sort. As I've just told Mr. Carter, he was a sensitive, hysterical type, when he was young."

"Did he outgrow it?"

"Entirely," said the Colonel decisively. "In later years he was one of the sanest and most unemotional men I've ever known, although lately . . ." He paused and shook his head. "I'll have to admit, the last few weeks he seemed a trifle upset about something."

"I wonder," Jimmy asked, "if you can remember anything about that day you talked together, the time he spoke of the 'fear of fear'? Did you notice anything unusual in the room, anything that might account for the state of mind?"

The Colonel shook his head. "No; nothing. Hold on, I did notice something—although I laid it to my imagination at the time—there was a distinct odor of jasmine in the room."

"Jasmine!" Jimmy exclaimed, but before he could ask more there was a noise at the door, and a sudden flare of light.

Insensibly the room had grown darker while we talked, until, at the moment of the interruption, we were in almost total blackness. Now the shaded lamps blossomed into light, and the shock was so great that it was almost like a physical blow. I was still blinking, half-blinded, when Singh spoke from the door.

"Captain Hemming to see you, sar."

And almost immediately a second voice:

"Sorry to disturb you, Colonel, but I'm the Chief of the Detective Bureau. I've come to see you about your brother's murder."

CHAPTER 5
THE BOLTED DOOR

If the Chief had intended to startle the Colonel by the suddenness of this announcement, his success was complete. For a perceptible interval the man stood, apparently stricken, the color of his face slowly changing from a healthy tan to a pasty white.

"My brother . . . did you say my brother's . . . murder?"

"I did. A post-mortem has been performed and the doctors report that he did not die a natural death."

The Colonel's face lost its unnatural pallor and flushed angrily. "By God, sir! You had the impudence to perform a post-mortem without notifying me?"

"It was not necessary to notify anyone. No death certificate should have been issued in the first place. The whole thing was most irregular."

The Colonel's temper was rising, and he was evidently upon the verge of exploding into one of his tirades when Jimmy saved the day. "I don't see anything irregular about it," he remarked. "Mr. Grant's own physician had warned him he was working too hard and would come a cropper if he didn't lay off. I should say he was quite justified in issuing the certificate."

The Chief glanced up, annoyed by the interruption, but something in Jimmy's eyes must have conveyed a message, for he held his peace.

The Colonel had recovered his composure. "May I ask how the doctors arrived at their idiotic conclusion?"

"You may. The post-mortem showed that there was no hemorrhage of the apoplexy type. The only blood clot was caused by a fracture at the base of the skull."

"The doctors think it was the fracture that killed him?"

"They're equally divided. Two of them believe it was responsible. The other two think it occurred at the instant of death . . . that his head struck something when he fell to the floor."

"And the cause of the death?" Jimmy was leaning forward eagerly.

"They were still trying to determine when I left. As soon as they decided the death wasn't natural, I came to have a look around. McCarthy is to bring word when they come to some conclusion." He turned to the Colonel. "Was it you who found your brother's body?"

"Singh and I together. We weren't surprised when he didn't appear at breakfast because he frequently worked all night and slept until noon. There's an electric bell on the desk which rings downstairs in Singh's room next door. It was understood that my brother was not to be disturbed until he rang. But, when he did not appear at lunch, we called him, and when he did not answer, we forced the door and found him on the floor . . . just back of those curtains."

Jimmy left the desk and walked with Captain Hemming to the other end of the room. For a moment he stood studying the velvet hangings which depended from dim rafters overhead, the great mirror in its frame of ornate gilt, and the heavily carpeted floor.

"Show us where you found him," Captain Hemming requested, and the Colonel complied.

"He was here . . . his feet toward the room, his head close to the base of that standing lamp." He was pointing to a tall wrought-iron affair which stood just inside the curtains.

The Chief examined the claw-footed base and nodded thoughtfully. "That could account for the fracture all right, if it struck at the base of his skull. Was he lying on his back?"

"Not exactly. His whole body was twisted as though by a convulsion. His knees were drawn up and his neck was strained back. His hands were clutching the bottoms of the curtains and his face—" The Colonel broke off and passed his hand over his eyes as though blotting out some sight. "His face was horrible."

"There was nothing anywhere about that seemed out of place? I mean, nothing which might have been used as a weapon?"

"No . . . yes, by Jove, there was! That stone god was lying on its side." He was pointing to a small crudely-carved figure of East Indian design which stood on a table under the lamp. From a little teak-wood shrine it grinned out at us with a vacant derision which was horrible, somehow, when one thought of what had passed before its staring, painted eyes.

Captain Hemming picked it up and hefted it appraisingly. "It could have been used," he said, "It's light enough to be easily handled, but heavy enough to do damage."

"Yes," Jimmy remarked, "it might have been used. At the same time, it's not particularly well balanced, and that table is close beside where Grant fell. It might just as easily have been overturned by his convulsion. However, it won't do any harm to have it gone over for fingerprints."

"Mine will probably appear," the Colonel pointed out. "I was the one who picked it up and put it back in the shrine."

"We'll count you out," Jimmy promised and, replacing the figure on the table, moved toward the center of the room. "You say the door was locked when you found your brother?"

"Yes; on the inside." The Colonel walked to the door and opened it. "As you see, there's no lock, in the usual sense of the word, just this bolt, which could only be operated from the inside. When we broke in, we tore it loose from the casing . . . the way you see it now."

"Any other way of getting into the room?"

"Absolutely none. That big window is built into the wall, while those ventilators up there are too small for a child to climb through—even if they weren't a good forty feet from the ground outside."

"Were they closed when you came in?"

"They were just as you see them now. Three closed and one open."

Captain Hemming dismissed the subject and started on another. "Did your brother have any enemies? Anyone who'd ever made a threat against his life?"

The Colonel considered for a moment, then shook his head. "No one I can call to mind. But he might have had contacts with people I knew nothing about. His work was of a private nature."

"So I've heard," the Chief observed dryly, "and I fancy he might have known a good deal about different people's affairs . . . more than they thought was healthy, perhaps."

"It's possible, but, in that case, I'd have known nothing about it. I managed his money but I never touched the occult side of his life."

"Didn't believe in it, eh?"

"Didn't believe in it," agreed the Colonel. He paused a moment and his eyes shifted quickly about the room. "But I must say the whole thing's a bit eerie."

"You mean," said Jimmy quickly, "that you believe there's something supernatural about his death?"

The Colonel looked confused. "Well, I wouldn't exactly say that, but you can see for yourself that no one could have got into this room—" He broke off as Singh entered with a short, heavy-set chap in a check suit and tie of vivid green.

"This is Sergeant McCarthy," the Chief told us, "one of my best men. I've assigned him to this case."

The Sergeant nodded amiably and I saw that he knew Jimmy, for he added a grin and an Irish twinkle of the eye to his nod. "I might have guessed you'd beat us to it, Mr. Lane. You've got a nose like a bird dog for murders!"

The Chief was speaking to the Colonel. "You can go back to your house now. If we want you again I'll send word." The little nod with which he ended the speech, though friendly enough, was a distinct dismissal and, for a moment, it looked as though the other would answer angrily, but with an effort he controlled himself, walked to the door and disappeared.

McCarthy waited until his footsteps had died away before he spoke. "The post-mortem's finished, Captain, and the doctors agree that Grant died a violent death all right, but they don't know as they'll ever be able to say for sure just how he was bumped off."

"But, good Lord!" Jimmy exclaimed, "that's absurd."

"Not as absurd as you think," the Chief explained. "The body was embalmed before we got hold of it and the only evidence left by certain poisons is a blood change. In an embalmed body all the blood has been removed and there is nothing for the toxicologists to work on."

"But I thought he died from a blow on his head."

"Two of the docs think he did," McCarthy said. "The others think he was killed by some poison and his skull was fractured when he fell."

"Isn't it possible to determine from the blood clot whether the hemorrhage occurred before or after death?"

"Sure it would be as a general thing, but if it was some poison that caused a convulsion, he might have fallen and cracked his head a minute before he died."

"I see." Jimmy's eyes were thoughtfully ranging the room. "Of course, the poison theory would account for the locked door. If it was slow in its action he would've had time to lock himself in before he felt its effects."

"But in the case of a slow poison, he'd have called for help when he began to feel sick," I objected. "There's not only a telephone but there's that electric bell which rings next door."

The Chief agreed with me. "I'll have a chemical analysis of the stomach made, of course; but, personally, I don't hold with the poison theory. I think he was struck on the head."

"Sure he was," agreed McCarthy, "and that Stoddard guy's the one who socked him!"

"Perhaps," Captain Hemming was plainly doubtful, "but I'll be hanged if I can see any reason for his doing it. He doesn't seem to have had any connection with Grant. However, we may find one when we get hold of him." He addressed McCarthy: "I'll show you where the body was found. Later you can have Singh and the Colonel up here and put them through a course of sprouts, but I'd like to go over the case with you before I leave."

As the two crossed the room and disappeared behind the velvet curtains I turned to Jimmy. "Did you find those papers in the files?"

"No; I never thought for a moment I would after the Colonel said he'd gone through everything."

"What are you going to do now?"

"You may be surprised at what I'm going to do," Jimmy told me grimly, and before I could question him the Chief returned with McCarthy.

"I'll send up the fingerprint men," he said, "but I doubt if you'll get anything at this late date."

"Me, too." The Sergeant's voice was rueful. "I sure hate these cases where everything's been straightened around. It's like trying to eat cold stew." The telephone on the desk rang stridently, and he turned to answer it. As he listened his face expressed, first astonishment, then delight. A moment later he hung up the receiver and turned to Hemming.

"Well, Captain, I guess Stoddard's guilty, all right. When they went to pick him up at his hotel in Pasadena they found he'd skipped out less than an hour before and they haven't found a trace of him. But the aviator who brought him up from the south, fellow named Hanson, has sure given us aplenty to go on. Says Stoddard came tearing into his aerodrome in Los Angeles about six o'clock Monday night and wanted to fly up here, top speed. They landed around nine, and Stoddard said he'd want to go back that same night, but he didn't know just when, so Hanson was to get his supper and be ready to start any minute. Well, Hanson did as he was ordered, and along about twelve-thirty Stoddard came skidding into the aerodrome in a taxi. He climbed into the 'plane and told Hanson to start right off."

"I don't see anything very damaging in that." Jimmy spoke casually, but I suspected he was more worried than he cared to admit. "It was after midnight and if I had three hours of flying ahead of me before I could get to bed I'd be in a hurry, too."

"Yeah?" McCarthy drawled. "Well, answer me these. Why did he order Hanson not to tell anyone he was in town? And why'd he go to a hotel instead of to his house?"

"You're sure of that?" the Chief asked quickly.

"Dead sure. They been checking up at Headquarters and they've found he took a room at the St. Francis. But he didn't sleep there. Just freshened up, put in a couple of phone calls and left."

"They're tracing the calls?"

"Sure. One was to some apartment hotel. The other was to this phone right here."

There was an interval of silence, and I saw that Jimmy was weighing some problem in his mind; evidently it was a difficult one for he turned, walked away toward the great window and stood looking out over the city below. After a moment he swung back.

"Look here, I think I'll tell you something about Stoddard. It's betraying a confidence, so I'm going to ask you to do me a favor in return."

"What's the favor?" the Chief asked warily.

"It's this: if I tell you something which makes it look as though Stoddard is guilty—guilty as hell—will you promise not to arrest him until you have absolute proof? I mean proof, not only of his motive, but of just how he committed the murder?"

The Chief considered, then he nodded. "All right. But it's understood that as soon as we locate Stoddard we'll keep him under surveillance, and if he tries to clear out, we're free to make the arrest."

"That's O.K.," Jimmy agreed. "I only want to fix it so that the newspapers don't get word of his connections with the case and, also," he grinned affectionately at the Chief, "so that you won't make a fool of yourself . . . as you undoubtedly will if I let you go off half-cocked."

"Thanks," grimly, "I'm waiting for your revelation."

For the space of five minutes Jimmy talked. At first I hoped that I was mistaken. Surely he would not betray Norah's confidence and retail her story to the police! But after a moment I saw, with sickening clarity, that he was doing just that. Everything she had recounted, the story of her girlhood, the story of her rise to fame, of her visits to Grant, and her secret engagement to Stoddard—all were re-told. He even, in some uncanny fashion, managed to echo the tones of her voice, convey her little tricks of expression, until I could close my eyes and see her again, sitting in front of the study fire and pouring out her story to Jimmy in whose honor she foolishly trusted. The thought was so infuriating that I could have struck him as he went on recounting, to the last detail, her troubles with Grant and her fears for her lover.

"Of course, when she found out he had been up here the very night of the murder she was terrified and tried to take back everything she had told us," he ended. "You can easily see why."

"Sure, I see. I also see why you were so generous about passing on the information. You know darned well we'd unearth it for ourselves just as soon as we traced that second phone call."

"Go to the head of the class," Jimmy chuckled. "But I beat you to it, and got your promise not to molest Stoddard."

"Good Lord, man, you don't expect me to leave him at large after all you've told me? Why, it's practically an airtight case."

"That so?" Jimmy picked up a pen at the desk. "If it's so clear, suppose you state it, and I'll put it down on paper."

"Wait a minute." The Chief closed his eyes and considered, then began dictating in short, crisp sentences:

"*1. Grant is threatening Norah Fallon.*

"*2. Stoddard is in love with the girl.*

"*3. He learns of the threats and comes to see Grant.*

"*4. They are heard quarreling as late as eleven-fifteen.*

"*5. The doctors state that Grant's death occurred about midnight.*

"6. *Stoddard arrives at the aerodrome at twelve-thirty.*

"7. *He has previously given orders that his presence in the city should not be made known, and avoided his own residence.*"

Hemming stopped dictating and struck his hand on the desk. "By George! The more I get into it, the clearer it is."

"That so?" Jimmy was regarding the paper with a little twisted grin. "Well, if I thought the case was clear against him you can bet your bottom dollar I'd never have told you what I did."

"You mean you think Stoddard didn't do it?"

"I mean I *know* Stoddard didn't do it."

"But how can you possibly know that?" The Chief was leaning forward across the desk and behind him, like a faithful shadow, McCarthy duplicated his pose, except that the worthy Sergeant's mouth was half-open. Regarding the two, a little dancing light came into Jimmy's eyes, a light I knew of old.

"I know he isn't guilty," he said solemnly, "because that solution of the murder wouldn't match the background."

"What?" The Chief was staring at him, bewildered, and Jimmy waved his hand toward the walls of the room.

"*Regardez vous.* The perfect setting . . . a séance room. Haunted by the spirits of the departed. Darkness. Mystery. A man murdered at midnight. Everything arranged for a ghost story. And you ask me to accept a commonplace solution revolving around blackmail! No; it won't do, I tell you. It'd be a sheer waste of gorgeous material."

"Are you telling me," the Chief's voice showed plaintive indignation, "that Grant was murdered by *spooks?*"

For a moment Jimmy's eyes lost their humor and his voice, when he answered, was grave. "I don't want to say what I think, as yet. The things I feel are all vague and shadowy. But if you'll let me go on with my investigations I may be able to tell you more . . . later."

McCarthy snorted. "Well, while you're ghost hunting, Mr. Lane, I'll get busy and dig up a few clues that'll tell us just how this Stoddard guy pulled the thing off."

Jimmy had risen and was gathering together the scattered sheets of my notes from the desk. "If you really want to solve this murder, Mac, take my advice and don't depend on the fingerprints and hairpin variety of clues. Look for something more intangible."

"Such as?"

"Such as," Jimmy glanced about, then smiled wickedly at the Sergeant, "such as the faint, elusive fragrance of jasmine."

Chapter 6
Dick Stoddard Tells His Story

"Just what did you mean by that idiocy about jasmine?" I asked. We were in Jimmy's car on our way down the hill, and the cobblestones were jolting even that marvel of upholstered softness.

In the half-light of a passing street lamp, Jimmy grinned at me. "Don't try to talk now," he admonished. "You're tired, you're hungry—and you've got a mad on. Oh, don't try to hide it. I know you'd like to choke me for giving Norah away."

"Really," Jimmy was right about the hunger, and in spite of every attempt to keep crossness out of my voice, it would creep in, "I must say you haven't much idea of honor."

"Not the slightest," he agreed cheerfully, "when it's a question of common-sense. Norah will probably try to murder me with the nearest paper-knife when she hears what I've done, but I think after you've had your dinner, and she's had a moment to think it over, you'll both agree it was the best thing to do."

"I don't see why. Even if the police were bound to find everything out, it would have taken them a day or so. Now that they know it, the poor fellow hasn't a ghost of a chance."

Jimmy was silent, and I thought he was regretting his rashness, but no, he was merely hunting for a cigarette.

"The trouble with you," he said at last, "and with Norah, too, is that you both think Stoddard is guilty."

For a moment I sat stunned at the realization, for, of course, he was right . . . at least so far as I was concerned. While I wrestled with the thought, Jimmy continued blithely. "Now me . . . I don't think Stoddard killed Grant, and I've a funny old-fashioned conviction that truth will out. Therefore, I don't in the least mind telling all the damning things I know about an innocent man."

"You're going to have a fine time convincing the police that he's innocent."

"I'm going to let 'em convince themselves. So long as they were bloodhounds, hot on the trail of facts, they'd be sure he was guilty. Now that I've saved them the trouble of digging up his motive, there's nothing left for them to do except concentrate on how he did the fell deed—and that's going to keep them very, very busy for the next twenty-four hours."

The car made a sudden turn and I glanced out of the window, then stared at Jimmy. "Where are we going?" I demanded. "This isn't the way to your house."

"No; it's the way to the dock. We're going out to the Wanderlust."

"What?" (The Wanderlust is Jimmy's yacht. Not the usual white-and-gold affair, but a sturdy little craft in which he prowls up and down the coast and out to the islands when the spirit moves him.) "I thought you'd let the Deans take her south."

"I did, but they got back to-night, and there's somebody on board I want to see."

Before I could ask any more questions the car had nosed its way down a side street to the channel; a launch was waiting, and five minutes later we climbed the ship's ladder and were on deck. The Deans were on shore, the skipper told us. The other guests were in the cabin, below. As we passed down the companionway I saw a little grin on Jimmy's face, and was not unprepared for the sight of Norah Fallon and a tall, good-looking young chap whom I recognized at once as Dick Stoddard. The two were already shaking Jimmy's hand and Norah was looking up at him gratefully.

"You're a genius," she declared. "Dick got away without a soul finding out."

"Thought he would," said Jimmy. "The Deans are a smart pair, and the wireless I sent 'em was a work of art, if I do say so."

Stoddard was speaking for the first time. His fair, wavy hair was rumpled and his eyes snapped with excitement. There was a frank boyishness about him that made him strangely likeable.

"It wasn't a patch on the message you sent me," he declared. "And it didn't come a minute too soon! I got out of the hotel just one jump ahead of the police."

I suppose Jimmy read disapproval in my face, for he grinned. "Carter, here, is shocked," he said. "He doesn't approve of assisting fugitives from justice. If he'd lived in the days of Torquemada he'd have handed his own grandmother over to the Inquisition if he thought it was required by law."

Jimmy always manages to make me look like a fussy maiden aunt, but I felt bound to protest. "I must say I don't think Mr. Stoddard has helped his case by disappearing in this fashion. You, yourself, heard the police cite it as an evidence of guilt."

Norah gave a little cry, but Jimmy raised his hand. "Don't let that upset you. In their present hysteria, the police would cite *anything* if only in hopes of making it stick. As it happens, I have a particular reason for wanting to see Stoddard before the minions of the law begin third and fourth degreeing him."

"You don't mean he's going to be arrested!" Norah cried, aghast.

"I don't believe so, but they're sure to want to talk with him. He'd better go to Captain Hemming of his own accord. I have the Chief's word that he won't bring any charges until they find conclusive evidence."

"Which they won't," said Stoddard promptly.

"Of course not," Norah seconded, and I saw that whatever doubts she may have entertained in regard to her fiancé had been set at rest. "Dick's been telling me what happened, and when you hear the story you'll see how perfectly asinine the whole thing is."

"Suppose you tell us while we eat," Jimmy suggested to Stoddard. "I've ordered the steward to serve a bite of dinner down here. Carter and I are famished."

"I'll be glad to," Stoddard said cheerfully, and while we pitched into our food he sat at the table and talked.

The information he gave us tallied so closely with Norah's that it is not necessary to set it all down. He had been attending a meeting of astronomers in Pasadena for three or four days; but on returning to his hotel, Monday afternoon, he found a letter in his mail from Harlan Grant. He knew, of course, that Norah had been consulting the fellow from time to time and had regarded it as something of a joke, but the letter was so full of veiled insinuations that he was brought up short.

"You saved the letter?" Jimmy asked quickly.

"Yes; it's in my suitcase. It won't tell you much. He merely hinted that he knew a lot of things about Norah's past life which were . . . well, discreditable." He paused and threw a quick little smile at the girl. "We've just had a heart-to-heart talk in which she's told me the whole thing.

It's absurd, of course, that the fellow should think it would make any difference to me."

"Of course," Jimmy agreed. "What did you do after receiving the letter?"

"I tried, first, to get Norah long distance, but she was out on location with her company, shooting some scenes, and nobody knew what time she'd be back. When I couldn't make connections, I decided the thing to do was to pile into an aeroplane and fly north. That would give me time to see this Grant fellow and probably Norah, then get back for a talk I had to give at the conference next day. So I chartered a 'plane and landed up here around nine p.m."

"Why'd you tell the aviator to keep quiet?"

"Because I didn't want the reporters on my trail. Norah and I were determined not to have a lot of silly chatter about our getting married, but we've got that confounded pearl necklace in our family, the one that's supposed to be given to every Stoddard bride, and I've got just enough fool sentiment to want her to have it. I hauled the thing out of the safety deposit last week to have it furbished up, and some sleuth-hound from the *Chronicle* got wind of it. I wasn't in any state of mind Monday night to give out sentimental interviews so I told the aviator to keep his mouth shut."

"And took a room at the St. Francis," Jimmy supplemented.

"Yes; and after I'd washed up, I tried to get Norah. She was still out and her maid didn't have any idea when she'd be back. If I'd known she'd gone to Grant's I'd have barged right up there, but when I phoned his house they told me he was having a séance and wouldn't be free until around eleven. So I had a bit of supper, and landed at his place about eleven-fifteen."

"Did you see anyone?"

"Only a spooky sort of Hindu who let me in."

"Singh," said Jimmy quickly. "Anyone else?"

"Nobody. Hold on! I did pass a woman on the stairs, a grey-haired flibbertigibbet sort of person who'd apparently been at the séance."

"Probably the nut Corrigan spoke of," Jimmy observed. "The one who heard you quarreling. Tell us exactly what happened when you talked with Grant."

Stoddard ran his fingers through his fair, curly hair, until it stood up on end, and grinned ruefully.

"I'm afraid nothing happened. I'd gone up there intending to punch the fellow on the jaw, but, hang it all, he wasn't the sort you could handle that way. I blustered at him a minute or two about blackmail and he let me get it all out of my system, then, cool as you please, invited me to sit down and talk it over. He protested that he wasn't blackmailing . . . just trying to help out. Some information about Norah's past had been brought to him by an entire stranger. Said it sometimes happens that crooks who didn't know his character and took him for the usual type of medium, brought him extraneous bits of information about celebrities and offered to sell them to him. Usually he threw them out, but he happened to be fond of Norah, in a nice fatherly way, and the stuff that had been brought to him was so raw that he felt something ought to be done about it. The fellow who had it in his hands would be just as likely to try to sell it elsewhere. As Norah's natural protector, he was appealing to me."

"Darn clever," said Jimmy.

"Wasn't it beautiful? Especially when you consider that the stuff was all in the room at that very moment."

"How do you know?"

"Because I saw it," Norah broke in. "He showed it to me when I was up there earlier in the evening."

"H'm." Jimmy was thoughtful. "How did the interview end?"

"Perfectly amicably. I explained I had to be in Pasadena in the morning and couldn't stop to dicker with his blackmailing friend. He promised to see the fellow and keep him quiet until I got back. In the meantime, he was to keep any word of this from getting to Norah. Naturally, I didn't want her worried."

"And all the time he was using the same stuff to try and make me marry him!" Norah exclaimed.

"Playing both ends to the middle," Jimmy mused. "He counted on your not saying anything to Stoddard and his keeping his mouth shut with you." He shook his head admiringly. "I'm sorry I didn't know that chap. He must have been a corker!"

"He was," Stoddard agreed. "Don't know when I've met anyone half so brilliant. After I'd blown up and cooled off, we really got quite friendly. The fellow showed a remarkable grasp of astronomical details . . . the sort of thing very few people understand. My particular line is light, you know and Grant seemed to have made a special study of what he called 'vibronica' both in relation to light and to sound. He'd worked out a fantastic theory about personality, or I suppose you'd call it the 'soul'."

"Can you tell me what it was?" Jimmy inquired.

"I'm afraid I can't give it to you as clearly or concisely as he stated it, but in a general way it was this; every one of us is composed of a body which is merely a chemical combination, easily reducible to recognizable elements. But inside of this tangible structure is something not so easily explained. It is this ego, this entity, which we, for want of something better, call the 'soul'. Grant contended that this 'soul' was nothing but a vibration, set up by some power which has never been clearly defined but has been recognized by every race of man under various names. God. Allah. Jehovah. He believed that this vibration, once set in motion, continues at its own particular velocity, and that velocity is what constitutes personality."

"You mean that no two people vibrate at the same rate, I suppose," Jimmy observed. "I've heard a similar theory."

"Yes; it's not new. But Grant had added a few frills. He told me he'd been experimenting for years on some method of catching these 'entity vibrations'

and transforming them into recognizable form. Just as sound and light waves are transformed in the radio and motion-picture."

"How did all this strike you?" Jimmy inquired. "Like a line of patter, or do you think he really meant it?"

Stoddard looked puzzled. "Hanged if I know. The fellow certainly was glib, but I couldn't help feeling he more or less believed the stuff. I could tell you more about it if a funny change hadn't come over him."

Jimmy glanced at me and I saw he was excited. "What sort of a change?"

"It's hard to describe. He'd been very keen while we were talking, but suddenly he got absent-minded. It was perfectly plain he wasn't thinking about what he was saying . . . and it was almost as though he were listening for something. I realized it was nearly midnight and that the man was probably tired and sleepy. So I reached for my hat."

"What did he do?"

"Rather clung to me; seemed to dread being left alone, but I told him the 'plane was waiting and I had to go."

"Was anything more said about Norah?"

"Not a thing. He seemed to have forgotten her entirely. But just as I got to the door he said a funny thing. I'd stopped long enough to tell him I was interested in his theories about the after-life, and that I had some ideas of my own—from a scientific angle, of course. We'd discuss it when I came back. He looked at me quickly and said, 'Yes, yes. That's what I want—a scientific explanation. There must be one, you know.'"

"Is that all he said?"

"Yes; all except 'good night'."

"You're sure he didn't say anything about the fear of fear?"

"The 'fear of fear'? No. Why should he?"

"No reason." Jimmy disposed of the subject and mused for a moment, then: "Did you meet anyone on your way out?"

"No one. Grant was going to take me to the door but I told him I could find my way. The fellow looked so exhausted I didn't like taking him down all those flights."

"Would it have been possible for there to have been another person in the house without your knowing it?"

"Why, yes, I should think so. There are three or four rooms on the second floor and some of the doors were closed. Almost anyone might have been hidden about the place. . . . But they couldn't have got at Grant. At least, not unless he'd wanted them to. After I left the room he closed the door and I distinctly heard him slide the bolt."

"H'm." Jimmy was thoughtful. "That would argue that the murderer was someone Grant knew and was on good terms with, since he admitted the fellow himself."

"I suppose so. But he must have had some premonition of trouble because if ever a man looked worried he did."

"How could the murderer have killed him, then got out of the room leaving the door bolted on the inside?" Norah asked.

"That's what I mean to find out." Jimmy rose to his feet. "To-morrow I'm going over every inch of that room."

"What are your orders for me?" Stoddard asked.

"You'd better sleep on board. We'll take Norah along with us and drop her at her hotel. To-morrow morning you might wander into Headquarters and give yourself up to the police."

"They won't twist his arms or give him the water cure?" Norah asked anxiously, and Jimmy laughed.

"You've been acting in too many movies. They're much more likely to offer him a nip of hooch and a good cigar."

Stoddard had been helping Norah into her coat; and now she turned and offered her lips to him quite frankly.

Jimmy grabbed my arm and dragged me up the companionway. "Now that," he said, "is what I call a profitable hour. I've learned a lot!" His voice was full of satisfaction, and I saw that he was smiling happily as he strode across the deck.

"You mean that Stoddard convinced you he didn't do it?"

"I was always sure of that. The thing I learned is that the Colonel wasn't lying about everything he told us."

Rapidly I ran back over the Colonel's words. "Oh, you mean about Grant's absent-mindedness?"

"Exactly. And all that stuff about his theories of the here and hereafter are important, too."

"But, good Lord," I protested, "you're not taking that stuff seriously? Why, the man was an admitted charlatan, little better than a blackmailer. All his talk about spirits must have been just his line of chatter."

For a moment Jimmy did not answer; he was standing by the rail looking out over the water where a thin veil of mist rendered the distant shore dim and ghostly. The tide was slipping along through the darkness with a soft whisper that was like suppressed sobbing, and somewhere, far off, a child or a dog was sending up a thin, persistent wail. He raised his hand and indicated the sound.

"That's a vibration," he said, "muffled because it has to find its way to us through the fog; and the sound of the water is deadened, too. How do we know Grant wasn't right in his idea that our essential selves are just vibrations?

Perhaps the souls of the dead are trying to make contacts with us and are held back by malign influences, or our own stupidity. And perhaps sometimes, when the conditions are exactly right, they do manage to break through."

"You mean you think Grant was murdered by a spook?" I was beginning when Stoddard appeared with Norah.

"I count on you to keep the police away from this girl," he told Jimmy.

"I think I can promise that. Of course, there's bound to be a little questioning about the hours she spent Monday night with Grant, but otherwise I believe they'll let her alone."

Stoddard shook his hand gratefully, and Jimmy was already half-way down the ladder toward the launch when he suddenly remembered something and called back. "There's one thing I forgot to ask. Did you notice any odor in the room that night when you were talking to Grant?"

"Odor? I don't think I know what you mean. We were both smoking, and the place smelled more or less of tobacco."

"That's not it." Jimmy waited while Stoddard crinkled his forehead in thought.

"Wait! Now you speak of it, I do remember something. Toward the end of the visit there was sort of a fragrance in the room. I spoke of it to Grant."

"Yes?" Jimmy glanced up quickly. "What did he say?"

"He looked at me in a funny way and said, 'Do you mean that you can smell it, too.' I told him I smelled it plainly, that it must be coming in from the garden."

"Why did you think it came from a garden?"

"Because, for some reason, it made me think of our garden at home."

"You don't know what reason?"

"No; I'm hanged if I do."

Norah stood up suddenly in the stern of the boat. "I bet I know why," she said. "It's because of that arbor by the pool . . . the one that's covered with jasmine."

CHAPTER 7
A VISIT TO HEADQUARTERS

It was midnight by the time we had dropped Norah at her apartment and reached Jimmy Lane's house. Instead of going sensibly to bed he insisted upon brewing strong coffee and sitting up before the fire in the study. While I wrote out the brief sketch of Harlan Grant's life which was given in the last chapter, he rearranged the notes he had been taking all day into coherent form. So many things had happened in the last twenty-four hours that I was mentally hazy and his brief recapitulation served to clarify things in my mind. For that reason I shall give it here:

Tuesday noon, November 15th
Harlan Grant, one of the most successful mediums in the West, is found dead in his séance room.

The body is discovered by his brother, Colonel Grant, and his East Indian servant, Singh, who have come to find out why he has not appeared at lunch.

The séance room occupies the entire third story of the house. There are no windows which can be opened and the only door is bolted so firmly upon the inside that the Colonel and Singh are forced to break it open.

Grant is found lying dead at the end farthest from the door behind a couple of long velvet curtains which cut off about a quarter of the room. He is on the floor close beside an iron lamp and a table with a small but heavy image of carved stone lying overturned upon it. His face is twisted into an expression of intense horror.

Dr. Waverly, an old friend who lives in the second house above, is called and issues a certificate giving the time of the death as around midnight Monday; the cause, apoplexy. He had been expecting something of the sort and repeatedly warned Grant that he was in danger of a stroke.

The body is removed to an undertaking establishment, where the undertaker discovers a fracture at the base of the skull. An autopsy is ordered.

Tuesday afternoon
The police start an investigation and discover that the last person to be seen with Grant Monday night was Dick Stoddard, a wealthy young astronomer who is supposed to be in Pasadena, but has come up to San Francisco in an aeroplane, remained there three hours, then flown South again.

A member of Grant's séance circle reports hearing Grant and Stoddard quarreling Monday night about eleven-fifteen.

Wednesday afternoon
The doctors report that Grant did not die a natural death, but are unable to agree upon the

cause. Two of them believe he was struck by some blunt instrument at the base of the skull, two others that he was poisoned and the skull was fractured when he fell, against the iron standing lamp. The toxicologists take over the investigation.

Wednesday evening
Stoddard returns via boat to San Francisco and tells his story. He testifies that he was with Grant from eleven-fifteen until twelve Monday night and they quarreled over some papers with which Grant was threatening to blackmail Stoddard's fiancé, Norah Fallon; that they came to an amicable agreement before he left, and that he heard Grant shoot the bolt in the door as he went downstairs.

Both Colonel Grant and Stoddard agree on two things: they state that Grant seemed nervous and worried about something, and that there was odor of jasmine in the room.

Norah Fallon and the Colonel have both got the phrase, "fear of fear", from Grant. In Norah's case it was scrawled on a contract, in the Colonel's it was spoken by Grant himself.

The situation looks bad for Stoddard. The police believe he is guilty of the murder but are holding off from an arrest until they can prove how he managed to murder Grant and yet leave the door bolted on the inside.

The inquest was held the next morning and Jimmy Lane attended it alone. We met at the club for lunch, and he gave me a vivid but not particularly enlightening account of the affair.

"As inquests go, it was a tolerable performance. Not as dressy as some I've attended, but fair to middling. Of course, the doctors all got on the stand and disagreed with each other about what the corpse died of. Two of 'em said it was the blow on the head. The other two politely indicated that they were liars, and claimed it was something mysterious which couldn't be accounted for, possibly some poison which would have shown in the blood if there had been any blood for it to show in. After they got pried loose from each other's throats, the coroner had Singh on the stand, then the Colonel and Stoddard. None of 'em offered anything new or startling."

"So they've dragged Stoddard into the case?"

"Only as a witness . . . the last one to have seen Grant. Just as I told Norah they were so glad to have him show up that they practically kissed him on the brow."

"Do they still think he's guilty?"

"They're too busy running around in circles to think anything. The official mind, Phil is utterly incapable of getting past a locked door. Every time they try to figure out a solution they run up against that brass bolt, and sit down to have a good cry."

"But, hang it all," I protested, "the bolt *is* there. You can't get away from the fact."

Jimmy had reached the dessert stage and was toying with a large wedge of mince-pie which a man of his plumpness had no business to have taken in the first place. He chose to ignore my remarks and finish this, then attacked a double portion of Roquefort cheese and six crackers smeared with butter and mustard. While consuming this devilish mixture, he ruminated aloud.

"You really oughtn't to have missed that inquest, Phil. It would have done your legal soul good. The coroner, twelve good men and true, and at least twenty witnesses spent the entire morning reaching the brilliant conclusion that Grant came to his death by hand, or hands, of person, or persons, unknown; and all of them left apparently feeling that something worthwhile had been accomplished. They might just as well have passed the time playing Ring-around-the-Rosie or Post-office."

"Was the Chief there?"

"No; but we had a chin on the telephone in regard to that beastly envelope full of notes about Norah. He's been darn decent . . . promised he'd let us know if they turn up."

"Where do you think they are?"

Evidently Jimmy had given this some thought for he frowned at his plate. "Hanged if I know. The Colonel may have taken them, of course, when he went through the files. Then again, there's Singh. He was evidently in Grant's confidence, and there may be others that we don't know about. I want to go up to the Chief's office this afternoon and look over a lot of people he's called in."

"Who's going to be there?"

"Waverly, for one. He's the physician who lives in the third house on the hill; queer old chap, they tell me . . . he's almost entirely stopped practicing and is doing research work on some Oriental disease. Grant knew him in India and the Chief hopes to get some dope from him. Then he's going to re-examine Stoddard and Norah."

"Will Chanda Steeb and her husband be there?"

"I doubt it. Steeb's a cripple, I understand, and never leaves the house. Makes you sort of sick to think of that nice-looking girl being tied up to a cripple, doesn't it?"

It did, but before I could express myself, Jimmy went on: "The Chief's also rounded up the gang who were at Grant's séance Monday night, and, from what I saw of 'em this morning, it ought to be as good as a play."

"Did any of them testify at the inquest?"

"Only the Lady Elfrieda. Oh"—at my look of inquiry—"didn't I tell you about her? It's Mrs. Elfrieda Jane Chapman, no less."

"You mean that nut who's always breaking into the papers?"

"I do. She's two-thirds crazy and one-third plain fool . . . just the sort of burbling idiot who'd fall for Grant. She's at the fat and susceptible age, and I gather she was half in love with the fellow. She's dirt rich, you know, and he advised her about investments."

"Did she have any information to give?"

"Lots of it, but it was all so mixed up with 'spirit messages' and sniffles over the 'dear departed' that it was impossible to make anything out. In spite of that, she's done a lot of damage to Stoddard. She was the one who overheard him laying down the law to Grant, and told the police about it."

"Does she actually think he did the murder?"

"No; her information about the quarrel was given purely accidentally. She's sure he didn't do it. She thinks Grant was bumped off by a spook."

"She's just the sort that would," I said disgustedly, but Jimmy shook his head.

"Don't be too smug," he advised. "When you've heard as much as I have, you'll begin to feel more respect for the spook theory."

He finished his infernal crackers, took a final sip of coffee, and accompanied me to the street where his car was waiting. Ten minutes later we were entering Headquarters. The place was like a beehive, or, I should say, a rabbit warren. All of the different conference rooms seemed to be filled with witnesses, segregated after some classification which McCarthy was at haste to explain.

"We got the nuts who went to the séance in there with the newspaper boys," he nodded toward a door. "Stoddard and the girl are down the hall where they won't be seen, and the Captain's got Dr. Waverly in his office. He said you were to go right in."

Captain Hemming greeted us briefly. Evidently he had had a hectic day, for he seemed worn and there was a litter of cigar ash about his chair. Dr. Waverly was sitting across the desk; a slight, sensitive chap, gentle-mannered and with a friendly expression. At present he seemed nervous and distraught, as though the last few days had been too much for him, mentally and physically.

"I've been talking to the doctor here," the Chief explained, "trying to get a line on Grant's past life."

"Were you intimate with him?" Jimmy asked, and the doctor nodded.

"Extremely, probably more so than anyone could understand who's never lived in India. When you're the only whites in a station with nothing but natives, you get very friendly with a man, either that or completely the other thing. At one time, Grant and I lived in the same station. When my wife died, the two of us moved into the same bungalow and we've been together, more or less, ever since."

"Was Grant in the Government service when you knew him?"

"Yes; after a fashion. Most of his time was spent among the natives. He was always interested in mysticism and the occult."

"Did you ever help Grant with any of his séances?"

"I can hardly say I *helped*, although I used to attend a good many of them."

"You believe they were genuine?"

"I know they were genuine," the doctor replied. "Grant often brought back my dead wife and she told me little intimate things that only she could have known. That's the main reason I have stayed near him all these years, so that I should not lose touch with her."

I saw that the Chief was looking annoyed by this conversation, but Jimmy leaned forward eagerly. "What form did the manifestations take?" he asked. "Did you actually see your wife?"

"No," the doctor spoke regretfully, "although he was able to get complete manifestations for a great many people, he was never able to make her visible to me. I could only get a message through his 'control'."

"Wasn't that rather strange?" For the life of me I couldn't help blurting it out. "If he managed to bring back the spirits of people who were strangers he should have been able to bring back someone he knew."

The doctor smiled sadly. "If you had studied spiritualism, Mr. Carter, you wouldn't be surprised. Frequently too great an intimacy makes it difficult rather than easy for a spirit to get through. It's possible that the very intensity of our desire prevented us from succeeding."

The Chief seemed anxious to get the conversation back to a more earthly plane. "Did you know Colonel Grant in India?" he asked.

"No; I never saw the Colonel in India. He and Harlan were at odds for a good many years. Didn't make it up until just before they came to this country."

"Do you know what they quarreled about?"

"It had something to do with the Colonel's marriage. His wife was a foreigner, and Harlan objected to her. Both he and the Colonel had quick tempers and they quarreled violently. Even after Mrs. Grant died they remained at odds until Chanda grew up, and reconciled them."

"Is Mrs. Steeb the Colonel's only child?"

"Yes; she was born in Chanda . . . a place in the center of India. Her mother died when she was a baby and she was brought up in a mission-school—which accounts for her little oddities."

"She's *odd,* is she?" inquired the Chief keenly, and the doctor hastened to explain.

"I've probably used the wrong word. It's just that she's different from most of the young women of to-day."

"What's her husband like?" Jimmy asked.

"Steeb's rather a difficult chap. He's a cripple . . . from infantile paralysis in his youth. It's made him abnormally sensitive and given him a horror of meeting people. He keeps himself shut away for the most part, on the third floor, in his laboratory."

"Just what is his line?"

"Research chemistry. He's been working on a new developing fluid for a company which manufactures motion-picture film. He thinks he's hit on a formula that will save an immense amount of money. I hope he's right because, so far, his work hasn't paid well, and they've had to live off the Colonel, which is difficult for Chanda."

"How on earth did a girl like that happen to marry such a fellow?" I asked. "It seems incredible."

"Not if you knew Chanda. She's the kindest person in the world . . . always bringing home starving dogs and cats to feed and care for. Otto was down and out, and she married him in exactly the same spirit as she'd pick up a maimed animal. She does everything for him—is his nurse, his secretary, and even assists him in his laboratory. Whatever work he accomplishes will be largely due to her. Not that he appreciates the fact. His physical condition has made him egoistical, and he's so insufferably conceited that he's almost impossible to live with."

"The Colonel must adore his son-in-law," Jimmy said ironically.

The doctor smiled. "Well, hardly; they fought like cat and dog the first year, and my friend Harlan sided with his brother. There used to be some pretty fierce encounters among the three of them, but lately they've been more friendly. Harlan confided to me one night that he'd begun to have a great respect for Steeb, really thought he was going to amount to something. I gathered that he and the Colonel contemplated backing him in his researches."

The Chief sighed with disappointment. "I was hoping, from what you first said, that he might have quarreled with Grant and been the one who polished him off."

"They might easily have quarreled," agreed the doctor, "but I'm afraid you'll have to cross him off your list. To my certain knowledge, he has never been in Grant's study. His crippled condition makes it almost impossible for him to get about."

"Who else is living in the two houses?" the Chief asked.

"Only the servants—Singh, and Lalah, his wife. Singh was with Harlan for over twenty years; and, during the time we were stationed in the same district, Lalah used to act as my wife's maid. Now she helps Chanda Steeb around the house. Singh's work was mostly with Grant in his researches, and handling the people who came to the house. He's really a brainy chap and from good people . . . had a year or two at Oxford when he was young. He was more of a secretary than a servant."

"Have you any reason to believe—" the Chief was beginning when the door opened and McCarthy came in apologetically.

"Sorry to bother you, Captain, but that Chapman nut insists on seeing you. Swears it's important."

The Chief sighed. "All right, send her in." And as Dr. Waverly started to rise, he shook his head. "Wait a minute, do you know this Chapman woman?"

"Only as I have met her at the Grants'. She was originally one of Chanda's friends. They were both interested in the question of International Peace, I believe, and got acquainted in that way. Later, Mrs. Chapman became one of Harlan's devotees."

"Do you think she's all there . . . mentally, I mean?"

The doctor chuckled. "I don't believe there's anything actually wrong with her, although she's of a more or less unbalanced type and apt to go to extremes. She was pretty much of a nuisance to Harlan . . . sentimental and all that. Used to use every pretext for hanging around him. He was constantly trying to get rid of her."

"Oh, he was, was he?" I saw that the Chief was interested, but before he could ask anything more the door opened and McCarthy ushered the Lady Elfrieda into the room.

CHAPTER 8
THE LADY ELFRIEDA

The Lady Elfrieda; it was Jimmy, with his fatal propensity for nicknames, that had bestowed the title and, because of its absolute incongruity, it was adopted by us all. She was a dumpy little woman with scrambled hair which wavered uncertainly between red and purple; she smiled perpetually and her voice babbled along in a ceaseless monologue, not quite normal in its incoherence. To hear her talk, everything was "sweet" and "lovely" in this best of all possible worlds, but there was a strained look about her eyes which belied her words. Not quite all on the surface, the Lady Elfrieda, I decided, and difficult to handle. That the Chief and McCarthy shared my opinion I was sure, but Jimmy seemed entranced by the woman. He hung upon her words as though they were precious pearls, encouraging her when the flood of her speech seemed to lessen. Not that she needed encouragement. She was talking steadily when she entered the room, emphasizing every fourth or fifth word irrespective of syntax, and she practically never stopped during the ensuing half-hour.

"Oh, Captain, I've been trying and *trying* to see you, but they simply *wouldn't* let me in—although I explained just how *important* it was—oh, I didn't know you had other people with you! How *do* you do, Dr. Waverly? And this is Mr. Lane, isn't it? They pointed *you* out at the inquest.

I've read practically every *word* you've written and seen *all* your plays, Mr. Lane, and I'd dearly *love* to talk with you some day about some perfectly *splendid* ideas. . . . I've always felt sure I could write if only I had *someone* to put things down for me. I have such *lovely* thoughts to give the world."

The Chief coughed. "No doubt . . . no doubt," he said, "but we haven't time to listen to them now, Mrs. Chapman. I'm extremely busy to-day."

The Lady Elfrieda abruptly switched her attention to him. "You really oughtn't to *allow* your psyche to be thrown out of tune by adverse vibrations, Captain," she said. "Oh, don't try to deny it, I can see that it *is!* You should cultivate a *serene* soul. Three minutes every hour of silent affirmation would do it, only *three* minutes out of each hour."

The Chief's psyche went even more violently out of tune. "Is that what you came in to tell me?" he roared.

"Oh, dear me, *no!* I came in to ask you not to bother that *nice* Mr. Stoddard because of anything I said. If I'd known you were going to take it in such an *unpleasant* way I'd never have said *anything* about his quarrel with Mr. Grant."

"You don't think he did it, eh?" The Chief was watching her keenly, and she shook her head.

"I'm sure he didn't. And I'm sure I know who *did*. Mr. Grant as good as told me the night he was killed."

"He *did?*" This was news with a vengeance; we all followed the Chief's lead and sat forward eagerly as she rambled on:

"Yes; he always *liked* to have me stay after the others had gone, but that night he seemed fearfully upset. I thought at *first* it was because he hadn't been able to get my son."

"Your son?" The Chief was bewildered.

"Yes; Ronald is what the unenlightened call *'dead'* although to me he's just vibrating upon another plane. Mr. Grant *frequently* got me into communication with him."

"You mean you actually *saw* him?" I blurted out.

"Oh, no; Ronald has passed over too recently to be able to get back to the earth plane, but *twice* we obtained materializations of my husband."

"I can testify to that," said Dr. Waverly. "I was present."

"This is all beside the point," snapped the Chief. "I want to know why you think Grant foresaw his own death."

"Oh, not his death, Captain!" the Lady Elfrieda protested. "It was just that he seemed to feel there were *unfriendly* forces around him. I'd been reading a great many reports on psychical researches in France, and Mr. Grant asked about them. He seemed *particularly* interested in the question of *malignant* spirits."

"And what are 'malignant spirits'?"

"Spirits that are not in *harmony* with the other world. Sometimes a soul fails to vibrate properly in the next plane. Then it may come back and do real *harm* upon this side. There are authentic cases of such spirits *murdering* people."

The Chief stared for a moment, then exploded: "You're trying to tell me Grant was killed by a spook with a grudge?"

"We don't call them *spooks,*" said the Lady Elfrieda with dignity. "We call them *'spirit entities'.*"

"Call them what you like," the Chief snapped, "so long as you don't do it around me. I've no time for such nonsense."

"Just a minute, Captain," Jimmy Lane interrupted. "I want to ask a question. Have you any idea who this 'malignant spirit' was, Mrs. Chapman?"

The Lady Elfrieda promptly transferred her affections to him. "I most *certainly* have. I think it was Amos Harcastle."

"Amos Harcastle? And who is . . . or, I mean, who was he?"

"He was Mr. Grant's *control*. Every medium has a control, a spirit who helps with the séances. Mr. Harcastle was a man who once owned those three houses on the hill. He died in the séance room."

"What?" The Chief's attention was attracted now, and the Lady Elfrieda's voice deepened with conscious importance.

"Yes; he died in the séance room . . . only it was a *long* time ago. Mr. Harcastle bought the three houses for himself and his two married daughters. He was a philologist and used that big room for his study. He was in there when he died."

"What did he die of?" I am sure at least three of us asked that question at once, and it was Dr. Waverly who answered.

"Nothing mysterious," he assured us. "The man was over eighty and he died of a heart attack. His daughter was in the next house and ran into the room in time to be with him when he died. Harlan once told me that was one reason for his buying the house. He had a theory that it was easier to connect with the spirit plane in a room where someone had died. Mr. Harcastle came back frequently and acted as his control."

"You actually saw him?"

"Oh, yes, several times—vaguely, and once with great distinctness. He was an old chap with a long white beard."

"—and a skull cap," the Lady Elfrieda finished for him. "I'm sure it was he who murdered Mr. Grant."

"Why do you think he wanted to murder him?" Jimmy asked before the Chief could explode.

"Because he was jealous of Mr. Grant for still being on the earth plane."

"Did Grant say anything about Harcastle Monday night?"

"No; but, as I told you, he asked me what I'd read about malignant spirits. Before we finished, Singh came up with word that Mr. Stoddard was waiting. So I went home."

"Without anything more being said?"

"Yes; except—he *did* ask me one very *strange* question. He asked if I thought women *ever* forgave an injury, or if they went right on hating the man who had hurt them."

Jimmy turned quickly to Dr. Waverly. "Did you ever know of Grant's having trouble over a woman?"

The doctor shook his head. "Never. Of course, he met a great many women in his work and he may have had friendships I knew nothing about, but I always supposed his relations with them were strictly of a business nature."

The Lady Elfrieda seemed about to speak, then changed her mind and there was a short silence, broken by the Chief.

"I can't see that anything you've brought us is important, Mrs. Chapman, except, possibly, the fact that Grant was worried about some woman. I'll have that lead followed up." He rose in polite dismissal, and the woman began gathering up an assortment of gloves, fur neckpiece, embroidered handbag, and pamphlets which she had dropped on the desk. These last she held out to the Chief.

"I brought them for you to study, Captain. They will show you how to tranquilize your vibrations, and tune them with the infinite."

Captain Hemming snorted and drew back as though they were red-hot.

"Thanks," he growled. "I'll be too busy for the next few days to do any reading."

"I won't." Jimmy Lane took the pamphlets from her hand. "If you don't mind, I'd like to look them over, Mrs. Chapman."

The Lady Elfrieda burbled happily. "If you're interested, Mr. Lane, I should simply *love* to have you come up to my house on Sunday afternoon. A little group of seekers meets there for tea. You, too, Captain . . . we'd be delighted to see you at *any* time, or any *other* friend Mr. Lane would care to bring."

The Chief made no direct reply. He had already disgustedly punched a bell, and an officer was at the door. "You may show this lady out," he said.

The man took the Lady Elfrieda's arm and steered her toward the door; on the threshold she paused. "It's been perfectly *delightful* to meet you," she declared chattily. "I can't *tell* you how I have enjoyed our little talk. I *do* hope we'll all meet again when we can have a *real* visit."

A moment later she was gone, and the Chief sank into his chair, mopping his brow.

"Now that," he said, "is what I consider a good half-hour wasted."

Jimmy Lane was glancing through the pamphlets. "I don't agree with you, Captain. It may sound mad, but I've a feeling that somewhere in what we've just heard there's a key to Grant's murder. If only," he shook his head gloomily, "if only we were clairvoyant, and could see where it lies."

It was a full hour before we got away from Headquarters. In the interval the Chief had rapidly disposed of six or eight witnesses, none of whom had anything new to offer.

Stoddard and Norah came first. They were looking much more cheerful than when we had last seen them, and Norah gave me the reason, *sotto voce*. "The Chief's been simply adorable. He's really a perfect old lamb."

Captain Hemming tried to pretend that he hadn't heard, but when he spoke I swear his voice was faintly reminiscent of the Lady Elfrieda's dulcet tones.

"Sorry to trouble you again, Miss Fallon, but there are still a few things we need for our records. Nothing that need worry you, of course."

"I'm not worried," Norah smiled up at him. "I'll be glad to tell you anything I can."

"Then suppose we get the question of time straight. We're checking everyone who was in the Grant house on Monday night. Will you start at eight and give us your program through midnight?"

"I had dinner at my hotel at eight—" Norah began, and as she talked I jotted down notes. To save time and space I shall give them here, along with those for Stoddard:

Norah:

8 to 9 p.m.	*Dining at hotel.*
9 to 9:30	*Visiting Grant.*
9:30 to 11	*At a movie.*
11 to 11:30	*In sweet-shop.*
11:30 through night	*In bed at hotel.*

Stoddard:

9 to 9:30	*Arrives at S. F. aerodrome.*
9:30 to 10	*In car on way to hotel.*
10 to 11	*At hotel. Phones Norah and does not get her. Phones Grant and makes appointment.*
11:15	*Arrives at Grant's. Meets Lady Elfrieda on stairs.*
11:15 to 12	*Talking with Grant.*
12 to 12:30	*On way to aerodrome in taxi.*
12:30	*Leaves for Los Angeles in 'plane.*

After jotting down these facts the Chief asked a few more general questions and was about to dismiss the two when Jimmy demurred.

"Just a minute; there's something I want to ask." And to Norah: "Do you know of any woman who had a grudge against Grant? Anyone to whom he'd done some injury?"

She looked surprised. "Why, no. He always had a lot of wild-eyed females around him. . . . I used to see them coming and going to his séances, but they all seemed to adore him. Hold on, I *do* remember, I heard him quarreling with one of them."

"When was that?"

"Some time last week. I went up there quite late, after one of his séances. There was a woman with him and she was acting absolutely crazy. I could hear her half-way downstairs."

"Could you make out what she said?"

"No; except that she was jealous of the other women at the séance. She gave me a perfectly poisonous look when I came in. She was a funny, dumpy little thing with dyed hair."

"The Lady Elfrieda!" Jimmy exclaimed, and turned to Stoddard. "You told us you met her the night of the murder. Did it strike you that she had been quarreling with Grant?"

"No; but I wouldn't have known it if she had. All I saw was a woman hurrying past me down the stairs."

"Did Grant look upset when you reached the room?"

"I'm afraid I was too upset myself to notice."

The Chief was impatient. "I wish you wouldn't waste time over trifles, Lane. I've still got a lot of people to see."

"Very well." Jimmy subsided.

Stoddard left with Norah, and was succeeded by a group of Grant's followers who were at the séance on the night of his death. Most of them belonged to what Jimmy calls the "scrambled brains" type, and their talk was reminiscent of the Lady Elfrieda who was, apparently, High Priestess of the Grand Cult. Her theory about Grant's having been murdered by a bad-tempered ghost seemed to have been accepted with weird variations by them all, and thirty minutes of their babbling reduced the Chief to a condition which bordered upon apoplexy. When Jimmy showed a disposition to question them about Grant's dealings with the unseen world, he simply blew up.

"Clear out the whole lot," he roared to his assistant. "I've had my fill of ghosts. I'm going to chuck the case until McCarthy gets back from Russian Hill."

"Russian Hill?" Jimmy pricked up his ears. "What's he doing there?"

"Examining the Grant family. We want to know exactly where everyone was at midnight on Monday."

Jimmy rose quickly. "In that case I'll beat it up to the hill. If I know McCarthy he'll have the whole family in fits by now."

"All right," the Chief agreed, not too enthusiastically, "only don't interfere. Mac's a good man, even if he is a bit heavy."

"Heavy!" Jimmy groaned. "He's positively elephantine. Every time he finds a poor little clue he sits on it as though it were an egg and he hoped to hatch out a solution . . . and all he manages to do is squash it flat! You should have picked out someone with subtlety and imagination for this case."

"You've got enough for us all," the Chief growled. "The way you wallow around among spooks and banshees anyone'd think you're intending to set up in Grant's place."

"Maybe I am," said Jimmy sweetly. "Anybody you want me to call back for you from the spirit plane?"

"Not unless you can get Grant to tell us who bumped him off."

Jimmy picked up the Lady Elfrieda's pamphlets and moved lazily toward the door, but on the threshold he paused. "After two hours of observing your methods, Captain, *dear,* I should say that's the only way you'll ever find out."

CHAPTER 9
THE GRANT HOUSEHOLD

The doctor had accepted Jimmy Lane's invitation to ride back to Russian Hill in his car, and five minutes later we were moving through the traffic on Market Street, bound for the Grant place. Waverly looked utterly exhausted. As he sank back on the cushions of the limousine he sighed deeply and closed his eyes.

"The excitement of the last two days has been too much for me," he explained apologetically. "I'm rather a quiet chap and the only company I normally keep is that of my microbes."

"I should think the germs of an Oriental disease would be exciting enough for anyone," I remarked.

"I suppose it does seem so, but I'm used to them, and my work is largely routine observation and the writing of notes."

"It's rather a dangerous type of research. How did you happen to select it?"

"It selected me," the doctor said gravely. "My wife died of an obscure form of cholera, and I have been dedicating myself to the work ever since. I shall probably never achieve anything of real value, but my notes may be helpful to younger men."

He closed his eyes once more, and I saw that he was too thoroughly exhausted to talk. Jimmy, too, seemed to have little desire for conversation and there was complete silence until the car reached the stopping place near the summit of Russian Hill. The chauffeur drew up to the curb and we started up the steep way on foot. It was late, and the world was drifting slowly into twilight. A fog was beginning to creep up from the bay, and the low, persistent moan of the fog-horn in the distance was sounding through the mist like the sad plaint of a lost soul.

Jimmy shivered slightly. "My word, that's a creepy sound. It gives you a nasty feeling that something unpleasant is in the offing, doesn't it?"

It did, but I forebore to say so—and we climbed the steps to the Colonel's house in gloomy silence. Before we reached the porch we could hear a man's voice from inside, raised in a continuous tirade. At our first touch on the bell, the door swung open and we saw the Colonel standing in the entrance hall; his face was mottled red, his eyes bloodshot.

"Ah, Lane. Thank God, it's you! There's a fellow here from Headquarters who's been deucedly impertinent. I hope you'll send him about his business."

Jimmy grinned. "Afraid I can't hurl him out, Colonel; but I may be able to tone him down. Where's he operating?"

"In the living-room." The Colonel led us across the hall to the doorway beyond. Through the wide arch the room was plainly visible, and it was here that I first saw Otto Steeb.

He was sitting in a wheel-chair at the far side of the room and, at first glance, I should have said he was a handsome man, with broad shoulders and a large, well-shaped head; but as I studied him more closely, I saw that his legs were wretchedly disproportionate, scarcely larger than those of a ten-year-old child. His arms were abnormally long and thin, and his hands, slim, flexible, stained with chemicals, seemed perpetually in motion. His face, when viewed in profile, was singularly regular in outline, but there was something malignant in the chill blue eyes with their sparse fair lashes; and the lips, full to sensuousness, had a sardonic twist which was vaguely disquieting. This was a mere fleeting impression, I am bound to admit, and probably an unfair one for the memory of our first meeting is, doubtlessly, colored by the character of the man as I knew him later. The Colonel performed the introductions a trifle curtly, I thought, and Steeb allowed his hard blue eyes to pass from one to the other of us without any attempt at greeting other than a slight nod, then he turned to the doctor at the door.

"I'm glad you've got here, Waverly," he said. "I wish you'd convince this fool," he jerked his head toward McCarthy, "that I've never been up in that room of Harlan's," His voice was low and guttural, with an occasional hissing sibilant which slurred the words between breaths. "Make him to understand that I could not possibly have climbed those stairs. He has got it into his stupid head that I had something to do with this murder."

"Nothing of the sort," McCarthy protested, "nothing of the sort." He turned to us for sympathy. "I'm only asking him a few questions, you understand. Just like I intend to ask all of the family, and he turns mad on me. Bellows like a bull. If he keeps on I *will* think he had something to do with it, you bet!"

The doctor came forward and assumed the role of peacemaker. From his gentle, placating manner I suspected that this was not the first time he had oiled troubled waters in the Grant family.

"Nonsense, Otto," he said, "there's no use your getting excited." And to McCarthy: "I can assure you, Sergeant, that it would be impossible for Mr. Steeb to climb the stairs next door without help."

McCarthy grunted. "All right, all right, I was just trying to get the position of everybody the night of the murder. Mind telling me where you were, Mr. Steeb?"

"Most certainly not. I had dinner on a tray in my laboratory at the top of this house, later Dr. Waverly came
up with Mrs. Steeb and the three of us talked for a short
time. After that, Mrs. Steeb and I put in several hours'
work on my notes. At about eleven, I went down to the
second floor to bed."

"Thanks." McCarthy wrote for a moment in his notebook. "That's all I want of you just now. I'd like to ask
Singh a few questions."

As he spoke he glanced across the room toward a shadowy corner, and, for the first time, I realized that the
East Indian was in the room. He had discarded his long
robes and was in a house-boy's suit of white drill, but he
retained his quiet air of dignity as he stood in front of the
detective. McCarthy regarded him keenly.

"You told a pretty straight story at the inquest this
morning," he said, "but there's a few more things I want
to ask you."

"Yes, sar."

"You testified that you didn't see Grant again after you
took Stoddard up to his room at eleven-fifteen. What did
you do immediately after that?"

"The master said he did not need me and I went for a
walk."

"What time did you get back?"

"About twelve-thirty, sar."

"Did you go into the lower house at all on your return?"

"No, sar, I sleep here in the house of Colonel Grant,
and I came straight home to bed."

"Did you see anyone who could verify that statement?"

"Yes, sar, my wife."

"And, of course, if you're lying she'll back you up."

"Yes, sar." Singh's voice was flat and metallic, utterly devoid of humor. "But I am not lying. It is as I have told you, after I left him with Mr. Stoddard I never saw Mr. Grant alive again."

"Very well." McCarthy was about to dismiss him when Jimmy spoke.

"Just a minute, Singh." The East Indian obediently faced him and he asked: "About the lady who was with Mr. Grant when Mr. Stoddard arrived—you remember?"

"Yes, sar. You mean Mrs. Chapman. She went out as I took Mr. Stoddard upstairs."

"You actually saw her leave?" Jimmy's voice was eager, and Singh started to reply, then hesitated in thought.

"No," he said slowly, "she passed us on the stairs, but I did not see her leave."

"Did you pass her on the first or second flight?"

"On the flight between the second floor and the séance room."

"How long were you in the room with Grant and Mr. Stoddard?"

"Perhaps two, perhaps three minutes."

"And after that you came straight down and went out?"

"It is as you have said, sar."

Jimmy leaned forward and spoke eagerly. "Then Mrs. Chapman might have remained in the house without your knowledge . . . in one of those rooms on the second floor?"

"Yes, sar, it is possible."

"Say," McCarthy broke in, "what are you trying to get at?"

"Nothing." Jimmy smiled quietly to himself. "Just a vague idea." And to Singh: "Thank you, that's all."

As the East Indian retired noiselessly into the shadows the Colonel spoke. "Is it necessary for this farce to go on any longer?" he demanded. "You can see you're getting nowhere."

The Sergeant shook his head doggedly. "I started out to find out where you all were Monday night, and I'm not going to leave till I've got that information. I'll take you next, Colonel."

"Oh, very well, very well." The Colonel was evidently making a violent effort to control himself. "Where do you want me to begin?"

"Start at dinner, same as Mr. Steeb. Where did you eat?"

"In the dining-room, of course. And, afterward, I went over to my brother's study for a little talk with him."

"What did you talk about?"

"Business mainly. Harlan left all his affairs in my hands, and we discussed the advisability of selling some bonds in order to raise money for a new invention we were contemplating."

"What time did you leave?"

"About nine. Miss Fallon arrived to see my brother, so we postponed our talk until the next day."

"What did you do next?"

"I returned to my house, and read in my room for several hours."

"Did you see anyone during that time?"

"Only my daughter and son-in-law. Somewhere around midnight I went to bed."

"Is your room on the side nearest the house next door?"

"Yes; because of the rise in the hill our house is over a floor higher than Harlan's, which brings the wall of my room next to his study. But if you're going to ask if I heard anything, I'll tell you plainly that I didn't. The wall between is very thick and not even a scream could get through."

"All right," McCarthy entered this in his notebook and turned the page. "Now who else is in the family?"

"No one, except my daughter, Mrs. Steeb. Surely you don't intend to annoy her at this time?"

"I don't know that this time is any worse than any other," snapped McCarthy. "Will you ask Mrs. Steeb to come in?"

For a moment I thought the Colonel's temper would break loose again, but before he could reply Steeb spoke to Singh who left the room. For a moment there was silence, then the door opened and Chanda Steeb appeared. She was dressed as before, in a straight woolen gown with white linen at the throat and wrists. It was a sort of uniform she had adopted, I discovered later. Although its color frequently changed, its general lines were always the same.

"This is my daughter, Mrs. Steeb," the Colonel said. And to Chanda: "The Sergeant would like to ask you a few questions."

She smiled at McCarthy and dropped into a chair. "I shall be glad to tell you anything I can, Sergeant."

McCarthy picked up his notebook and moved toward her, a slight deference showing through his brusqueness. "I'll make it as snappy as I can, Mrs. Steeb. All I want is an idea of what you did on Monday night."

"Monday night?" She paused a moment, her brow wrinkled in thought; then: "To begin with, I had supper here with the family. That must have lasted until about eight. Then I went up to the laboratory with Dr. Waverly and we talked to my husband until somewhere around nine. After he left, I remained working on notes, with Mr. Steeb, until eleven. Then father and I helped him downstairs and he got ready for bed."

"You went to bed at the same time?"

"Not immediately. Sometimes my husband does not sleep and I have to get him a hot drink, so I always read until I am sure he won't need me. That night he seemed restless, so I read until around twelve."

"And you didn't hear anything?" McCarthy was watching her keenly.

"Nothing from the house next door. But I heard Singh come in for the night."

"What time was that?"

"Some time after I had gone to bed, twenty minutes to half an hour, I should say."

"Which would make it about twelve-thirty." McCarthy wrote the time down, and nodded to Chanda. "That's all I need from you, Mrs. Steeb. Now, Dr. Waverly, just as a matter of form, y'understand, I'd like to take you."

"Certainly." The doctor drew out a little card. "I've already jotted my movements down to save you trouble. I had dinner over here with the family, then, as Mr. Steeb has told you, I went up to the laboratory and talked for half an hour or so up there. Following that, I returned home and began going through some old trunks and letters. That took longer than I expected and I didn't get to bed until around midnight."

"Any one in the house except yourself?"

"No one. There's a sort of a charwoman tends to it during the day, but she goes home at night. I'm afraid you'll have to take my word for my movements during the evening. I've no way of proving that I wasn't in and out of the house a dozen times."

"No, no," McCarthy protested, "I wasn't meaning that, Doctor." He took the card and slipped it into his notebook. "I guess this takes in everyone except that maid of yours, Mrs. Steeb."

"Lalah?" Chanda stared at him, then gave a little laugh. "Oh, I can answer for Lalah. She was busy in the kitchen during dinner, and was cleaning it up until eight or nine; after that, she sat in my bedroom making over one of my dresses. At about eleven o'clock I sent her to bed."

"You're sure she went there?"

"Absolutely sure. She's extremely shy and never goes out. I know she was in her room when Singh got home because I heard them talking."

"Where do the servants sleep?"

"At the back of the house, just off the kitchen. Their window is directly below mine and I frequently hear the murmur of their voices."

McCarthy made a note or so, then closed his book. "That's all," he said, "unless Mr. Lane has something he wants to ask." He turned to Jimmy who was standing at one side of the room, his eyes fixed with an almost hypnotic gaze upon the Colonel's hands where they gripped his cane. "Anything more you want to know before we go up to the séance room, Mr. Lane?" McCarthy repeated.

"Yes," said Jimmy slowly, "just one little thing. I'd like to know how well the Colonel plays golf."

CHAPTER 10
BLACKMAIL

"What made you ask that idiotic question about golf?" We were in Grant's house, climbing the stairs toward the séance room, and McCarthy was out of earshot on the flight ahead. "Did you have something in mind, or were you just trying to get the Colonel's goat?"

"A little of both. There was a bag of golf clubs in the hall and it suggested a wild idea which may not mean anything."

We reached the top of the stairs where an officer was guarding the door. "The Captain's inside," he said. "He's expecting you, Mr. Lane."

"Good." Jimmy hurried into the room and grinned at Captain Hemming. "I thought you'd decided to lay off the case for a while."

"I thought so, too," growled the Chief, "but it wouldn't let me alone. I knew I'd never be content with a second-hand report, so I came up to go over the place again."

"Looking for the secret passage?"

"Something like that. But I'll be hanged if we can find anything." He was standing at the farther end where the mirror had formerly been framed by bookcases. Now the shelves had been pulled from the wall, disclosing an unbroken expanse of plaster. 'This is the only wall that could possibly have an entrance," he pointed out, "because the other three are on the outside of the building."

"This is against the house next door, isn't it?" Jimmy asked.

"Yes, but those bookcases haven't been moved for years, judging by the dust and cobwebs, and the wall back of them is as solid as granite."

"How about the mirror?" Jimmy was regarding the huge affair of French gilt that reached from the ceiling to within three feet of the floor. "If you'd read the proper books, Capt'n, you'd know there is always a knob concealed in the frame of the mirror."

"Sure," the Chief agreed with a chuckle. "And when you twist it the glass swings out silently and discloses a hidden staircase. But this one doesn't work that way, see? It's been screwed into the wall with heavy bolts; and I'm dead sure it never did any swinging because the paint that was used to gild the frame has dripped and stuck to the plaster. If it had ever been pulled loose the drops would be broken."

"How about the glass itself?" Jimmy was investigating as he spoke. "No; the same thing applies there. The gilt has run down on to the glass as well."

The Chief was testing the hardened paint with his knife. "The drops are old," he said. "That mirror must have been there for a long time because the stuff's badly oxidized."

"It's been up about six years," McCarthy told us. "The Colonel said his brother got the mirror when they wrecked an old house down town. It was brought around the Horn in a sailing ship."

Jimmy was looking at the glass with interest. "It's rather a fine specimen," he said. "They don't make them like that any more, with those heavy candelabra built into the frame. That's another reason why you can be sure it's solid, Captain. Those brackets are wired and to move it the wires would have to be pulled out."

"Yes." The Chief sighed. "I guess we'll have to give up any idea of an entrance being made through the wall." He spoke briefly to his men, and they began moving the book-cases back against the plaster while Jimmy glanced about the room.

"A trap-door is out of the question," he said, "because the carpet is tacked down solidly all the way around."

"Yes; and the side walls are plain plaster, while that window at the end is built in, with no opening of any sort."

"How about the roof?"

"Nothing there. We've had a man look it over."

"How'd he reach it?"

"From a window in the house next door. But even from the roof it's impossible to get in here. A cat couldn't get through those ventilators."

Jimmy had sunk down lazily on a divan. "I don't know what all the snorting's about. The question isn't how some-body got into the room. It's how he managed to lock the door behind him after he left."

"That's just the point," said the Chief despairingly. "That door's not the sort you can play tricks with. Grant didn't depend upon an ordinary lock and key, but upon a bolt."

Jimmy rose from the couch and moved across the room. For a moment he regarded the bolt thoughtfully. "It's the sliding type," he observed, "and the

door fits tight, without a crack. I don't believe even Philo Vance could figure out a way of locking it from the outside."

"No," agreed the Chief, "not even a burglar with a com-plete set of tools could handle it, but we've discovered one

odd thing . . . look here." He reached up on the outside
and touched one of the carved panels. It slid to the left,
disclosing a small pane of glass three or four inches square.

"A peep-hole!" Jimmy exclaimed.

"Yes; that Hindu servant insists that 'the master' had
it put in so that he wouldn't be disturbed when he was
concentrating. Personally, I believe it was used for those
séances of Grant's."

"Probably." Jimmy was examining the thing carefully.
"But I don't see how it can have had anything to do with
the bolting of the door. You can see the glass has been
built into the woodwork so there's no way of opening it."

"I've already figured that out." The Chief slipped the
wooden panel back into place and joined us on the inside
of the door.

"The whole thing is beyond me," he confessed. "If it
weren't, I'd have put Stoddard under lock and key long since."

"Then you owe a debt of gratitude to that door," Jimmy
said. "I tell you frankly, Captain, if you throw Stoddard
into the hoosegow, you'll live to regret it."

"Hang it all," the Chief exploded, "you talk as if I
wanted to prove him guilty! Matter of fact, I like the chap
as well as you do. I'd be glad to discover anyone else who
could have polished Grant off."

"If that's all that's worrying you," said Jimmy calmly,
"I can make you a present of several."

"Such as?"

"Well, to begin with, such as the Lady Elfrieda."

"You're kidding?"

"Never more serious in my life. She was up here just
before Stoddard. Singh admits that he didn't see her leave
and she might have been hiding in any of the rooms on the
second floor. I say might, but it's practically certain she
was, because if she'd gone straight out, she wouldn't have

heard Stoddard arguing with Grant."

"You're right, at that! The row didn't start until after Singh left."

"Which was two or three minutes after she was supposed to have gone. Perhaps she had some reason for wanting to finish her talk with Grant and waited until Stoddard left, then climbed the stairs again, knocked on the door, and got Grant to admit her."

"What could have been her reason for killing him?"

"Jealousy. We've already been told she was crazy about the fellow, and I should say he was pretty much of a ladies' man. At least, his standing order to Singh not to disturb him in the morning until he rang looks as though he were in the habit of having visitors that might not want to be seen. Also we know he was trying to make love to Norah. Perhaps the fair Elfrieda got her back up about something and did him in."

"How'd she do it?"

"You wouldn't expect me to know that when the experts themselves disagree, would you? If I were to make a guess, I'd say she lured him to the far end of the room, then struck him on the back of the head with that little stone image. You'll remember the blow was at the base of the skull, about where a rather short woman would strike a man as tall as Grant."

"But how did she get out and lock the door behind her?"

"That, my dear Watson, I leave you to figure out for yourself, but the difficulty is no greater than in the case of Stoddard. Mind you, I'm not saying she did it. There are still several others."

"What others?"

"Just as a venture, I should say everyone in the family, with the possible exception of Steeb. McCarthy has just been going over their movements on Monday night, and there's not a single one of 'em with a real alibi for the time between twelve and twelve-thirty. Singh was out walking and could have come up here without being seen. The Colonel says he was in his room reading, but it would have been easy for him to have slipped down the stairs and into this house. The same thing applies to Chanda Steeb and Dr. Waverly."

"Why do you exclude Steeb himself?"

"Because the man's a cripple and couldn't have climbed the stairs, otherwise I'd cheerfully add him to our list."

"But there's the question of motives—" the Chief began.

"Yes; and there's frequently nobody in the world with as much reason for wishing a man dead as his own immediate family."

"If I'd been given my pick of the lot," said McCarthy savagely, "I'd choose the Colonel. With that temper, he's a born killer."

"Yes," Jimmy agreed, "it could easily have been the old boy. We know that he was talking with Grant earlier in the evening about business, and it's possible they had a quarrel which was interrupted by Norah's arrival. Suppose, for example, that the Colonel had been speculating with his brother's funds and Grant was demanding an accounting. The Colonel might have waited until after everyone was gone, then come up to finish the argument. It's darned easy to imagine his flying into a rage and striking Grant with the closest thing at hand which was probably—"

"His cane," McCarthy broke in excitedly. "I've never seen him without that stick of his, and it could crack a skull same as you'd crack a nut with a hammer. I'll bet that's why you asked what you did about his playing golf, Mr. Lane."

"You've guessed it, Mac. That was in the back of my mind. A blow at the base of the skull such as that might have been struck from below at the end of a swing, similar to a drive in golf."

"Very clever," admitted the Chief, "but it doesn't tell us how he got out of the room and yet left the door bolted on the inside."

"No," Jimmy began, then paused. "By Jove! It does give me an idea! I wish you'd send for Singh."

As an assistant left the room to fetch the servant, Jimmy moved toward the door and began inspecting the bolt, his eyes alight with some inner excitement. "It's quite possible that this was not locked on the night of the murder."

"Not locked?" The Chief was plainly bewildered. "But we know that it was. Both the Colonel and Singh insist that they found it that way the next morning."

"The Colonel may be lying and Singh may be taking his word. It all depends on who came up to call Grant Tuesday noon, and who held the handle while they were forcing the door."

"I don't get what you mean."

"You will in a minute. Suppose the Colonel killed his brother Monday night . . . then went downstairs, leaving this door unlocked. Suppose the next day when Grant did not appear for lunch he saw to it that he was the one to come up and investigate. When he called Singh to help break in he had only to hold the handle of the door tight, with the metal tongue in a locked position instead of turned back, in order to make it seem like a bolted door to the other."

"But the bolt is torn loose from the doorjamb."

"Yes; but we've no way of knowing that it wasn't done deliberately the night before—with the trick I've just told you in mind. Or it might even have been done after the body was discovered."

"By God, I believe you're right!" McCarthy struck his hand against his thigh. "The Colonel has always been my candidate."

"Hush!" Jimmy was listening. "Here's Singh now. We'll see what we can get from him."

The East Indian was already on the landing at the head of the stairs, his linen suit gleaming ghostly white against the blackness of the stair well. "You sent for me, sar?" He addressed the group impartially, his dark face imperturbable as ever.

"Yes." Jimmy motioned him into the room. "There's one or two things that we'd like to ask about the morning when you and Colonel Grant found the body."

Singh had moved across the threshold and was standing just inside the door. "I will tell you what I can, sar."

"Then tell me who first came up to call Mr. Grant."

"It was the Colonel. When the master did not appear at lunch he said he would come up here and find out what was the matter."

"Then he called you to help him break in?"

"Yes, sar. The door was bolted and he could not open it alone."

"I suppose," Jimmy was lighting a cigarette with great casualness, "I suppose you tried turning the handle?"

For a moment the man hesitated, then shook his head. "No, sar. The Colonel was already battering against the door and I did not stop to try it."

Jimmy and the Chief exchanged glances. "Did you notice the bolt after you smashed in?" Jimmy asked. "I mean if it was broken?"

"No, sar. I was thinking only of the master and then, too, as soon as we were in the room Mowgli jumped on me."

"Mowgli? Who is that?" the Chief questioned.

"Mowgli is Mr. Grant's monkey, sar."

"You mean to say there was a monkey in the room?"

"Yes, sar. He was beside the body when we broke in."

"Where is he?" Hemming was plainly excited. "I want to have a look at him."

"I will get him."

Singh moved noiselessly from the room and for a moment everyone talked at once. I suppose our minds were reverting to "The Murders in the Rue Morgue", with its gigantic and murderous ape, for at Singh's re-entrance there was a unanimous gasp followed by involuntary laughter. Cuddled down on Singh's shoulder was a tiny marmoset no larger than a six-months-old kitten. Looking at it, I suddenly remembered the strange spider-like shadow that had seemed to run up the ivy-covered wall the first night we had come to the house.

"So you're Mowgli!" Jimmy put out his hand and the little creature twined a tiny brown claw about the index finger. "I'm afraid you're too small to have committed a murder."

The native rolled his eyes and for the first time his teeth showed in a quick smile. "No, sar, Mowgli would not have hurt the master."

"All right," Jimmy seemed to have lost interest in the little beast, "you can take him away, Singh."

"Very good, sar." The East Indian left the room, and, as his steps died on the stair, McCarthy spoke excitedly.

"I've got it, Chief! It was the monkey pulled the bolt and locked the door! You needn't laugh," he swung on Jimmy who had dropped into a chair and was shaking helplessly. "I've read lots funnier things than that."

"So have I," Jimmy agreed with him. "I've not only read 'em, I've written 'em. But we're not dealing with fiction right now, worse luck! This is cold, hard fact."

"Well, what's wrong with my idea?" McCarthy's voice sounded grieved, and Jimmy patted his arm comfortingly.

"Nothing. It's a grand thought and if I know my Conan Doyle, Sherlock Holmes got there before you. The only trouble is, in this case, the bolt is not only heavy but also fits tight in its socket. You can see for yourself what a

lot of force it would take to slide it. That little creature
has almost no strength in its paws and couldn't possibly
manage it. In addition to that, you've got the difficulty of
training a monkey to shoot a bolt and then being sure he
does it at exactly the right moment."

"Well . . . perhaps you're right." McCarthy was plainly
loth to give up his idea. "But it would sure help a lot if it
was so."

The Chief dropped down into a chair. "I've got to get
back to Headquarters," he said. "Before I go let's run over
this thing and see where we stand. Ignoring the question
of motives there are a number of people who might have
come into this room last night and committed the murder."

He picked up a pencil and began to write:

1. *Colonel Grant.*
2. *Singh.*
3. *Mrs. Chapman.*
4. *Stoddard.*
5. *Dr. Waverly.*
6. *Lalah.*
7. *Chanda Steeb.*
8. *Otto Steeb (?)*

"I put a question-mark after Steeb because we know
that he was incapable of climbing the stairs. Of this entire
list, we have an explanation which covers the bolting of
that door only in the case of Colonel Grant. I'm bound
to admit that your theory sounds plausible to me, Lane.
It's the nearest approach to an explanation which has been
devised as yet."

"It seems feasible to me, too," Jimmy confessed. "But,
of course, there's a lot we want to find out before we
spring any accusations. In the first place, I'd like a report
on Grant's relations with his family as a whole; second,

on his money affairs and his will; finally, I want to know more about the Colonel's past in India."

The Chief looked doubtful. "That will take a good deal of time. Especially the stuff about India."

"Not necessarily. I'll put Corrigan on the trail and if that red-headed Irishman doesn't sleuth some facts out of the Indian colony, I'll eat my hat."

"Very well, I'll leave that to you. Meantime, my men can check on the other things." The Chief rose and was picking up his hat when the telephone rang. He answered it, and, a moment later, when he turned to us, his brows were drawn down into a puzzled frown. "Now that," he said, "complicates things a bit more. It's your friend Stoddard calling from Headquarters."

"Headquarters? You don't mean to say you've had him taken up?"

"No; he hurried down there with some news. It seems that girl of his has just received an anonymous letter."

"About those papers of Grant's." Jimmy spoke positively and the Chief looked surprised.

"How did you know?"

"Merely a guess. I've been expecting something of the sort ever since we found they were gone. Did the letter suggest they might be returned to her?"

"Yes; at a price. It told her to hold herself ready for a message which would be sent later."

"Hurrah!" McCarthy was executing a triumphant double shuffle on the carpeted floor. "Now all we got to do is to nab the bird who wrote that letter and we'll have the guy who did the murder."

Jimmy, picked up his hat and was moving toward the door; on the threshold he paused.

"I hate to dash all your pretty hopes, Mac," he said, "but you're doomed to disappointment. The fellow who did this murder is too clever to be caught."

"Don't worry, we'll catch him all right," said McCarthy. "With that letter we can't go wrong."

"You may get the man who wrote the letter," Jimmy told him, "but, take my word for it, if he's stupid enough to let himself be caught that way, he's too stupid to have committed this murder."

A moment later he was running down the stairs.

Chapter 11
The Colonel is Suspected

When we reached the street we found that darkness had fallen and the fog had grown so thick that the street lamp was only a luminous spot in the midst of ghostly greyness. The cypress trees above the retaining wall were weighted down with moisture which dripped like tears from the ends of their branches. Seen dimly through the mist, they resembled grotesque, crêpe-veiled mourners at a wake, and the distant moan of the fog-horn formed a dirge-like accompaniment. As we moved down the pavement Jimmy looked back at the house and shook his head.

"I don't like it, Phil," he said. "I don't like it at all. This whole business has got me worried."

"You mean this development about Norah?"

"Good Lord, no! There's nothing remarkable about that. So long as those papers were kicking around we could expect someone to make use of them. What I mean is the place itself, and the feeling it gives me of ominous presentiment. It's too much like a stage set for a play. So far, we've had only one act—but something tells me there is more to follow." He broke off with a forced laugh at his own expense. "Don't listen to me, Phil, I'm as nervous and as full of fool intuitions as a woman. When I've got one of Friday's dinners inside me I'll feel better."

At the apartment we found Norah waiting with Stoddard. Friday was setting places for four.

Over the fruit cocktail Norah gave us an account of the blackmailing letter. "It came in the noon mail," she said, "but I was out with the company and didn't see it until I reached home."

"Have you got it with you?" Jimmy asked.

"No; the police wanted it to look over, but I'm afraid they won't find much. It's typed on ordinary paper with a purple-black ribbon and the envelope, unfortunately, was destroyed."

"How did that happen?"

"Well, being in the movie business, I get an awful lot of mail and my maid usually opens it for me. The envelopes that have no addresses she chucks out. By the time I discovered what was in the letter, the envelope had been burned."

"The police may be able to get something out of the typing," I suggested. "They have experts who can identify machines."

"Yes," the girl sounded dubious, "but there must be an awful lot of typewriters in a city as large as San Francisco."

"Not many in the Grant house," Jimmy said meaningly.

"You think the letter came from there?"

"Not a doubt of it, but which of 'em sent it—that's the question."

"I think it was that horrid Colonel," Norah declared.

"What do you know about him?"

"Nothing, except that he's got a perfectly vile temper. I heard him cursing Harlan Grant once when I came up to the séance room, unexpectedly, and another time I thought I saw him strike Singh, but I can't be sure whether it was him or his brother. They looked rather alike and the hall was dark."

Jimmy suddenly changed the subject. "About that maid of yours, how long has she been with you?"

"I don't know exactly . . . I should say about two years."

"I suppose she knows a lot about your private affairs?"

"She certainly does. Clara's more than a maid . . . she's a sort of secretary and dresser combined. Buys my clothes, orders train tickets when we're travelling, and manages things for me generally."

"You said you couldn't remember how you got started going to Grant. Isn't it possible she suggested it?"

Norah looked astonished, then thoughtful. "I think you're right! I got Clara when I was playing in San Francisco and, I remember now, it was she who told me about Grant. He'd given some good advice to a woman Clara worked for."

"I thought so." Jimmy nodded wisely. "It's not particularly important, but that's probably where Grant got his information about you."

"I'm sure of it!" Norah's eyes were snapping dangerously. "Clara used to drive up there with me sometimes and she often talked with Singh while she was waiting."

"She was probably slipping him information . . . for a consideration," Stoddard remarked disgustedly. "Personally, I never liked the woman, even tried to get Norah to discharge her. By Jove!" he exclaimed suddenly, "don't you think she may be in cahoots with the one who's doing the blackmailing?"

"Possibly. She may have burned that envelope by chance and then, again, it may have been prearranged. We'll just keep an eye on her and see if she communicates with anyone from the Grant house."

"Don't you believe it's the Colonel who has those papers?"

"I'd like to think so," said Jimmy musingly, "because he's the easiest man to pick, but if you've ever read a detective novel you know it's always the guy you never thought of who's guilty."

"Then it's the doctor," I said. "Nobody's mentioned him."

"It might be, at that. He was pretty much in Grant's confidence and he had access to the study after his death. He could easily have taken the stuff from the files. That's the main trouble with the problem," he added irritably. "In the twenty-four hours before the police came on the scene almost anyone might have got at those files."

Something suddenly flashed across my mind. "Do you remember that night we went up there to see the Colonel the night after Grant's death? There was a light in the study."

"Yes; I've been thinking of that. I shouldn't be surprised if the papers were taken at that time."

"Then it couldn't have been the Colonel because he appeared from the next house, you remember."

"I remember perfectly," said Jimmy, and grinned in a way which told me he was thinking of the Colonel's language. "But I also remember that we rang for about five minutes before he showed up. He had plenty of time to slide out the back door and through his own house. Anyway, we know the Colonel went through the files—he told us so himself."

"It might just as easily have been Singh," Stoddard suggested. "He must have known a lot about Grant's affairs."

"Yes," Jimmy agreed, "I shouldn't be a bit surprised to find that Singh was at the bottom of the thing . . . or the Colonel . . . or the doctor, so far as that goes. Even the Colonel's daughter might have slipped into the room and helped herself."

"What about fingerprints?" Stoddard asked. "Are we going to get anything out of them?"

"Afraid not. McCarthy says they're all over the place, but they're all legitimate. Of course, the family were in and out of that room constantly and those séance people were there all evening."

"How about that stone god?"

"Nothing there—not even the Colonel's. But it's not a good surface—too porous for prints." Jimmy sighed and shook his head over the excellent *chicken à la King* which Friday had just placed before him. "I suppose we'll have to be patient until we get a little more evidence."

"Well, I'm the baby that's got it for you!" Everyone jumped when a voice spoke from the door, and Norah dropped her fork, then laughed nervously as Corrigan came into the room. His plump face was damp and he blinked tiny drops of moisture from his eyelashes as he stood looking about the room. "Beastly fog outside," he began, "like cotton-wool." He suddenly caught sight of Norah. "Beg pardon, J. L. . . . didn't know you were having a party."

"It's not a party," Jimmy explained. "It's more in the nature of an inquest. This is Miss Fallon."

"You needn't introduce her," Corrigan chuckled. "She's God's gift to the newspaper boys. When all else fails we can always dig her picture out of the morgue and run a yarn about the death of her pet seal or how she's turned down another million-dollar motion picture contract."

"Thank you," said Norah smiling on him cheerfully. "I'll remember you next time and give you a—what do you call it?—a 'scoop'."

"You don't need to. I've got enough stuff on this murder to keep me writing for the next ten years . . . provided I'm ever allowed to spill it."

"Which you won't be," said Jimmy calmly, "if I have my way. Did you get what I wanted?"

"Sure did," Corrigan advanced to the table, his round face wreathed in smiles at the sight of food, as Friday automatically set a place for him between Jimmy and Stoddard, "I've been digging around among some old-timers

from India and what I picked up on your friend the
Colonel is aplenty."

"Tough hombre, eh?"

"A ten-minute egg! And you were right about the commission, J. L.; he isn't a Colonel, and never was one."

Jimmy explained to us quickly, "There's always been
something fishy about the Colonel. His carriage isn't that
of a man who's spent thirty years in the Army." He turned
to Corrigan. "So he's not an officer at all?"

"Not any more. He got as far as a captain, but they
broke him for bashing a non-com. over the head with a
walking-stick. That was 'way back in the 'nineties and he's
been hanging around India ever since."

"Doing what?"

"Lending money. He specialized in broke subalterns
and half-pay officers with sick wives at something like
seventy per cent. per annum. Of course, he didn't sport
the 'Colonel' over there; that was a brilliant inspiration
on this side."

"Sounds like a regular blackguard. Did you find out
anything about the daughter?"

"Yes . . . all good. She seems to be straight as they make
'em. She didn't have much to do with her father until they
came over here because she was put in a mission-school
when her mother died."

"Who was her mother?"

"Nobody seems to know much about her, except that
she was foreign . . . by that I mean not English. The girl
must be a peach. The fellows at the club said she'd often
stood up against her father when he was coming down
heavy on some poor devil who owed him money."

"How about her husband?"

"Steeb? Oh, he appears to be all right . . . although how
he managed to marry her is a mystery. They tell me he's a

regular devil to live with, but mentally he's considerable of a man."

"And the doctor?"

"Nothing much to report on him except that he served his time in India, then retired and followed Grant over here. I couldn't get a lot on the servants, either. Singh has been with Grant ever since early days in India. Lalah, his wife, acted as lady's maid—'*amah*' they call it over there— to Mrs. Waverly, the doctor's wife, but whether that was before or after she and Singh were married, I don't know. Of course," he added, "none of the people I talked to were at all intimate with the Grants. Most of 'em would be glad to see the 'Colonel' hung, drawn and quartered."

Before he could continue, Friday entered from the hall. "Beg pardon, Mis't Lane," he said, "but there's a gent'man as wishes to see you. He says he's from Police Headquarters."

"It's just me, Mr. Lane." McCarthy's voice spoke over Friday's shoulder, and at Jimmy's invitation he came into the room, hat in hand. "I don't like to butt in at meal-time like this, but Captain Hemming sent me up with some information you wanted."

"Good boy," Jimmy approved. "We'll take our coffee in the study and talk things over."

I could see that McCarthy was bursting with news and we were barely seated before he began: "I guess you were right, Mr. Lane. It looks as if the Colonel is the guy we're after."

"So you've changed your mind about our friend Stoddard, here?"

McCarthy looked embarrassed. "Oh, come now, I never really thought that it was Mr. Stoddard. I had my eye on the Colonel all along, and what we've dug up to-night just about clinches it." He paused and brought out a paper from his pocket. "To begin with, we've got hold of a copy of Grant's will and we find all his property goes to the Colonel."

Jimmy leaned forward and I could see that he was interested. "All of it?" he asked.

"Yeah; the whole works. He's executor, too, which means that it goes into his hands at once. After him it goes to the Steebs, and in case of their dying, it's to be split between Dr. Waverly and that pair of East Indians."

Jimmy opened a box of cigars and passed them around while he digested the information, then: "Did you find out anything about the Colonel's business affairs?" he asked.

"We sure did, Mr. Lane." There was a triumphant ring to McCarthy's voice as he carefully selected a cigar and, with equal care, put it away in a battered cigar-case. "We sure did. The Colonel was telling the truth when he said he had charge of all his brother's money affairs. They kept their securities in the same safety deposit box and their cash in a joint account. Usually they had a fair balance, but of late the Colonel's been drawing it out. Last week he took a bunch of securities and tried to raise money on 'em in a hurry."

"Did he get it?"

"Not as much as he wanted. Some of the stock had been bought when it was high and the market break brought it 'way down so the bank wouldn't allow him as much as he paid. He was pretty sore about it. Went into one of his rages and damned the management right and left. I guess you see what all this looks like, Mr. Lane."

"Yes." Jimmy was smoking thoughtfully. "It looks as though he'd been playing the market and got called for more margins. Did you manage to find his broker?"

"Not his latest. He did business with several at different times. He was always having rows and walking out. But I'll bet we find he was trying to raise money on his brother's stuff in order to cover some little flyer of his own."

"It's possible," Jimmy agreed. "The Colonel told us he was talking to his brother in the séance room Monday night about selling some securities." He turned to Norah. "You were the one who interrupted them. Did they look as though they'd been quarreling?"

Norah wrinkled her brow in thought. "I really can't say. I heard the Colonel's voice, but then the door was open and he always roars, even when he's perfectly amiable. Singh was walking ahead of me, and if they were fighting they had time to stop it before I came into the room."

"Perhaps they didn't get to fighting until later," Stoddard suggested. "The Colonel might have gone up to the room again after I left for the aerodrome. If he tried to get Grant to turn over his securities and Grant refused, I can easily imagine the old boy flying into a rage and doing him in."

"So can I, Mr. Stoddard," McCarthy agreed. "Only I think it went farther than that. I think Grant had just discovered that the Colonel was playing fast and loose with his money and was threatening to do something about it. The Colonel figured he'd have to bump him off to keep out of jail. Since he was the one to inherit, and was executor for the estate, nobody would ever know what a mess things were in . . . provided, of course, he managed to put over the idea that Grant died a natural death."

I saw him glance toward Jimmy Lane as though for approval, but Jimmy was once more in his favorite position, prone upon the hearth-rug. His eyes were half-closed, watching the smoke rise from the fire, and he seemed not to have heard. McCarthy's voice changed a trifle, became argumentative.

"I haven't told you everything we discovered, Mr. Lane. We've knocked the Colonel's alibi all to thunder. He wasn't in bed at twelve o'clock on Monday night. He was at the drug store."

Jimmy sat up a trifle. "Who says so?"

"The druggist. I've had a man making inquiries around the neighborhood and the druggist told him the Colonel came into his shop around twelve the night of the murder."

"He's sure?"

"Dead sure. He always closes at midnight and he was just locking up when the Colonel came in and bought some veronal."

"Veronal!" Norah exclaimed, and we all sat forward.

"Yes; on a prescription from Dr. Waverly. He told the druggist he'd been sleeping badly for several nights and he'd asked the doctor to do something about it. Of course, that was only an excuse. What he really used it for was to slip an overdose to Grant."

"What did he slip it in?" (I think it was Corrigan who asked the question.)

"In coffee or wine. Probably took it up with him. It would have been easy for him to carry off the glass or cup afterwards, and we've already explained how he worked the bolt on the door."

"That all sounds good to me." Corrigan was enthusiastic. "Have the M.D.s found any trace of veronal?"

"The toxicologists' report on the stomach isn't in yet. That stuff always takes time, but I bet they find it."

"How do you explain the blow on his skull?" Stoddard asked.

"The veronal made him dizzy, he keeled over and struck his head against the floor lamp," McCarthy explained. "That's easy."

"Too easy," said Jimmy from the hearth-rug.

"What do you mean?"

"I mean nobody'd be such a fool. Figure it out for yourself. Every argument you've used against the Colonel he put into your hands himself. He told us perfectly frankly that he was talking with his brother about selling some stock. He went openly to the drug store nearest his house, where he was sure to be known, and bought veronal on the very night his brother was killed. Nobody but a half-wit would go about a murder that way."

"Well," McCarthy was stubborn, "perhaps he isn't quite right in his head. Those rages of his come darn near insanity."

"They do," Jimmy agreed. "And they are also the best argument against your theory. Like Stoddard, I can imagine the Colonel flying into one of his rages and hitting his brother over the head hard enough to kill him, but I can't imagine his going out and deliberately buying poison for a premeditated murder. It doesn't go with his type."

"Type or no type, the Colonel's the boy for me," said McCarthy. "And the Chief feels the same way."

"You mean he's planning to arrest him?"

"No; but he's had a couple of men tailing him ever since this afternoon, but they'll keep him in sight until we get everything straight."

Jimmy's face twisted into an expression of worry. "Of course, by all the laws of common-sense, it ought to be the Colonel," he admitted. "He's certainly the one with the most obvious motive. According to the will, the doctor doesn't stand to gain anything by Grant's death, and Singh would lose an excellent position. The Steebs seem to be out of it, too. They won't inherit until the Colonel dies."

"Besides, he couldn't navigate those stairs," I pointed out.

"And she couldn't have faked the bolted door," Norah added.

"Which brings us back to the Colonel again. He's the only one who could have managed the door." Jimmy frowned unhappily and stared at the fire. "I wish I didn't have this wretched feeling of dissatisfaction. I think it's because the whole thing's too flat. It doesn't satisfy me artistically."

"What do you mean?" McCarthy growled.

"I told you when we first started that this case had the perfect background for a mystery yarn, and that I'd never be content with a solution which didn't fit the background. What you're offering me is too banal, too commonplace. What's become of the sinister spirits that haunted the séance room? Where's the expression of horror on the dead man's face? How have you explained the 'fear of fear', and the ghostly fragrance of jasmine . . . ?"

McCarthy groaned impolitely. "He's off again! Honest, Mr. Lane, I sometimes think you're getting ready for a nice quiet padded cell."

"I'm sure of it," Jimmy agreed promptly. "And you can order me a straight jacket if I don't begin to see light on this case soon. I tell you plainly, Mac, I can't . . . simply can't accept a solution which doesn't match the rest of the story."

"Bet you a million I've got it!" Corrigan suddenly brought forth.

"Got what?"

"The solution that explains everything. It wasn't the Colonel who murdered Grant; it was Steeb!"

"How'd he do it?"

"With a chemical! We know he's a chemist and we also know he used to fight with Grant. That ventilator in the top of the séance room isn't big enough for anyone to get in, but it would be big enough for a hose to go through. He might have run it out of his laboratory window."

"Say!" McCarthy whistled. "That isn't such a bad idea at that! There's a lot of poisons that when they're inhaled only show in the blood stream. The embalming made it impossible to test for them."

"I know it," Jimmy spoke slowly and seriously. "I've already been up that alley and it's very attractive, but it doesn't lead anywhere. In the first place, Steeb and Grant had made up their differences and were getting along famously; in the second, it would take a regular acrobat to run a hose out of a third story window, carry it across a roof and push it through a tiny ventilator under the eaves. Steeb not only isn't an acrobat . . . he's an almost helpless cripple. Finally, there's the question of the monkey. . . ."

"What monkey?" Corrigan demanded.

"You weren't with us this afternoon so you don't know that Grant's little marmoset, Mowgli, was found close beside the body . . . alive."

"You're sure he was there all night?"

"Absolutely, And marmosets are peculiarly delicate. If anyone had forced a chemical through that ventilator, Mowgli would have been the first to die."

Corrigan sighed with disappointment. "I'm sorry. It would have made such a bully front-page story . . . and it ties up with the jasmine odor you're always talking about. Some gases smell like flowers."

"You're thinking of cyanide. But it smells like peach blossoms, not jasmine. Besides, the jasmine odor is just another argument against your idea."

"What do you mean?"

"It was noticed by a number of other people. If Steeb was going to use a gas to kill Grant, he'd hardly have sent it into the room when others were there."

"I'm afraid you're right," Corrigan agreed, and McCarthy grinned.

"If you don't look out, Mr. Lane, you'll bring yourself right back to the Colonel. Near as I can make out, the one thing you've got against him is the fact that he's the only guy who could have done it!"

"You're dead right, Mac. It's sheer perversity on my part and—" Jimmy stopped as the telephone shrilled, and rose to answer. "Hello, hello. Oh, yes, Colonel . . . what can I do for you?" For a moment he listened; then: "Yes, of course I'll be there . . . shall we say two o'clock?" He hung up and faced McCarthy with a grin. "Perhaps it isn't going to be so disappointing as I thought," he said. "The plot is taking another twist."

"What's the Colonel want?" McCarthy asked gruffly.

"He wants to give me some information of the very *greatest* importance. I'm to see him to-morrow."

"If it's so important, why doesn't he see you now?"

"Because . . ." Jimmy paused, and his grin widened, "because he wants to be sure the doctor is out of the way. It seems that what he has to tell is something which will implicate our grey-haired friend."

CHAPTER 12
CHANDA STEEB ASKS FOR HELP

When Jimmy Lane made his visit to the Colonel's house the next afternoon I was with him. There's no doubt about it, my practice would have suffered from neglect if it had not been for my partner, but this whole affair had taken such a firm hold upon my imagination that I greeted Jimmy's suggestion that my vacation be taken now with quite immoral enthusiasm.

"You know you're enjoying yourself," he said. "If you went away on a trip you'd only lie on your back and read detective stories, such times as you weren't ruining your digestion with hotel food. This way you can live the detective stories and eat Friday's cooking. Now what could be sweeter?"

I had long since moved over to the room in Jimmy's house which I had frequently occupied before my marriage, and Friday was excelling himself in the dishes he set before us. There was something not quite normal about Friday these days. Usually he served the meal and retired to the kitchen where he waited until recalled by a bell; now, I noticed, he hovered over the table and listened to the conversation with a sort of horrified attention.

"It's the spooks," Jimmy explained as we were driven toward Russian Hill. "Friday is one-third Harlem and two-thirds pure Congo. This case has got him howling to his own particular voodoo for help. Yesterday I found this in my pocket." He brought out a little twisted tuft of bone and feathers and displayed it in the palm of his hand. "When I asked him about it he admitted he'd got it from Mammy 'Stazia, his pet witch lady. It's a charm against 'hants' and I promised to carry it every time I went to the Grant place." He chuckled as he spoke, but after he had returned the thing to his pocket his face grew grave. "I wish to heaven I saw some light in this muddle," he said. "I'm still completely at sea."

"Why don't you try making it into a scenario?" I inquired. "That's the way you solved the Lopez affair."

Jimmy shook his head. "This is a different type of story, Phil. It doesn't depend upon melodramatic action, but upon atmosphere. It would take an Arthur Machen to really do it justice. Nobody else could quite catch the peculiarly eerie feeling of horror that hangs over it."

I looked at him shrewdly. "You've got something up your sleeve," I accused, "something you're holding out on me."

"No; upon my word, I haven't. It's just that no theory we've worked out yet *feels* like the truth."

"Perhaps what the Colonel has to tell us to-day will help."

"I hope so," Jimmy spoke despairingly, "but I'm not counting on it, Phil. I'm not counting on anything."

At the Colonel's house Singh admitted us, impassive as always, then vanished into the shadowy hall as Chanda Steeb came swiftly from the stair.

"I should like to speak with you just a moment," she said in a low voice, "I've something to say before you see my father."

She led us into the little study at the end of the hall. It was much as it had been on Tuesday night except that a portable typewriter was lying, case open, upon the desk.

Jimmy's eyes leapt to the machine and I knew the question of the blackmailing letter was uppermost in his mind.

Chanda Steeb drew the curtains at the door, then turned to us quickly. "I want to ask your advice about father," she said. In the full afternoon light I saw that her face was pale, her eyes deep shadowed and full of care. "I . . . I don't trust the police," she continued. "But you seem kind and understanding."

"I hope we are, Mrs. Steeb." Jimmy smiled and drew forward the desk chair, but she remained standing, her hands clasped nervously upon her breast.

"It's about father," she repeated. "I'm frightfully worried. He hasn't been himself since Uncle Harlan's death."

"But surely that's perfectly natural," I suggested. "It must have been a pretty bad shock."

"Yes," she agreed, "but father isn't an affectionate person. He and Uncle Harlan were friendly but they weren't devoted. I'm sure his death wouldn't normally have upset him like this."

"But it wasn't a normal death," I pointed out. "He was murdered."

"I know." She hesitated, then seemed to decide upon frankness. "I think that's the trouble. Father's got an absurd notion that the police blame him for Uncle Harlan's death." Jimmy was silent, and she looked at him quickly. "It *is* absurd, isn't it?" she asked. And when he still did not answer: "Surely you don't . . . you can't mean they are suspecting him!"

The horror in her eyes brought him out of his abstraction, but I noted that he answered for himself, not the police. "No; I don't believe that your father was responsible for the murder."

The girl sighed with relief. "I knew it was ridiculous," she said, "but I can't convince him of it. He has a perfect obsession that two men are watching him all the time."

Jimmy glanced at me with an almost imperceptible grin and I knew he was thinking of McCarthy's smug assertion that the Colonel would suspect nothing, then turned again to Chanda Steeb.

"You say it's worrying him?"

"Frightfully. He hasn't slept and he spends all his time peering out the windows to see if the men are in sight. That's the reason I'm telling you about it. I'm afraid if he keeps on imagining this awful thing he may try to do something desperate."

"Just what do you mean?"

She raised her tortured eyes to ours. "I mean suicide. He spent last night and this morning going over all his affairs and putting them in order. When he went next door for a moment I looked through his things and found— this." She held out a little box to Jimmy who inspected it with an expression of relief.

"It's only veronal," he told her. "Nothing that need worry you. He's been taking it on Dr. Waverly's prescription."

"He's been buying it on his prescription, but he hasn't been taking it. I heard him walking up and down his room all night. If he'd taken anything of the sort he'd have been asleep, wouldn't he?"

"Yes," Jimmy agreed, and she went on quickly:

"That's what frightens me. I'm afraid he may be accumulating enough for an overdose—" She stopped and looked at us pitifully. "Oh, you don't know how hard this is for me, but Mr. Steeb is in no condition to be worried and I feel so helpless. . . ."

"Of course." Jimmy patted her hand paternally. "Still, I think you're unduly alarmed. Your father is naturally upset by what's happened and you've let your imagination work you into a panic."

She sighed with relief, and I saw that the unnatural tension was leaving her face. "You're probably right. Just telling you about it has made me feel better." She turned suddenly as a voice called from the stairs:

"Chanda!"

"It's father," she said. "Please don't let him know we've been talking, and thank you for being so kind." She pressed his hand and went out of the room quickly as the call was repeated.

For an instant Jimmy listened at the curtains, then, like a flash, returned to the typewriter on the desk. A couple of sheets of manuscript were lying beside it. One of them was crumpled and torn, obviously a discard. With a quick movement, he folded the paper and stuffed it in his pocket as the Colonel came into the room.

I suppose his daughter's picture of him as nervous and distraught had made me expect some visible change in his appearance, but he looked as grimly unmoved as ever. If I had not twice seen him in the midst of a rage I would have said the man was incapable of emotion as an iceberg. His greeting consisted of a more or less perfunctory nod and he dropped on to the worn leather cushion of the desk chair with something very like a snarl.

"It's my confounded knee," he explained, touching the stiffened joint with his stick. "Been getting worse all week; since last night it's been downright devilish."

"Rheumatism?" Jimmy asked politely.

"Touch of arthritis. Dr. Waverly's been trying to fix me up but hasn't managed to do anything. Never was much good as a physician, always too busy messing with microbes and spirits."

There was unconcealed contempt in the Colonel's voice, and Jimmy glanced up quickly. "I believe it was the doctor you wanted to talk about to-day," he suggested.

"Yes." The Colonel paused and traced the design on the carpet with his cane. His voice, when he spoke, was undecided. "When I gave you a ring last night I'd fully made up my mind to tell you something. But since then I've been thinking it over and I don't know . . ."

I was watching the fellow keenly as he talked. If his hesitation was assumed it was, at least, well done. He seemed to find great difficulty in choosing his words, and whole phrases were repeated twice, as though his mind was troubled by some doubt.

"I don't know whether it's wise to say anything or not. Fact is, I'd hold my tongue if it weren't that I've a pretty good idea the police are suspecting me of the murder." He paused and glanced up sharply as though to see the effect of his announcement, but Jimmy was apparently too busy looking for his cigarettes to answer. "I see you haven't anything to say to that," the Colonel remarked, "and I suppose if you're in the know you couldn't very well give me a hint, but there's been two fellows wandering around the neighborhood whom I never saw before and, last night, when I went out to the tobacconist I distinctly saw one of them following me."

Jimmy found his case and offered it. "Perhaps," he said, "it's because you lied about your whereabouts at midnight Monday."

The Colonel paused to light a match before he answered. "So they've found out about that, eh? Well, I'm not surprised. I was a fool to lie but I thought it might prevent my being drawn into the mess."

"I understand perfectly. But, as you say, it was a fool thing to do. When the police discovered you had been on the street at twelve o'clock they naturally drew their own conclusions."

"And made me the murderer! Pretty clear case of putting two and two together and getting fifteen. What?"

"Perhaps," Jimmy agreed with a grin which was disarming in its frankness. "But you needn't blame me for the performances of the police department. I don't agree with them, you know."

"Never thought you did. Know a man who has sense when I see him. That's the reason I want to tell you what have on my chest. Now that I don't lose anything by admitting I was on the street at five minutes past twelve Monday night, I don't mind telling you I saw someone go into my brother's house at that time."

"You know who it was?"

"No; I was crossing the street at the corner and from there the porch is more or less obscured by hanging vines. But the door opened and closed."

"You saw it by means of the light in the hall?"

"Yes; when the door opened it threw an oblong block of light out on the walk. At the time I didn't think anything of it because Singh goes in and out at all hours."

"But you don't think now it was Singh?" Jimmy asked quickly.

The Colonel shook his head. "No; I think it was Dr. Waverly."

"Have you any particular reason for thinking that?"

"A very good one. As you know, the doctor's house is next to mine. As I came across the street, I noticed that the lights were on in his living-room, which gave me the idea of dropping in on him for a moment. He'd been giving me some advice about my knee and I thought I'd stop and tell him the way the infernal thing was behaving. When I got up on his porch I was able to see into the front room, and I discovered it was empty."

"You didn't ring the bell?"

"No; it was after midnight. I was afraid the doctor might have gone off to bed without remembering to turn off the lights. Besides, there was something else that prevented my ringing."

"What was it?"

"The fact that he'd evidently been occupied with some business of his own. You remember he said he'd been going over old letters?"

"Yes," Jimmy nodded, "I do."

"Well, it wasn't only letters he'd been going through. I could see from the window that there were several trunks in the middle of the room and a lot of things which belonged to his dead wife were strewn about . . . dresses, and things of that sort. I concluded that, even if he was awake, he wouldn't want to be disturbed so I went on home to bed. Later on, when I thought it over, I decided it was the doctor I had seen going into Harlan's house."

"Why didn't you mention it before?"

"I couldn't without admitting that I was out on the street. Under the circumstances, I preferred to keep still."

"But Dr. Waverly had no reason for killing your brother."

"He had a better reason for killing him than any other man."

The announcement came so coolly that for a moment its real importance did not penetrate to my brain. When it did I gave an involuntary exclamation.

"Good Lord, man . . . they were devoted friends!"

"Yes," agreed the Colonel, "but there's one thing which will part the best of friends—and that's a woman."

"A woman?" Jimmy betrayed real excitement. "You mean to say there's a woman in this case?"

"I do," the Colonel nodded. "And what's still stranger . . . she's been dead for over ten years."

"The doctor's wife!"

"Exactly, the doctor's wife. I have reason to know that she was madly in love with my brother for some time before she died and, I believe, that is the reason the doctor killed him."

Jimmy was staring at the man astonished. "Why should he wait ten years?"

"Because he didn't know it ten years ago." The Colonel shook his head gloomily. "There's no one so blind as a devoted husband, Lane. The three of them were living together in one of those little settlements in India, the only whites in a hundred or so miles. It was a cholera year and Waverly had to be away a good deal, up and down the country. My brother was no saint where women were concerned and Mrs. Waverly was a pretty little fool. You can imagine the result. I don't know how long the affair would have gone on behind the doctor's back if Mrs. Waverly hadn't suddenly died. As luck would have it, the doctor was away at the time and he never learned the truth."

"But what makes you think he's discovered it now?" Jimmy demanded.

"Because of those old trunks. After his wife's death such of her things as weren't burned were saved by Singh's wife, Lalah. She was Mrs. Waverly's *amah,* you know, and she put everything away for the doctor to look over when he came back."

"And you think there may have been incriminating letters among her things?" Jimmy asked.

"Not a doubt of it. Harlan told me once that those wretched trunks hung over his head like a sword."

"You're sure the doctor had never been through them before?"

"Absolutely sure. He worshipped his wife, and my brother played on the fact. He used to get spirit messages from her for the doctor almost every week. Of course, it was easy to quote all sorts of intimate details . . . knowing what he did of the woman."

"Of course." Jimmy's lip curled in disgust and I knew he was experiencing the same anger that affected me at the thought of a man who would use his knowledge in such a way.

Evidently the Colonel had no such feeling for he went on serenely:

"He prevented the trunks being opened for years. But recently the doctor hasn't been well and he felt he wanted to dispose of his wife's things in case of his death."

"So you think the doctor found some letters in those trunks which opened his eyes to the relationship between your brother and his dead wife; the shock was too much for him and he temporarily went berserk?"

"That's what I believe," the Colonel said firmly. "I've believed it from the very first, but knowing the provocation I've said nothing about it."

"After all, it's only a conjecture," Jimmy observed. "It would be a shame to cast suspicion upon the man if he's innocent."

"*If.*" The Colonel raised his eyebrows. "I suppose you realize where that places me, Lane? If he's innocent I must be guilty."

"Not necessarily," Jimmy disagreed. "There's still another member of your household who might be responsible."

"You mean Singh. I've thought of him, too, but it doesn't make sense. He was getting a good living out of my brother's business. Tips, and that sort of thing, from the people who came up to the séances, and I can't see him deliberately cutting off his revenue."

"No?" Jimmy rose and stretched. I saw that something was in the back of his mind as he moved toward the door. "Well, perhaps you're right about Dr. Waverly, Colonel, but I hope not. I'd much rather think an outsider came in and killed your brother."

"So should I." The Colonel pulled himself erect with difficulty. "I'm not particularly fond of Waverly, but, hang it all, the man's been in and out of the house here for years and I don't relish the thought of his going to the penitentiary."

"Or being hanged," I suggested, but he shook his head quickly.

"He'd never hang for it in this country. The 'Unwritten Law' and all that. Am I right, Lane?"

"Yes," Jimmy's voice had a peculiar intonation, "yes; you're quite right, Colonel."

We were moving toward the door, but at the threshold he paused. "And, by the way, before I forget it—d'you mind telling me who uses the typewriter?"

"Typewriter?" The Colonel stared. "Why everyone in the family."

"You all go in for literature?"

"Well . . . not exactly. But every one of us has something in the way of a hobby or business which requires written stuff. My son-in-law, Steeb, makes notes on his experiments, and Chanda sometimes re-types them for him. I use it for business letters, and even Singh was in the habit of using it for my brother's work."

"Do any of you use the touch system?"

"Only Singh. The rest of us pick at the keys with one finger, but my brother had him trained in business college."

"Thanks." Jimmy spoke lightly but I knew something pleased him. "I think that's all I need to-day. Carter and I will just run down to Police Headquarters and see if anything new has developed."

As we moved down the steps I turned to him quickly. "What did you find out?" I demanded. "Don't deny it! I know by your voice that you got hold of something."

"Right as usual," he agreed. "I discovered that blackmailing letter was from Singh."

"Then you think Singh did the murder?"

"I do not. At least, I've no reason to think so."

I sighed with disappointment. "I'm sorry. I'd hoped against hope that it wasn't the doctor, even after what the Colonel told us."

Jimmy was regarding me with a quizzical smile. "Don't let the Colonel's yarn warp your judgement, Phil."

"You mean that you don't believe him?"

"I mean that I don't know what to believe. The story was good . . . but it was almost too good. And why didn't he tell it before?"

"He didn't want to admit that he was out on the street at twelve."

"So he says . . . but how do we know for sure? And then there's the matter of his knee. . . ."

"His knee?"

"Yes; he mentioned it twice, if you remember. Went out of his way to tell us how bad it was, and, only ten minutes before, his daughter said she'd heard him walking the floor all night. Does a man with a bad knee stalk up and down for hours?"

"But why should he lie about it?"

"Hanged if I know. Hanged if I know anything about anything! But I don't like the Colonel's sudden frankness about his brother's *amour* with the doctor's wife. It looks too much like a large and odoriferous herring drawn across the trail."

"But only this morning you said—"

"If you'll kindly oblige me by forgetting what I said this morning, or any other time, you'll do me a favor." Jimmy's tone was irritable. "Nine times out of ten I'm wrong."

"You mean—"

"I mean I believe the Colonel's the boy we're after. Just now he's my favorite candidate."

CHAPTER 13
THE SECOND MURDER

At Headquarters we learned that the Chief was away on business connected with another case. The news was something of a shock to me. For the last three days my mind had been so full of the Grant murder that it was hard to realize there were other cases on the calendar as important, if not as mysterious, as the Russian Hill affair.

Jimmy left an urgent invitation for the Chief to drop in and enjoy one of Friday's dinners, phoned a similar one to Corrigan, then drove on home. I dropped into my neglected office and found so much to attend to that it was nine o'clock before I reached the house. Dinner was long since over. Jimmy had retired with the Chief and Corrigan to his study where they were going over a series of notes which he had typed during the late afternoon. Since they give a very fair statement of the case at that time, I shall copy them here:

The Grant Murder
Harlan Grant murdered in his séance room a little after midnight on Monday night.
Body discovered Tuesday noon by his brother, Colonel Grant, and his East Indian servant, Singh.

*The door is bolted upon the inside and they
are forced to break in.*

*Grant is found lying upon the floor, at the
end of the room farthest from the window. His
face is twisted into an expression of horror, and
there is a fracture at the base of his skull.*

*Dr. Waverly, his family physician, pro-
nounces it death from cerebral hemorrhage. A
post-mortem is performed and there is a diver-
gence of opinion. Two doctors claim that he
died from the fracture at the base of the skull,
two others that he was poisoned and the skull
fracture was caused when he fell. Toxicologists
report no poison found in stomach. Impossible
to test for blood poisons because of embalming.*

Possible Suspects

Colonel Grant:

*Had motive because all brother's property was
left to him. It was known that he had been trying to dispose of securities for some time.*

Was on street at twelve Monday night.

*Might have gone up to see brother, quarreled
with him, struck him on head with cane, and
left room, leaving door unlocked. Could have
faked locking of door the next day by holding
handle while pretending to break in.*

Dr. Waverly:

*Had motive only if Colonel's story is true and
he had just discovered former relations between
his dead wife and Grant.*

*Lights on in his house at twelve o'clock Mon-
day night. May have been man seen by the Colonel going into Grant's house. Could have gone*

up, quarreled with Grant, killed him, and then returned home. No explanation, as yet, of how he could have locked door.

Stoddard:
Motive: blackmail threat that Grant was holding over Norah Fallon.

Was known to have been in the Grant house as late as twelve o'clock. As in the case of doctor, no explanation of how he could have locked the door behind him.

Singh:
Motive uncertain, but might have killed Grant in order to cash in on blackmailing material in files. Also might have been some quarrel between them we know nothing about.

Was known to have been on the street at twelve o'clock. May have been man Colonel saw enter house. Same difficulty as to the locked door that we have in the case of Stoddard and the doctor.

"I haven't put the Steebs down," Jimmy explained, "because we haven't been able to find any motive for them. Also, we'd still be faced with the question of the door."

Evidently Jimmy had retailed the Colonel's story about his brother and Mrs. Waverly, for Captain Hemming's first observation was a reference to that affair. "The case still seems strongest against the Colonel," he said. "Even with the stuff he's told us about the doctor, I'm inclined to suspect him."

"Same here," Jimmy agreed. "I don't like the patness with which he sprung that yarn after he began to realize we were suspecting him. And then, of course, there's nothing in his story which tells how the doctor could have locked the door behind him."

"I can tell you!" In his excitement Corrigan fairly leaped from his chair. "It was his germs! He inoculated Grant with some disease that didn't take effect until after he'd gone."

"And that didn't show up in the post-mortem!" Jimmy snorted. "I suppose the doctor trained his germs to kill Grant then fly out the window."

"Perhaps he used some form of poison that wouldn't work until after he'd left. I know there wasn't any found in his stomach, but it might have been given by hypodermic."

"Without Grant's knowing?"

"Couldn't the doctor have tricked him?"

"He could, but he didn't," the Chief spoke up from the other side of the fireplace. "I thought of that and had the doctors look for a break in the skin such as a hypodermic needle would make, but there was nothing of the sort."

"There's another reason against that theory," Jimmy observed. "You must remember that if the Colonel is right—and we're basing our entire assumption of the doctor's guilt on his story—then he must have only just discovered Grant's relations with his wife. Can you imagine a man in that state of mind stopping to figure out a complicated form of murder involving trained germs, or a mysterious poison and a hypodermic needle?"

"No," Corrigan admitted, "I can't."

"Neither can I. I can easily picture his reading the telltale letter, rushing over to Grant's, getting into a violent quarrel and hitting him over the head with the stone god. But that still doesn't explain the locking of the door."

"Which brings us back to Stoddard," the Chief observed, referring to the list. "I thought you were convinced of his innocence."

"I am. But I put him down because I wanted to play fair. There's no doubt about it, Stoddard had a perfect motive and an excellent opportunity."

"What about Singh?" Corrigan asked. "I see you've got him down as the one who's blackmailing Norah."

"We are practically certain he is the one," Jimmy explained. "I got a sample of typing from the Grant machine and it matches with the typing in the letter. A corner of the 'G' is broken off and the 'O' is a trifle out of alignment. The experts at Headquarters said that the letter was written by someone who used the 'touch system' and Singh's the only one who knows it in the Grant household."

"Which doesn't necessarily make him guilty of the murder," the Chief pointed out. "The hope of realizing profits on blackmail is rather a weak motive for a killing. He's much more likely to have seen a chance to carry out one of Grant's little schemes after his death and have seized it."

"That's my theory, too," Jimmy agreed with a nod. "He must have known most of Grant's business, and it wouldn't have taken him a minute to slip that envelope out of the files."

"Would it make any difference to you if I gave you a motive for his killing Grant?" Corrigan asked suddenly.

"Of course it would." The Chief looked a trifle annoyed. "Have you been withholding information?"

"Not exactly. It's something I learned only this afternoon." Corrigan paused for a moment and scratched Ruggles's ears as the pup lay luxuriously across his knees, then he went on, slowly: "I dropped in to see an old Anglo-Indian friend of mine, Major Cole. He talked a lot about Grant, but the only thing *new* he had to offer was about Singh. He says the fellow isn't of the servant class at all. He's an aristocrat. What's more, the Major is ready to swear that Singh was once an officer in the Army. He has a theory that Grant was holding something over Singh's head . . . something that kept the fellow faithful to him. He says it's no secret among the Indians here that Singh hated his master."

For a moment there was silence while they digested this, then Jimmy gave a low groan. "What a fool I've been! What a blooming, blasted fool not to see that Singh could have faked the locking of that door just as easily as the Colonel!"

"But it was the Colonel who tried it first."

"We have only *Singh's* word for it. Don't you see? If Singh was lying and he, himself, was the one to go up first, all our theories are reversed. Singh could have committed the murder and then pretended, the next morning, that the door was locked. It all depends upon which was the first to go up to the room Tuesday noon."

"That ought to be easy to find out." The Chief glanced at his watch. "It's only eleven. Why not call the Colonel and see what he has to say about the opening of that door?"

"I believe I will." Jimmy was crossing to the telephone, and later we had grim reason to remember that he actually had his hand on the receiver when Friday opened the door and announced Norah Fallon. I sometimes wonder what would have happened if Jimmy had put through that call. It might have made the moment's difference that would have saved a life. Then again, it might not. As always in real life, nothing warned us of impending tragedy and Jimmy abandoned the telephone to greet Norah.

I believe I have said twice before that Norah was beautiful, but the statement bears repeating. Just now she was in a dark-green coat with fur that framed her face and neck in a standing ruff of shining black. Her hat, too, was green, with a black buckle above one eye which gave it an indescribably jaunty air; but there was nothing jaunty about the girl herself as she stood looking about the room.

"Is Dick here?" she demanded, and when Jimmy shook his head she burst into speech. By the time my slow wits managed to catch up with her I discovered she was talking about a blackmailing letter. Not the one we had seen, but a second, apparently from the same source.

"It was left in my mail-box some time this evening," she said. "A perfectly horrible letter that threatened all sorts of things."

"What sort?" Jimmy asked. He was trying, unsuccessfully, to take her coat and lead her to a chair.

"That they would give that envelope full of stuff about me to the newspapers, and what was worse—would tell our connection with the case, I mean Dick's and mine, unless we left three thousand dollars in a certain spot in Golden Gate Park. Dick says even if we do it they'll never return the papers. He thinks they'll just take the money and go right on blackmailing us. He' says we've got to do something drastic."

The Chief looked distressed. "I suppose he's gone down to Headquarters to see me," he said. "I'd better call and have him come up here." He was reaching for the telephone when Norah shook her head.

"He hasn't gone there," she said positively. "I'm sorry, but he doesn't think an awful lot of the way the case has been handled so far. He said if we gave the police this second letter they'd only bungle it again . . . said he was going to handle the matter himself."

"But what is he planning to do?" Jimmy demanded.

"I don't know," her eyes were full of vague terror, "but I'm afraid he's gone to see the Colonel."

"The *Colonel?*"

"Why, yes. Of course, we know that horrible old man must be sending those letters. He's the only one who could possibly—" She suddenly faltered at Jimmy's expression. "You . . . you don't think it is someone else, do you?"

"We're sure it is," Jimmy told her, and exchanged a despairing glance with the Chief who had risen and come forward.

"What makes you think he went to see the Colonel?" he asked. "Did he tell you he was going?"

"No; but he left the hotel almost an hour ago and after he'd gone I began to worry. I tried to get him at his home but he wasn't there, nor at his club."

"But that doesn't prove he's gone to see the Colonel."

"I know, but just before he left he told me to go to bed and not worry because, by hook or crook, he'd have those papers in the morning. I was too mixed up to think clearly at the time, but afterwards I realized he must be planning to go up to Russian Hill and get them to-night." She broke off and wrung her hands with a little helpless gesture. "Oh, please . . . please go up there and stop him. I'm afraid of that terrible place."

"Don't worry," the Chief spoke comfortingly, "we've got men watching the Colonel. They'll see that nothing happens."

"Yes," Jimmy echoed the assurance, "they won't let him get into any trouble." But I noticed he was crossing to the closet where he kept his hat, and the Chief was about to follow when the telephone rang. For a moment, no one moved to answer. We stood eyeing the thing as though it were a poisonous snake, then Jimmy crossed to his desk and picked up the receiver. From the expression on his. face it was plain that something horrible had happened, but just how horrible we did not suspect even when he hung up the receiver and stood staring at the floor like a man who is suddenly stricken. For the space of a breath he stood so, then he swung around and put his hand over Norah's; his eyes were very kind as he looked down at her, kind and pitiful.

"It's no use trying to keep it from you, my dear," he said, "because you will have to know sooner or later."

She caught her breath in a little gasp. "It's Dick! He's been hurt!"

"No; it's the Colonel. He's been killed . . . and Dick has been arrested for the murder."

CHAPTER 14
THE YELLOW GHOST

It was misting when we reached the street and climbed into the police car. There are three hills between Jimmy Lane's apartment and the Grant house, but the land might have been as flat as a pancake for all the attention the driver paid to them. The car roared up breathless ascents and coasted down sickening declines at a speed which should have been terrifying, but which seemed, at the moment, all too slow.

Jimmy was sitting beside me in the tonneau with Ruggles in his lap; the pup had followed when we hurried out the door and, much to my surprise, Jimmy did not send him back. He rode now, one hand upon the dog's collar, his eyes fixed upon the darkness ahead, and, from his expression of utter weariness and despair, I knew he was blaming himself for the new disaster which had fallen upon Dick Stoddard.

"It's impossible that Stoddard should be guilty," he said, "utterly . . . madly impossible."

"I wouldn't be too sure until we get there," the Chief warned gloomily. "You don't know anything about the circumstances."

"I don't need to know. He might, conceivably, have killed one man accidentally, but two— Why, the thing's fantastic! It belongs in the category of bad dreams."

The Chief did not reply and it was apparent that he, too, was bewildered by the turn of events. Even Corrigan, who was accompanying us on the strict understanding that no story should go forth unless it was o-kayed by the Chief, was brooding glumly in his corner.

Nothing more was said until we reached Russian Hill, where we found officers guarding the door of the lower house. That it was the lower house and not the Colonel's surprised us, but there was no doubt the excitement centered there for a babble of voices sounded from within. In the upper hall a police surgeon was talking with Dr. Waverly who was dressed in pyjamas and a woolen bathrobe.

"Where is the body?" the Chief demanded, and, without speaking, the doctors turned and stepped aside so that we had a clear view of what lay on the floor between them.

I had been expecting that the body would be upstairs, in the room overhead, and the sight of it came as a double shock. It was lying at one side of the staircase, face down, arms extended, the head twisted at a grotesque and unnatural angle.

"Neck's broken," the police surgeon explained. "Snapped off short from the fall."

McCarthy bustled forward from the rear of the hall. "He was thrown from that landing up there." He pointed to the square space at the head of the stairs. "Stoddard was choking him when he fell over the banister."

"How do you know?" Jimmy asked quickly, and McCarthy turned to the police surgeon.

"You tell 'em, Doc, you can make it clearer."

"There are unmistakable marks of strangulation," the surgeon explained, "protruding eyeballs, tongue swollen, and congestion. Also, there are the marks of Stoddard's fingers on his throat."

"How do you know they are Stoddard's?"

"Because he admits it," said McCarthy.

"He admits *killing* him?" I have never seen such blank astonishment as showed in Jimmy's face.

"No; he hasn't confessed to the killing, but he's admitted that he choked the Colonel. What he says is—"

"Never mind that now," the Chief interrupted. "We'll hear his story in a minute. What I want to know is how this could happen when you were supposed to have men watching the place."

McCarthy flushed. "I did have men watching, Captain. The Colonel stayed in his house all day, but at ten-thirty he came over here and went upstairs. Then, in about half an hour, Stoddard came along and rang the bell. The boys didn't have orders to stop anyone from going in so they let him get by."

"How'd he get into the house?"

"The Colonel opened the door himself, Kellogg says. He's the man I had on the front of the house. Wilson was on the back. I landed a moment later to give them some orders and I couldn't help wondering what Stoddard was doing up there, so I moved up on the porch to listen at the window. I heard a lot of arguing going on 'way off upstairs. It finally got so hot that I'd just about decided to break in when it quieted down again. I didn't hear anything for a minute or two, then someone started coming downstairs. Whoever it was only got about halfway down, then started back up again. I guess it was about two minutes later, there was a sort of moan, then the most *godawful thud*. Of course, I started for the door, and just as I was getting it open Stoddard came running downstairs full tilt. He grabbed me, kind of crazy-like, and sung out: 'There's a man hurt upstairs, I got to get a doctor!' 'Course I wasn't going to let him get away so I sent Kellogg for Dr. Waverly and made Stoddard go upstairs with Wilson and me."

McCarthy paused and looked around, to make sure of our attention, before he continued. "The lower stairs were kind of dark but there was a light in the hall, and when I got up there it didn't take a minute for me to see that the Colonel was dead."

"Was he lying exactly as he is now?" Captain Hemming asked.

"Yes; the doctor didn't have to move him because a baby could see there was nothing to be done. His neck is twisted clear back."

"What did you do next?"

"Took out a pair of handcuffs and slipped them on Stoddard, then went down and called Headquarters."

"Without looking into the study upstairs?" Jimmy asked.

"Sure. Why should I look in the study?"

"To see if there was anyone there."

"There wasn't. Wilson looked later."

"After the culprit had got away," Jimmy suggested, and McCarthy shook his head.

"Nobody could have got away, Mr. Lane. There's only one staircase in this house, and the telephone's right on the landing. I could have seen anyone coming down from the study."

Captain Hemming seemed annoyed by the interruption. "What did Stoddard have to say?"

"Nothing. Just seemed kind of dazed, as though he couldn't make out what had happened."

"I thought he admitted something about choking the Colonel."

"That was later, after the doctor got here. You see, everything sort of happened at once. While I was phoning Headquarters Kellogg got back with the doctor. They went on upstairs, and I followed to see that the body wasn't moved. Stoddard went with me and when Dr. Waverly discovered fingermarks on the Colonel's neck, he said: 'I made those, I was choking him.'"

"I say!" Jimmy lighted a cigarette and glanced toward Hemming. "That doesn't sound very much like a guilty man."

"Why not?" the Chief snapped. "He was caught with the goods, probably thought it would pay better to make a clean breast of it."

"But he didn't," said McCarthy. "I thought for a minute he was confessing and I guess he realized it because he turned on me pretty sharply, and said: 'I was choking him but I didn't throw him down the stairs. That happened afterwards.' 'After what?' I asked. And he said, kind of dazed: 'After I'd left.'"

It was Jimmy's turn to be impatient. "Why don't we get the story from Stoddard instead of listening to it second-hand?"

The Chief nodded and turned to McCarthy. "Fetch him, Mac."

"O.K., Captain. I got him in a room down the hall."

As he left the group, Jimmy moved away toward the body of the Colonel. For a moment he studied the prone figure, then spoke to the police surgeon. "You're sure that congestion was caused by choking?"

"Yes; it's a plain case of strangulation . . . only partial, however. Death was caused by the broken neck, not the throttling."

"I see." Jimmy turned and looked up at the landing. "But I don't understand how he happens to be lying face down. If anyone was strangling him, the movement would naturally be backward."

"He might have turned over as he fell," Corrigan suggested.

"Not in that space." Jimmy pointed out the closeness of the ceiling overhead. "He is an extremely tall man, and a complete revolution would have been impossible. It looks to me as though he took a straight dive forward over the railing."

"Perhaps Stoddard was strangling him from behind."

"In that case, the thumb-marks would be on the back of the neck, wouldn't they, Doctor?" Jimmy asked, and the police surgeon nodded.

"You're right. The thumb-marks are directly in front. Any strangling that was done must have been with the two men facing each other." He was about to add more when the Captain raised a warning hand. Stoddard was coming down the hall with McCarthy. The change in him was terrible to see; he was looking dazed and uncomprehending, as though roused from a recent sleep. His blond hair was standing on end and his usually immaculate linen was rumpled and soiled. At sight of Jimmy his eyes brightened and he would have hurried forward if it had not been for the detective.

"Thank God you've come, Lane!" he said. "Perhaps you can get these fellows to listen to how it all happened."

"That's what I'm here for," Jimmy assured him, and the Chief added quickly:

"All we want is the truth, Mr. Stoddard."

Jimmy glanced at him with a slight smile. "I'm afraid, Captain, you won't like it when you get it. I warn you it won't be what you're expecting." And to Stoddard: "Don't waste time trying to conceal why you're here. Norah's already told us you came to see the Colonel."

"Good. Then you know that another of those damn letters came this evening. It gave us just twenty-four hours to act, and I decided to tend to it myself. I was a fool, of course, but it seemed to me the quickest thing would be to come up here and see the Colonel."

"But he wasn't the one who was blackmailing you."

"So I found out later. But at the time we both thought it was he. I was afraid if I phoned ahead he'd be warned, so I came up to catch him unaware. I was expecting t to find him at his own place, but when I got here there was a light in the upper window of this house and I rang the bell on the chance he might be here."

"And he was."

"Yes; he came to the door himself. I'm bound to say he seemed perfectly friendly and willing to talk. I suppose that should have warned me that he wasn't the fellow sending those letters, but I was obsessed with the idea and didn't stop to use my head. I made some sort of excuse for wanting to see him and he took me up to the study on the third floor."

"Did he close the door?"

"No; he left it wide open."

Jimmy nodded to McCarthy. "That's how you were able to hear them."

"Did he hear us?" Stoddard asked. "Then he knows what we were quarreling about. The Colonel insisted he didn't know anything about that envelope full of stuff that was in Grant's files. I thought he was lying and we had it hot and heavy. You know what the Colonel's temper was like. When I called him a blackmailer he went mad with rage and flew at me with that stick of his. For a moment it looked as though he was going to get the best of it, but I managed to get him by the throat and choke a little sense into him. It was along about there that I made up my mind he wasn't the one who was sending those letters."

"What made you realize that?"

"Because I went pretty far with that choking business . . . farther than I intended. When he got back his breath he swore on his honor that he'd never seen that envelope of stuff and hadn't sent those two blackmailing letters. He'd had a pretty bad shaking up and there was something about the way he talked that made me feel he was telling the truth. Not only that . . . he told me he was perfectly sure who was guilty."

"He meant Singh, of course," Jimmy interpolated.

"Yes; Singh. The Colonel said he was about the room a good bit the day after Grant was found dead and it would have been easy for him to have taken the envelope from the files. He was furious at the fellow and offered to help me get the stuff back, so we parted perfectly good friends."

"Did he come down to the door with you?"

"No; I left him sitting at the desk and came down myself. Only . . . I didn't leave at once. While I was walking downstairs I suddenly remembered the way Grant had fooled me Monday night, pretending not to have that envelope full of stuff when all the time it was in his files. I realized the Colonel was his brother and it made me think the envelope wouldn't be much safer with him than with Singh. He'd said something about going through Singh's office on the second floor, and I thought I'd just take a look for myself. I was half-way down the lower flight of stairs before I got the idea, then I stopped and went back to the second floor."

"Did you find anything?"

"Yes; I found the stuff about Norah. It was in a drawer of Singh's desk, tucked in between some other notes. I don't suppose he dreamed anyone would break in there and look for it."

"Never mind about that," Captain Hemming ordered impatiently. "Tell us about the Colonel."

"I was coming to that. As soon as I found the envelope I started for the door, but before I reached it there was a sound in the room overhead."

"What kind of a sound?"

"Well, first, I heard the Colonel speaking very low and indistinct, as though he were at the other end of the room. Then, suddenly, there was a horrible sort of scream and the sound of footsteps running. Immediately the door of the study flew open and the Colonel burst out of the room."

Stoddard broke off and frowned, as though he despaired of finding words to describe what he had seen. "The Colonel burst out of the room," he repeated, "and ran out on to that landing overhead. There's a bright light by the door and I could see his face plainly. I tell you, it was so contorted with horror that it wasn't like a human face . . . it was like a fantastic mask. It was as though he'd seen a ghost . . . not the usual sort of ghost . . . but something so hideously, unnatural that his brain refused to accept it. As he reached the landing he gave a sort of convulsive shudder and a ghastly moan that sounded as though it was torn from his throat, then pitched forward over the rail and landed, face downward, on the floor below."

Stoddard stopped and steadied himself as though the mere recounting of the scene was too much for him. The rest of us stood silent, hypnotized by the horror that was in his voice. Captain Hemming was the first to speak.

"What did you do then?"

"Nothing for a moment. Things like that don't happen to you every day, you know, and I was actually frozen with astonishment. Then I went down on my hands and knees and tried to lift him, but as soon as I'd raised his shoulders I saw that his neck was broken, so I laid him back again and made for the stairs with some wild idea of getting a doctor. At the front door I ran into McCarthy. I suppose he's told you the rest."

"Yes," Captain Hemming agreed grimly. "McCarthy arrested you and locked you into that room where you've spent the last half-hour thinking up this fairy-tale."

"Fairy-tale!" Stoddard glared at him. "Good God, you mean you think I'm lying?"

"Of course I think so!" The Captain's voice was angry, and I saw he was fighting stubbornly against the spell of horror which Stoddard had cast upon us. "Nobody could believe such a fantastic yarn."

"Just what is your theory, Captain?" Jimmy asked. "What do you think happened?"

The Captain spoke slowly, as though he were struggling to convince himself. "It's pretty plain what happened. Stoddard, here, came up to get those papers. The Colonel refused to give them up, and he was leaving. Probably, as he says, he got halfway down the second flight when he decided to go back and make another attempt. When he returned to the study he found the Colonel had taken the envelope out of some hiding place and was looking at it. He tried to take it away by force and, in the course of the struggle, the two went through the door to the landing where the Colonel was overbalanced and fell over the rail." As he talked, the Captain's voice grew firmer. It was plain he was beginning to be impressed with his own logic, and he finished almost cheerfully. "You really killed the Colonel accidentally, but you were afraid we wouldn't believe it so you figured out that wild yarn about his seeing a ghost and breaking his own neck, isn't that about the size of it, Mr. Stoddard?"

Dick Stoddard shook his head. "It isn't," he said, "but I can see that you've got everything fitted in so it's convincing. I know my story sounds impossibly fantastic, but it's the truth. If you won't accept my word . . ." His voice died away and he stood staring at the Chief helplessly.

Instead of coming to his rescue Jimmy Lane moved down the hall and beckoned to McCarthy. As the captor of the murderer there was a look of smug satisfaction upon the Sergeant's face and a hint of swagger in his walk.

"Want to know anything, Mr. Lane?"

"I do. I want to know how soon you went into that room at the head of the stairs after the Colonel's death?"

"Not for twenty minutes or maybe half an hour."

"I suppose," Jimmy's voice held a note of sarcasm, "it never occurred to you that it might be a good thing to search the room from which the Colonel had just come?"

"Can't say that it did, Mr. Lane. I'd already got the murderer and I knew there couldn't be anyone else in the house."

"Yes; I see." Jimmy paused a moment in thought, then: "Where's the other man who was with you?"

"Wilson!" McCarthy called, and a man detached himself from the group at the other end of the hall. "Wilson, Mr. Lane wants to talk to you."

"Glad to tell you anything I can, sir," the man answered willingly enough, but I noticed that his eyes shifted nervously and he flinched at Jimmy Lane's first question.

"Did you look into the room upstairs to-night, Wilson?"

"Yes, sir, I did. Right after we came up. The Sergeant told me to go up on the landing and measure how far it was to the floor. As I went past the door I happened to glance in."

"Did you see anything?"

The man hesitated. "Well . . . no, sir. I wouldn't exactly say . . ."

"Which means that you did," Jimmy interrupted. "What was it?"

"It was . . ." he spoke slowly, as though searching words for a difficult description, "it was something . . . yellow."

"What d'you mean," McCarthy growled, "'something yellow'?"

"I don't know," declared Wilson wretchedly. "It sounds crazy, but there was something yellow at the dark end of the room."

"You mean by the curtains?" Jimmy asked.

"Yes, sir. There wasn't any light there, you understand, but I got a sort of feeling of something yellow."

"Do you mean it was on the floor?"

"No . . ." Wilson again fought for words, "it wasn't on the floor, and it wasn't anything I could describe exactly because I only seen it out of the corner of my eye as I hurried past the door. But I got the idea there was something yellow between those curtains, something about as tall as a short man."

"How did you see it if it was dark?" McCarthy demanded, and Wilson was genuinely puzzled.

"I don't know, Sergeant. Honest, I don't know any more than you do. I only got the feeling it was there and that it was yellow. But when I come back into the room it was gone."

"You mean you went into the room later?" Jimmy asked eagerly.

"Yes; as soon I could get away I went up and looked again. Funny thing, I ain't usually scared of anything, but I was so sort of upset when I come into the room that my heart was pounding like it would bust. But there wasn't nothing there . . . nothing there at all."

"Was this, this *thing* you're trying to describe at all like a ghost?"

Wilson glanced up quickly and I saw that his eyes held terror, combined with something like relief; he seemed almost glad to have his thoughts brought into the open.

"Yes," he said. "I didn't like to say so because it sounded so crazy, but that's just what it did look like, Mr. Lane. All sort of thin and misty, like a yellow ghost."

CHAPTER 15
RUGGLES COLLAPSES

It must have been ten minutes before anyone became coherent after Wilson's statement fell like a bombshell in our midst. The Chief was annoyed, almost abnormally so, I thought, and McCarthy surreptitiously crossed himself. For a time everyone talked at once, then Captain Hemming took charge of the situation and ordered Stoddard taken to Headquarters. Corrigan went with him, also McCarthy, who superintended the removal of the Colonel's body, which had been photographed while Stoddard was telling his story. With the departure of the coroner's men, the house became quiet and we had time to catch our breaths.

"Where is the Colonel's daughter?" Jimmy asked Wilson. "Hasn't she been told about this?"

"Yes, sir. She got here right after Dr. Waverly."

"How'd she stand the shock?"

"Pretty well, considering. It was that East Indian maid of hers who collapsed. Mr. Steeb went to pieces, too, and Mrs. Steeb had to go back and take care of him."

"He wasn't here, of course?"

"No, sir. They said he was in the other house, in bed."

"How about Singh?"

"He came over before Mrs. Steeb but the Sergeant sent him back. Didn't want a lot of people mussing around."

"Good!" Captain Hemming nodded, and gathered up his hat. "I don't think we need bother the Steebs to-night. As a matter of fact, there isn't much more to be done. It looks as if we've got a pretty straight case against young Stoddard."

I glanced at Jimmy to see how he was taking this, but he was, apparently, not disposed to argue. "Do you mind if we remain a little longer?" he asked the Chief. "I'd like to take another look around."

"Why no. You can't do any harm so long as you don't touch anything. At the same time, I can't see that you'll do any good. What's your idea, Lane?"

"Haven't any," Jimmy admitted. "But, unfortunately, I'm not like you officers of the law. I can't bring myself to discard evidence just because it doesn't fit some cast-iron theory."

"Well," Captain Hemming was shrugging on his heavy coat and drawing the collar up around his neck, "I wish you luck! If it's that stuff of Wilson's that's worrying you, my advice is to forget it. The explanation is so simple that it's laughable."

"Yes?" Jimmy was regarding him keenly. "I suppose you mean that unshaded light on the landing?"

"Oh, you've thought of that, have you?" The Captain's voice sounded a trifle disappointed.

"I have," said Jimmy, and I heard him chuckle as Hemming went down the stairs.

I waited a moment for the explanation. When it wasn't forthcoming I asked irritably: "What's that unshaded light got to do with Wilson's spook?"

"It's a little optical illusion that the Chief thought wouldn't occur to me," Jimmy explained. "Have you ever stared at a flame for a moment, then looked at a dark surface?"

"Of course. . . ." Suddenly I caught his meaning., "You think that Wilson was looking up. at the landing and printed the light upon his retina so that the 'something yellow' he saw was nothing more than a reprint of the light against the curtains?"

"No," Jimmy corrected me, "that's what the Chief thinks. It's too early to say what *I* think. First, I want to look into that room above." But, instead of immediately climbing the stairs, he stood a moment lost in thought, then called Wilson. "You're dead sure nobody could have got out of that room upstairs without being seen?"

Wilson was positive. "Not unless he could fly, sir. From the time the Colonel fell, there was never a minute when somebody wasn't either in the hall or on the stairs."

"Good." Jimmy turned to me with one of his incomprehensible requests. "I say, Phil, do you mind going downstairs and getting Ruggles? We need a little expert bloodhounding."

Ruggles had been tied on the porch, and through the window I could see him sitting, a shaggy figure of dejection, his nose pressed tightly against the door. At sight of me he changed instantly into the personification of joy, and I had to suppress his yelps of delight with a firm hand across his hairy nose. The pup under one arm, I returned to the second floor where Jimmy was putting Wilson through some sort of a test. The detective was standing at the bottom of the stairs staring up toward the light on the landing overhead.

"I want you to concentrate on it for a moment," Jimmy said, "then run to the top of the stairs and look into that room just as you did to-night."

Wilson obeyed, and a moment later his voice came from above: "No, sir. It don't look the same . . . not the same at all."

"In what way does it differ? Can you tell us?"

"Sure I can tell you. This here is round and hard and bright. It stays in one place, just like the light. The other

was sort of tall and wavery like . . . sort of like somebody
in a yellow veil. And while I was looking it moved."

"Good," Jimmy showed satisfaction, "that eliminates
the light theory. Come on, Phil, it's time we looked into
that room."

It wasn't until I was actually climbing the stair that I
realized the enormous excitement under which I was labor-
ing. What Jimmy expected to find in the room overhead I
had no idea, but whatever it was, my heart was pounding
like a trip-hammer and my hands were shaking as we entered the door.

The place was exactly like it had been on our last visit
except that only one light illuminated the room. This was
on the desk, and its green glow barely served to brighten
the space by the window. The other end was, for the moment, only a cavern of darkness; but, as my eyes became
accustomed to the gloom, I picked out the gilded mirror
glowing dimly beyond the hanging curtains of dark velvet.
Jimmy glanced at this and then toward the desk lamp.

"You can't get any reflection of that light in the mirror
from the door," he said thoughtfully. "And even if you could,
it would reflect green instead of yellow." He crossed to first
one then the other of the davenports and regarded them
intently for a moment, then moved on toward the curtains.

The heavy folds of velvet were half-drawn, cutting off
the room at either side so that the shadows lay beyond
them, thick and dark and strangely disturbing. I found my
heart pounding again, but this time its pulsation was slow,
not fast. It seemed to be marking some deadly rhythm with
its muffled beat. There was a queer heavy feeling stealing
over me, a conviction that something infinitely evil and
malignant lurked in the shadows of the room.

Ruggles was shivering with excitement under my arm.
He was barking sharply and looking toward Jimmy with

those strange speaking eyes of his which were brown with golden lights. Jimmy took him from me and planted him firmly upon his feet. I saw that he was holding a pistol and that it was pointed toward the curtains.

"Go seek!" he ordered. "Good boy! Go seek!"

It was the old game of hide-and-seek, Ruggles's favorite, and one that he often played with Jimmy or with visitors at home. There it ended in a wild romp with the pup barking madly at the door or curtain behind which, his keen sense of smell told him, his playfellow was hiding. To-night it seemed horrible, somehow, and indecent, to see Jimmy put the quivering terrier on the floor and, pistol in hand, bid him "go seek".

The dog darted behind the curtains and his little yelping bark came to us from a shadowy corner. Suddenly the sound died away and there was silence. As Jimmy started forward, the dog reappeared. I think I have said that Ruggles laughed as easily and as readily as any human being. In front of the crackling fire in Jimmy's study I have seen him throw back his head and stretch his mouth into a grin which was reflected, in his twinkling brown eyes. If you can believe this, perhaps you can believe what I tell you now. When he reappeared from behind the curtains his little whiskered face showed horror, a horror that was expressed by a whining protest in his throat. For a few tottering steps he came toward us, his body shivering so violently that it seemed impossible he could keep his feet; then he dragged himself toward the door, still at that hideous, crawling pace, only now his head was twisted back over his shoulder as if in deadly terror of some unseen thing which pursued. Before he reached the threshold his four legs crumpled and he went down in a little heap. The low whining in his throat died away and only his eyes, wide and staring, showed that he still lived.

In an instant Jimmy was on his knees gathering the pup
in his arms. I believe he was crying, I know that I was . . .
crying and swearing, too. Somehow, between us, we got
him out into the hall, down the stairs and into one of the
bedrooms. I think leaving the dog there with Wilson was
the hardest thing either of us ever did, but there was no
time to be lost. On the run we pounded up the stairs and
back into that abominable room.

Ignoring the Chief's order about touching things, Jimmy pressed the button at the door and lights flashed upon
the walls. Together we advanced on the curtains and threw
them back to their farthest limits so that every inch of the
room was illuminated. There was nothing visible, nothing
which could remotely explain Ruggles's terror.

I think both of us were a little mad. We pounded the
walls, sounded the mirror, and Jimmy again examined the
drops of gilt upon both sides of the frame to make sure
that they remained unbroken. But it was all useless. There
was no opening in the walls, the ceiling above, or the
floors beneath that would admit so much as a rat, let alone
a human being. At the end of ten minutes we gave up the
search and sank down on a davenport. Wilson had come
up from below to report that Ruggles was himself again,
though pitiably shaken and weak. He had left him tied to
a leg of the bed in Grant's room and his little whimpering
cries, coming up from below, did nothing to help our state
of mind.

Wilson took out a large handkerchief and passed it over
his forehead which glistened with little beads of sweat. "I
wish I'd never been put on this case," he declared. "It . . .
it's got me going, Mr. Lane."

Jimmy made no answer. He was sitting, sunk down
among the cushions of the davenport, his face looking
strangely white against the dark tapestry. His eyes were
upon the velvet curtains, which hung like black palls

against the bare white walls of the room. Below, the faint whining had grown into a steady wail, like the sobbing of a frightened child. Otherwise the house was silent, with a sort of monstrous quietude, as though all motion had stopped and the world hung suspended, waiting for some abominable thing to take place.

For a long moment Jimmy's troubled eyes passed over the curtains, the floor, and the mirror which reflected the room with a sort of scornful detachment, then, at length, he answered Wilson.

"It's got me, too," he said softly. "It's hideous beyond anything I've ever encountered. Up to ten minutes ago I believed that we had only to stretch out our hands and we'd lay them upon a flesh and blood murderer, but now . . ." He hesitated, as though he dreaded to go on, and Wilson asked in a voice which trembled slightly:

"You mean . . . you think it wasn't flesh and blood, Mr. Lane?"

"What can I think? We know that no human could have got in or out of this room to-night. And what mortal thing could have put that look upon the Colonel's face, and driven a dog half-mad with fear?"

Desperately I tried to bring my mind to some semblance of reason, to catch hold of the realities of life. "Surely," I protested, "surely you don't believe in spirits?"

Jimmy rose, and I saw that his eyes were dark with pain. "There are more things in Heaven and earth than we dream of, Phil. After what we've seen to-night, who am I to say that spirits do not return . . . yes; and commit murder, too?"

CHAPTER 16
THE DOCTOR'S WIFE

It was almost light when we reached home Saturday morning. Both of us were exhausted and, without any discussion, we dropped into bed and slept heavily. At one o'clock I woke to find Friday shaking me firmly by the shoulder.

"Mist' Lane wants fo' you to get up, Mist' Cartah. He's jus' settin' fo' his breakfast an' Miss Fallon is comin' fo' a talk."

Instantly the whole hideous pageant of the night before flashed across my mind. "How is Ruggles?" I demanded, and Friday frowned.

"He's up an' aroun' but he's mighty poorly. Ah reckon that little dog seen somethin' las' night that sits heavy on his mind." He shook his head at me reproachfully. "You and Mist' Lane hadn't ought to of take him to that house. Dogs is lots smarter than folks is and their eyes is sharper. They can see things we cain't. If that dog could speak, Ah reckon he tell you-all things would make your blood run cold!"

From his ominous tone and the way he shook his head as he withdrew from the room I gathered that Jimmy had told him the story of the night before, although I couldn't for the life of me see why. He enlightened me at the breakfast-table.

"I wanted to get Friday's reactions," he said quite soberly. "Those fellows are a lot simpler than we are, Phil, and nearer to the heart of things. Sometimes they feel truths instinctively that we, in our infinite wisdom, are too ignorant to admit."

"You're not talking about spirits again, are you?" I demanded irritably. Already the sober light of day had brought back my sanity and I was prepared to discount our terror of the night before. "I was hoping you'd have acquired sense by morning."

"I haven't acquired anything," said Jimmy sadly, "except a whale of a headache and a great distaste for the whole affair."

"Have you heard anything from Stoddard?"

"Not directly, but I communicated with his lawyer this morning, and with Norah. She's coming over now to give us the full particulars. I understand they've locked him up, but so far the Chief's kept it quiet. The morning papers carry only stories about the Colonel being found dead. I'm afraid the news about Stoddard's arrest will break this afternoon. . . . Hemming's promised to keep Norah's name out of it as long as possible."

"Pretty decent of him, considering the fact that he's sure Stoddard is guilty."

"I don't know how *sure* he is," Jimmy said. "I had him on the phone, too, and while he still insists that everything's against the boy, I've an idea that somewhere inside of him he feels it doesn't make sense."

"Do you think so, yourself?" I asked.

"Know so," he snapped. "It's idiotic anyone should think Stoddard did it."

"But all the evidence . . ." I began, and Jimmy interrupted.

"Oh, I'll grant you the evidence about the Colonel's death. But, how about his brother? No one has ever explained how Stoddard could have locked that door behind him."

Of course. I had forgotten that cursed door. It actually took me a moment to recollect the particulars surrounding Grant's death.

"I remember, we decided that the only one who could have managed the door was Singh or the Colonel," I said slowly. "I suppose now that the Colonel is dead you're looking toward Singh?"

Before he could answer Norah's voice spoke from the door. "Who's talking about Singh?"

Jimmy rose to greet her and brought her back to the table, where Friday poured a cup of coffee and hovered solicitously about with muffins and marmalade. She accepted the coffee but waved aside the food and turned to us eagerly.

"Do tell me, have you learned anything new about Singh?"

"No." Jimmy looked at her sharply. "Why do you ask?"

"Because something has happened. You remember what you said about my maid . . . that she was probably the one who gave Grant his information? Well, you were right. This morning, after I'd left the house to start here, I discovered I had a pair of mismated gloves, so I turned and went back to the apartment. I wasn't intentionally quiet, but when I let myself in, Clara didn't hear me. She was at the telephone talking to Singh."

"What did she say?"

"Not very much because she caught sight of me in the mirror over the table almost at once. But I heard enough to know that she was giving him 'Hail Columbia' about something."

"He was probably breaking it to her that he'd lost those papers and the scheme was off," I observed, and she nodded.

"That's what I figured, too. I suppose she was to get part of the money."

"What did she say when she saw you?"

"She pretended she'd been talking to the cleaners, about a suit that hadn't been sent back, and I pretended to believe her. But I heard one thing: she ordered Singh to meet her this evening."

"Where are they to meet?"

"That I didn't catch. Just the time . . . eight o'clock. Oh, don't you suppose something can be done about it? Singh must have been the one who committed those murders!" She waited a moment, then, as Jimmy did not answer: "Don't you think he is?" she demanded.

Jimmy looked down at his feet where Ruggles lay, twitching and shaking nervously in his sleep; at sight of the pup an expression of pain crossed his face, and when he answered, his voice was very grave.

"I can't tell you what I think, Norah. Up to last night I believed that when the case was solved, the explanation would be so simple that we'd all laugh at our own stupidity, but now . . . my mind is in chaos. I tell you frankly, there are things which I can't explain except in a way which my common-sense refuses to accept."

"You mean you think there was something . . . something supernatural about it?" Norah asked in a half-whisper.

"I hate the word 'supernatural'," Jimmy protested. "Let's call it 'unnatural' . . . that is, outside the limits of what we usually encounter in the course of everyday life."

"But what are we going to do?" Norah demanded helplessly. "You can't tell that to the police, they'd only laugh at you. And in the meantime Dick—" her voice broke over the name, "Dick is locked up in that horrible place, and he's forbidden me to go near him for fear of the reporters. I can't stand it much longer! I can't!"

She was crying now in earnest, and Jimmy rose hurriedly from his place and put his arm comfortingly about her shoulders.

"Don't," he protested, "don't lose your courage. Nothing is going to happen to Dick, I can promise you that."

She looked up, her eyes shining through tears. "Then you do know who committed those murders?"

"On my word of honor, I don't know any more than you do. But I'm certain it wasn't Stoddard. Somehow I'll convince the police."

"What are you going to do?"

For a moment Jimmy did not answer. He had turned away and was studying some notes which were jotted roughly on the back of an envelope. In the strong light of the afternoon sun his face showed unusual strain; the fresh color was gone from his cheeks, and his eyes, usually twinkling with humor, were heavy and dark-circled. There was a gravity about his whole demeanor which was so unlike him that he seemed a different and much older man.

"There are a number of things I want to find out," he said, "and still others that I'll get Corrigan to look up for me; but, first, I think Carter and I will go to Russian Hill."

"And see Singh?" Norah asked eagerly.

"No," Jimmy shook his head, "I'm not interested in Singh for the moment. I want to see Dr. Waverly and ask him a few questions about his dead wife."

The doctor was at home and admitted us himself. If he was surprised at our visit he showed no signs of it. He was looking a trifle pale and I noticed his hand shook as he greeted us, but that might easily be explained by the strain of the last few days. He led the way into his living-room, a square apartment with a fireplace at one end and a desk by the window. It must have been, normally, a cheerful, comfortable place but now it was in complete confusion. Before the hearth an open trunk strewed its contents over the chairs and floor; an embroidered shawl, a feather fan, and a pair of slippers that had once been gold were tossed upon the couch, while the desk was stacked with several packets of old letters, and a little leather-bound diary. The doctor apologized in his gentle voice.

"You'll find the place rather upset, I'm afraid. I was going through some things which belonged to my wife when this terrible tragedy happened next door."

Involuntarily my eyes sought Jimmy's but he was looking at a portrait on the wall. "Was that Mrs. Waverly?" he asked.

The doctor nodded. "Yes; it was painted only about a year before her death. The artist was visiting India; he saw her at a costume ball and asked her to sit for him."

"She was very beautiful," Jimmy observed, and I agreed with him.

Unless the painter was an arrant flatterer, the woman of the portrait must have been singularly lovely. She was dressed in a costume of the *moyen âge* (Mélisande, I believe, was the character) and her dress of gold brocade was spread out about her like the petals of a flower; above the pearl-embroidered bodice her shoulders rose in a divine curve to her neck and throat, which were beautifully modeled, as were her lips. Her eyes were deep blue shadowed with heavy lashes, but the thing which caught and held one was her hair. It flowed from under a chaplet of pearls rippled over her shoulders to the pointed waist of her bodice and fell in swirling tendrils upon the embroideries of her skirt like a cascade of living gold. The painter had caught, somehow, the vital quality of that hair and had played upon it until it became the theme of the picture.

The doctor seemed to read our thoughts. "It wasn't a wig," he said quickly. "She was in fancy dress but her hair was her own. It was exactly like that, pale gold and so heavy that when she loosened it at night it hung about her like a veil to her knees." He was gazing up at the picture with a look which was strangely intent, as though he had forgotten our presence and was lost in recollections of the past.

In a low voice Jimmy asked, "How long has she been dead?"

"Ten years . . . but it seems only yesterday. I was not there when . . . when it happened, and she has always seemed alive . . . until the other day when I opened that trunk and saw her things. It is as though she had only just died."

Words are poor things at times and I cannot give any idea of the mournfulness of the man, the utter desolation of his voice. It was as though everything which bound him to the earth had been swept away, leaving him helpless and bewildered. A minute passed, two minutes, and he still stood, apparently unconscious of our presence, then suddenly he roused himself.

"I'm sorry, gentlemen, I'm very inhospitable. Won't you sit down?"

We dropped into chairs to left and right of the hearth while the doctor bent over and lighted the fire which was already laid. "I'm glad you've come," he said. "I wanted to ask you about the latest developments of the case. The papers this morning said very little, but I gathered from the police last night that they were arresting young Stoddard. Is that so?"

"Yes," Jimmy replied. "Stoddard is being held."

The doctor shot a quick glance at him. "Do you think he is guilty, Mr. Lane?"

Jimmy side-stepped the question by returning it. "Do you?"

"I don't know." The doctor's eyes were troubled. "The evidence against him is pretty clear but he doesn't seem like the sort of chap who would deliberately murder two men. At the same time, there isn't anyone else who could have done it."

"Except Singh," I suggested.

He swung around quickly. "You've thought of him?"

I glanced at Jimmy Lane; he seemed amiably willing for me to go ahead, so I nodded. "Yes; we've figured that he and the Colonel were the only ones capable of faking the locking of the door." At some length I explained the method and he listened with an interest which was obviously heightened by some secret thought. "Singh told us that the Colonel was the first to go upstairs to call Grant," I finished. "But he may be lying. We were just going to call the Colonel and learn what he had to say when word came that he'd been killed."

For a moment there was silence and I saw that the doctor was thinking deeply, then he apparently came to some decision.

"I don't want to cast suspicion upon an innocent man," he said; "at the same time, I don't want to withhold information which may lead to the guilt being thrown unjustly on young Stoddard. I think perhaps I should tell you that there was no love lost between Singh and my friend Grant."

"We've already been told something of the sort," I said. "Corrigan found it out from a member of the Anglo-Indian colony. He said that Singh hated his master."

"It's true," the doctor told us. "Lalah, Singh's wife, frequently came to me with her troubles. Harlan was hard to get along with, overbearing and inclined to be cruel. I can't say that he treated Singh well. He used to speak of him as 'that nigger', and I've even seen him strike the fellow. Singh isn't from the servant class, and he resented such treatment . . . no doubt of it."

"Then why did he stay?" Jimmy asked, and the doctor shook his head.

"I've never quite understood the relationship between the two men, but I'm afraid Harlan was holding something over Singh. He once told me he had Singh's life in the hollow of his hand and, occasionally, he used to threaten him in a veiled sort of way. He paid him very little, and Singh depended upon tips for the largest part of his wages. When you really come down to it, Singh had more reason than anyone for committing the murder."

"But why should he kill the Colonel, too?"

"I can't tell you that," the doctor admitted. "They certainly disliked each other and the Colonel used to roar at him now and then . . . but that's scarcely sufficient reason for murder."

"Unless the Colonel had discovered something and was about to give him away," I suggested.

The doctor threw me an approving glance. "That's possible," he agreed. "In fact, I should say it's more than possible . . . it's probable. Certainly it sounds more likely than that young Stoddard killed them both."

Jimmy had been sitting back in his chair, his eyes upon the fire; to all appearances his mind was far away from our discussion, but the question he asked was entirely pertinent. "If it was Singh who killed the Colonel, how do you account for the story young Stoddard told?"

The doctor shook his head. "I don't," he said frankly, "any more than I can tell you how Singh committed the murders themselves, that is, if he did commit them. I am only saying that he seems a likelier man than Stoddard."

There was an interval while Jimmy considered this, then he changed the subject abruptly. "I wish you'd tell me something about Lalah. Was she with your wife for a long time?"

"No," the doctor shook his head, "only a year or so. She was already married to Singh when Grant came to the station, and when my wife's *amah* left she offered her services. She was with my wife when she died."

"Was Mrs. Waverly's death sudden?" Jimmy asked.

"Very sudden, and I was too far away to be reached. By the time I got home she was already buried." The doctor's voice was low and his eyes were again seeking the portrait which hung, dimly beautiful, on the shadowed wall beyond.

As though to distract him Jimmy made another sudden transition. "I wonder if it would be possible for us to talk with Mrs. Steeb again?"

"Why, I fancy she'll be able to see you. When I was there an hour ago she seemed to be bearing up very well. That silly maid, Lalah, had gone completely to pieces, and Steeb is in a state of collapse, so she has to nurse both of them."

"You say that Steeb has collapsed?"

"Well, 'collapsed' is probably the wrong word.' As a matter of fact, the fellow is almost insanely lively. He's always been more or less neurotic and this thing has provided him with an obsession. He claims that this business is only half through and that someone is trying to wipe out the whole family. His latest plan, I believe, is to lock himself in his laboratory and have food passed through a hole in the door."

"Perhaps," I said hopefully, "perhaps he knows of some mysterious enemy the family had in India."

The doctor smiled a trifle wanly. "I'm afraid you've been reading 'Dr. Fu-Manchu' or 'Sherlock Holmes'. Those things don't happen in real life. And, besides, if Harlan Grant had possessed any such enemy you can be sure he would have told me. We were extremely intimate for years."

"That reminds me," Jimmy exclaimed suddenly, "of a question I meant to ask earlier. Did Grant say anything to you about the fear of fear?"

For a moment the doctor considered, then nodded. "Yes; I believe he did . . . but it was some time ago."

"Just what did he say?" There was a hint of eagerness in Jimmy's voice and he leaned forward to catch the doctor's reply.

"As I remember it, we were discussing his mother's death. She was a medium, too, you know, and she was found dead with an expression of terror upon her face. I was telling him that in cases of apoplexy the features are often distorted into a grimace which may be construed either as anger or fear or horrible laughter, depending upon which facial muscles are affected. Harlan seemed relieved by my explanation. He told me that he was only a boy at the time she died and that the whole thing had preyed upon his mind until he became convinced that she had seen something horrible. For years he lived in constant fear of some day seeing something so terrifying that he would die of sheer-fright. It was this which originally had led to his researches in India." The doctor paused, and Jimmy leaned still farther forward in his chair.

"You were the first to see Grant after he was found dead in his study, would you say that his expression was one of horror?"

"Undoubtedly that is how it would be described."

"Didn't you connect it in any way with the conversation you have just repeated?"

When the doctor answered his voice was very low. "If I did I tried to put it from me as absurd and fantastic. At the time, I had no reason to suspect that the death was anything but natural. I merely thought that he had died from a brain lesion, in the same fashion as his mother."

"And later," Jimmy pressed, "when they declared that it was murder, what did you think then?"

The doctor's hands went to his head and I saw that they were trembling violently. "I tried not to think," he cried. "Don't you see what untold horror it opened to the imagination? I deliberately forgot everything connected with it until last night."

"You mean when you saw the Colonel?"

"Yes." The other raised tortured eyes. "Call it due to strangulation if you like, I swear to you his expression was the same as that of my poor friend."

CHAPTER 17
IN THE LABORATORY

Dr. Waverly himself took us into the next house, unlocking the door with a key which hung upon his key-ring. He established us in the living-room then went in search of Chanda Steeb. When he returned she was with him, immaculate, as always, in her simple, straight gown. To-day the white collar and cuffs were missing and the dress was of unrelieved black; between the somber high collar and the curve of dark hair the creamy oval of her face showed like a tragic mask.

She gave a hand to each of us, then dropped wearily into a chair. "Dr. Waverly tells me that you want to ask some questions," she said. "Do you mind being as quick as possible? I can't leave Mr. Steeb for very long."

"How is he to-day?" Jimmy asked sympathetically, and a shadow crossed her face.

"Not at all well. I want him to see a doctor, but he refuses . . . he's a little difficult at times."

"The eccentricity of genius," he suggested, and she nodded.

"He really *is* a genius, you know. Only few people appreciate it because chemistry isn't a showy thing like music or art."

"You help him, I understand."

"Yes; I keep his notes and do the unimportant routine work that would merely waste his time." She made a deprecatory little gesture and changed the subject. "What do you wish me to tell you, Mr. Lane?"

"First, I should like to know where Singh was at the time of your father's death last night."

"Singh?" She looked puzzled. "Why, I suppose he was in his room."

"You said, I remember, that his room was directly under yours. Did you hear his voice?"

"No; because I wasn't in my room. Mrs. Chapman was here—"

"The Lady Elfrieda!" Jimmy gasped, then, at her expression of astonishment: "Just a fool nickname we've given her," he explained. "Do tell us what she was doing here at that hour."

"It wasn't very late," Chanda protested, "and there was nothing unusual about her being here. She's president of the League for International Peace, and I've been acting as secretary. I wasn't able to attend the meeting last night because of Uncle Harlan's death and Mrs. Chapman dropped in to give me the minutes."

"What time did she leave?"

"I can't tell you exactly, but it was some time after my father went over to the house next door. He passed through the hall and called to me that he was going to work in the study. After that we talked for about fifteen or twenty minutes, I should say, then she left and I went up to my room and got ready for bed. Next, I began to heat some milk over a little stove we have in the bathroom. It was while I was there that I heard my father scream."

"You heard him?" Jimmy stared at her. "You actually *heard* him scream?"

"Yes, then a moment later, I heard the sound of his fall."

"By Jove, that's queer! Did your husband hear it, too?"

"No; he was asleep on the other side of the house. He'd slept very little for the past few nights and I'd persuaded him to go to bed early."

"What did you do after you heard the scream?"

"I ran into the hall and discovered Lalah was coming up from her room. I told her to have Singh go over to the house next door and find out what had happened."

"And did he go?"

"Not at once. I suppose he stopped to dress. It was at least three or four minutes before I heard him leave. In the meantime, Mr. Steeb had wakened. I didn't want to alarm him unnecessarily so I went into his bedroom, and I was there when Singh came back. One of the detectives was with him and they told us what had happened. I left Singh with Mr. Steeb and took Lalah next door with me."

"What happened when you got over there?" From the casual tone of the question I knew that Jimmy had forgotten Chanda Steeb's relationship to the dead man and how harrowing the experience must have been for her. But almost immediately he remembered and there was sympathy in his face as he listened to her brave attempt to answer.

"My father was lying in the upper hall, just as he had fallen. Dr. Waverly was there with two or three detectives and Mr. Stoddard was just being locked into one of the bedrooms. I wasn't there long because Lalah had foolishly gone upstairs into that study of my uncle's and it threw her into a fit of hysterics. She had to be carried back here and put to bed."

Jimmy was plainly interested by something in this recital. He addressed his next question, not to Chanda, but to Dr. Waverly.

"Did you see the maid when she was having her attack?"

"Yes; I took charge of her until she quieted down."

"Did she speak of seeing anything in the séance room?"

"Why, no." The doctor looked puzzled, then seemed to realize the purport of the question. "Oh, I understand. You thought she might have seen someone in the room when she went up there, but it's impossible. Nobody could have got either in or out of the house. I know because Singh and I helped the detectives check the windows and doors immediately after the murder."

"Singh helped them check?"

"Yes; the man they called Wilson was busy upstairs with McCarthy so Singh and I went around with Kellogg to look at the windows and doors."

"How did you find them?"

"They were all fastened on the inside except the window by the front door which was open but had a locked screen. Both McCarthy and Kellogg were standing there at the time of the murder so it would have been impossible for anyone to have escaped that way."

"You're sure none of the windows were open?"

"Absolutely certain. After Harlan's death, the place was closed and locked upstairs and down, and has remained so ever since."

There was an interval of silence while Jimmy mused over this, then he turned to Chanda Steeb. "I wonder if I might see your father's bedroom?"

"Why, of course you may."

"I've got to ask your help, too, Dr. Waverly. Would you mind going next door and," he drew out his watch, "in exactly five minutes, trying to reproduce the sounds that occurred last night?"

"I don't believe I understand what you mean."

"I mean that I wish you to go into the study, stand at the end farthest from the door, where Stoddard believes the Colonel was standing, and then give a loud scream. After that I want you to run quickly out the door, on to the landing, and throw something heavy over the balustrade, something approximately the weight of the Colonel. There's an ancient leather chair by the door which I think will do nicely. Wilson's over there on guard and he'll help you."

"I'll do the best I can." The doctor looked a trifle doubtful but he compared his watch with Jimmy's and left for the house next door as Chanda Steeb led the way upstairs.

The Colonel's room was a pleasant, sunny place with high windows which looked out on the street. Toward the rear, a door led to a clothes-closet and, beside it, a second door disclosed a bath. Like the rest of the house, the room was filled with heavy Victorian furniture. There was an enormous bed with a hideous headpiece of carved walnut, equally ugly chairs and a bureau and wardrobe to match. The room was large but even in its generous space the massive pieces seemed to be crowding upon each other.

"My word," Jimmy exclaimed, "I haven't seen furniture like that since I visited my great-grandmother in Vermont."

"It's awful," Chanda said, "but my father liked it. He picked it up with a lot of other pieces when they auctioned an old house down-town. They told him it came around the Horn in a sailing packet." As she spoke she moved toward the bathroom. "I'm afraid the five minutes is almost up. If you'd like to stand where I stood when I heard the scream last night it was right here."

Jimmy nodded and took his place inside the door of the bathroom which also opened into the hall. He stood with his eyes on his watch and we waited beside him. One minute passed . . . two . . . then suddenly we felt a dull shock. I say "felt" rather than "heard" because it was more a vibration than a sound.

"There's the chair dropping!" I exclaimed; and then, in surprise, "I didn't hear any scream, did you?"

"No," Chanda Steeb looked astonished, "I didn't hear a thing."

"It's not important." Jimmy's voice was casual, but I sensed some emotion back of it. "The doctor probably didn't call loud enough. We'll get him to do it over." He was starting toward the door when there came a strange, prolonged whistle from above.

"That's my husband calling me," Chanda Steeb explained. "Will you excuse me for a moment?" She ran past us toward a staircase beyond and the instant she disappeared Jimmy was across the room tugging at the heavy bed.

"Quick!" he commanded. "Help me!"

Bewildered, I joined him. "What on earth are you trying to do?"

"Trying to find out if there's any opening between this room and the house next door."

"But you've already looked at the other side of the wall."

"Yes; but I've got to satisfy myself from this side, too."

With considerable difficulty we pulled the bed away from the wall and disclosed an expanse of unbroken plaster.

"Nothing here," Jimmy admitted. "We'll try the wardrobe." With desperate strength, we shoved the bed back and made for the massive clothes-press which stood three or four feet to the left. But the thing defied our strength. Tug as we would it refused to budge and the ring of dust and lint around its base showed that it had not been disturbed for months, or years.

Chanda Steeb's footsteps were already sounding on the stair and we turned guiltily to face her. "My husband is anxious to see you," she said. "Would you mind going up to his laboratory?"

"We'd be delighted," Jimmy exclaimed. "I've been hoping we might talk with him." He was moving eagerly toward the door, but she stopped him with a gesture.

"You'll remember that he's really not himself, won't you?" she begged. "He hasn't been normal since Uncle Harlan's death."

"Of course," Jimmy assured her, "you can trust us to understand and make allowances."

With a little grateful smile she led us up the stairs which I saw were an exact duplicate of those leading to the séance room next door. I was not surprised, therefore, to find the room overhead was of the same proportions as Grant's eyrie and had windows similarly placed, except that there were three small movable sashes instead of one huge pane of glass. In every other way the room was a direct contrast; in place of the luxurious furnishings of the study, there were crude work-tables and benches arranged about the walls with shelves that reached to the ceiling. At one end a low sink was close beside a row of Bunsen burners and on the far side a complicated series of jars and coils seemed to form some sort of a condenser.

The room was so large that the far corners were in shadow and the effect of the chemical apparatus was slightly fantastic, like the grotesque drawings of medieval alchemy. Steeb himself fitted perfectly into the picture. He was seated in his wheel-chair, dressed in a long bath-robe of dark wool which was not unlike the gown of an ancient wizard. The change in the man since we had last seen him was shocking. His leonine head seemed, some-how, to have shrunken; the temples were hollow, the jaws unshaven, the corners of the nostrils pinched and white. Even the lips had lost their color and his eyes were deep-sunk and bloodshot under his thatch of unkempt hair.

"Come in," he ordered in a surly voice, and, as we com-plied, "close that door behind you . . . quickly!" Before we could obey he was speaking again: "I have sent for you to ask what you have discovered about these murders."

"Nothing, I'm afraid," Jimmy told him regretfully. "We are still all at sea. Of course, the police have arrested Stoddard—"

"But you think he is not guilty, yes?" Steeb interrupted. "You think he could not have killed them?"

"I don't think he did the killing."

For a moment Steeb regarded Jimmy keenly, then: "You are sure it is not Stoddard; that means you have some idea . . . some suspicion of another, yes?"

"Unfortunately, I have no suspicion whatever."

"But, two men, two strong men like that do not die without some cause. There must have been someone to kill them."

"I'm not even sure of that," said Jimmy quietly.

"You think," Steeb was leaning forward, staring at him, "you think it was something not human?" Suddenly his face contorted, his hands beat together, and he raised his voice in a frenzied bellow. "Bah! You are a fool . . . a dunderhead! You will let us all be murdered while you sit back and do nothing because you believe in spirits—"

Jimmy interrupted him coolly. "I'm not sure what I believe, but I should be interested to hear your ideas on the subject, Mr. Steeb."

The man dropped back into his chair and I saw that his face had gone extraordinarily pale. "I . . . I," he stammered, "I have no ideas. What should I know—up here all day, alone, with only what they choose to tell me? Why should you ask me, a helpless cripple who knows nothing?" His voice had grown thin and high with a note of hysteria, and Chanda Steeb advanced to the arm of his chair.

"Please . . . please, Otto! You mustn't get excited. Mr. Lane only came up because you asked him."

"Yes," Jimmy spoke reassuringly, "I had no intention of questioning you, Mr. Steeb. I merely thought you might have some theory that would be helpful."

Steeb still seemed suspicious. His eyes darted quickly about from one to the other of us, and he shook his head obstinately. "I have no theory," he repeated. "I know nothing about it. I spend all my time up here experimenting, discovering things that should revolutionize the world, while the rest of you are down in the streets grubbing for money . . . money . . ." His voice was rising again, his hands clutching the arms of the chair, while his body was shaking convulsively with a rage so intense that, if I had not known his affliction, I would have said he was about to spring to his feet. "All of you with money!" he cried. "And I . . . I who have genius . . . I who am greater than any of you, am forced to whine for pennies like a beggar in the street!"

Chanda Steeb was behind him now, pressing her hands against his shoulders. "Don't, Otto, don't talk like that. Mr. Lane will misunderstand."

Jimmy, indeed, had risen from his chair and was staring at the man with an expression which I would have given much to read. There was astonishment in his face, and wonder, mixed with a sort of growing horror. Words seemed to fail him for a moment, then:

"We shouldn't have come," he said quietly. "Dr. Waverly warned us that you weren't well."

"Dr. Waverly!" Steeb's eyes flew quickly toward the door. "Where is Dr. Waverly?"

"In the next house. We can send Singh for him, if you like."

"No!" A quick movement sent Steeb's wheelchair back to within a foot or two of the wall, "No; I don't wish to see Dr. Waverly! I wish to keep away from everyone . . . *everyone.*" As he spoke his face was so ghastly that I feared he would collapse. Chanda Steeb evidently shared my fear for she threw us a little pleading glance.

"I think," she said, "if you don't mind, you had better go."

"Of course." Jimmy moved toward the door and I followed suit. "I'm sorry that our visit should have upset him so, Mrs. Steeb."

"It's not your fault. He insisted upon seeing you." She glanced again toward her husband who was lying with his eyes closed, his head against the back of his chair, in a half-faint. "Will you excuse my not going down with you to the door? I'm afraid to leave him alone when he is like this."

"Don't think of coming down. We're perfectly capable of letting ourselves out." Jimmy pressed her hand comfortingly, and a moment later we were on the stairs which led to the lower hall. He was glancing toward the Colonel's room, evidently meditating another foray in that direction, when he discovered Dr. Waverly waiting on the stairs.

"Did you hear anything!" the doctor asked eagerly.

So much had happened in the last ten minutes that both Jimmy and I stared at him stupidly for a moment before we remembered his errand next door.

"Yes," Jimmy told him at last, "we heard the dropping of the chair, or, I should say rather, we felt the jar. But we didn't hear your voice. Are you sure you shouted out loud?"

"As loud as I could. Do you want me to try it again?"

"No," Jimmy seemed to dismiss the subject from his mind as unimportant, "we'll forget it for the present. There are several other things I want to ask . . . if we can find a quiet place." He glanced around, then drew us into the little study at the end of the hall where we had sat during our first interview with the Colonel.

The room was exactly as it had been that day and I could not help picturing Colonel Grant as he had sat in the desk chair, his leg extended, hands clasped upon the head of his cane. The scene was so clear in my mind that Jimmy's voice came as a shock.

"First, I want to know about the Colonel's leg."

"The Colonel's leg?" The doctor stared at him. "Just what do you mean, Mr. Lane?"

"I mean the leg that was giving him so much trouble. Did you ever examine it?"

"I did." The doctor was bewildered but courteous. "It was an ordinary case of arthritis."

"You're very sure it was genuine?"

"Absolutely genuine. The suffering was intermittent, but at least three days before his death the knee joint was badly swollen."

"Which made walking difficult?"

"Yes; extremely so."

Instead of continuing the subject Jimmy made a sudden switch. "How about Steeb; have you ever examined his legs?"

"No." The doctor shook his head. "He had infantile paralysis in his childhood and has been as you see him for years. Except for various nervous troubles, which are directly traceable to his crippled condition, he's had no real illness since I came to San Francisco, and, even if he had, I doubt if I'd have been called in. He's always been abominably aloof and unpleasant. Possibly because he has a jealous hatred of anyone who is fond of Chanda."

"Then you can't tell me for certain whether or not his legs are entirely paralysed?"

"Yes; I can answer as to that. They're shrunken and weak, but only partially paralysed. He's able to get in and out of his chair and to go from room to room with the aid of canes." He seemed suddenly to realize where his answers were tending, and broke off. "You mustn't get any wild ideas from what I'm saying, Mr. Lane. To climb even one flight of stairs without help would be quite beyond him."

Jimmy nodded without speaking and I saw that his thoughts were already elsewhere. "As to Singh's wife,

Lalah," he asked, "just what would you say was the cause of her collapse last night?"

"Why, shock, of course. She's been upset ever since Harlan Grant's death and the sight of the Colonel's body was too much for her."

"But she wasn't looking at the Colonel when she went to pieces," Jimmy pointed out. "I distinctly remember Mrs. Steeb saying she was in the séance room."

"That's true, but it doesn't change my diagnosis. She's suffering from a form of hysteria produced by shock."

"'Hysteria produced by shock'," Jimmy repeated and lapsed into a silence which was so protracted that I thought he had forgotten his surroundings. In the end he came to himself with a sigh. "Deeper and darker," he said wearily. "It grows deeper and darker every step we take," then to the doctor: "Can you tell me where Singh is hiding himself?"

"He isn't exactly hiding, he's with his wife. I've been intending to look in and see how she's feeling. If you wish, I'll send him in."

"Please do. In a world of chaos only one thing stands out as absolutely proven . . . Singh is the fellow who's been blackmailing Norah Fallon. I yearn to exchange a few words with him."

"Very well." The doctor rose briskly. "I'll send him to you."

He was as good as his word, and a moment later Singh was in the room. His entrance had been as silent as a shadow but we were warned by the little whistling sound made by Mowgli, the marmoset, which was riding on his shoulder.

"You wished to see me, sar?" he asked in his flat, emotionless voice, and Jimmy nodded.

"I do," his tone was faintly sardonic. "I have a message for you, Singh. A message from a lady." If the man was startled he gave no sign; instead, he merely inclined his head politely and waited. "It's from Miss Fallon's maid, Clara. She regrets exceedingly that she cannot meet you at eight to-night for she has been unavoidably detained by the police." There was an interval of silence while the Hindu stood, still unmoved. Jimmy regarded him impatiently. "You don't seem to be interested in the message," he said at length. "Is it possible that you don't realize what it means? We're on to you and your little blackmailing friend, Singh. We're on to you completely."

Singh's face was still impassive, but he nodded slightly. "Yes, sar. I quite understand."

"And what have you to say for yourself?"

For a space of half a minute Singh studied the wall over Jimmy's head, then he spoke quietly. "I have nothing to say, sar . . . I must think."

His imperturbability was plainly getting on Jimmy's nerves.

"I advise you to do it quickly," he snapped. "If you don't, you may find yourself thinking in jail."

As though he had not heard, Singh closed his eyes and went into some sort of quiet contemplation, the marmoset cuddling down on his shoulder in unconscious imitation. In the end he spoke. "I will see you, sar, at eight o'clock to-night."

For the fraction of a second I thought Jimmy would answer angrily, then he controlled himself, and asked: "Why eight o'clock?"

The man glanced over his shoulder toward the stairs and sank his voice to a half-whisper. "I have something of importance which I must tell you, and it is better I should not say it here but at the place where you live."

"Why not go with us now?"

"Because I wish to bring my wife. She has been ill and it will take me a little time to prepare her."

Jimmy looked at him keenly for a moment, then nodded. "Very well, eight o'clock it is!" He was starting toward the door when he evidently thought better of it and came back into the room. "See here, Singh. . . . I want you to give me at least a hint of what you intend to tell us tonight. It will show that you mean to play straight."

Singh looked at him with his sharp, black eyes, then nodded slowly. "It is fair," he said, "I will tell you this much: I was not speaking the truth when I said I did not see my master, after I took Mr. Stoddard to his study upon Monday night. I was up there later . . . at midnight."

"Midnight!" Jimmy's face lightened. "Then you saw—"

"Yes, sar. I believe that I saw who was with him when he died."

CHAPTER 18
SINGH MAKES A CONFESSION

Singh's appointment was for eight o'clock, which gave us time to refresh ourselves with baths and with dinner. While we waited in the study I tried to draw Jimmy out about his impressions of the afternoon. He refused to speculate upon what Singh might have to tell us, but upon the subject of the Steebs he was more communicative.

"They're a queer pair," he said. "Darned if I can make 'em out . . . and yet I've a feeling that they ought to fit into this affair somewhere."

"You mean you think they may have had something to do with the murders?"

"It's possible. The man is obviously terrified . . . almost insane with fear. But, whether he's frightened because he thinks the murderer will be after him next, or because he's got some guilty knowledge and suspects he'll be found out, I can't say."

"But he couldn't have been in the séance room. The doctor said it would have been impossible for him to climb those stairs."

"The doctor merely said he couldn't have climbed them *without help.*"

"You're intimating that his wife may have helped him? But that's absurd! Why, the girl's a perfect saint."

"There's a pretty thin dividing line between saint and sinner, Phil, and Steeb seems to have her thoroughly under his thumb. Oh," he raised his hand quickly to forestall my speaking, "I'm not saying that Chanda Steeb would deliberately assist in a murder, but if she found her husband had committed one I could imagine her shielding him."

"But what possible reason—"

"The root of all evil: money, my son. Didn't you hear Steeb's harangue about his poverty? To an ego such as his, even murder might seem justifiable if there was a great scientific discovery at stake." He shook his head impatiently. "What's the use of our speculating? Singh will be here soon, and what he has to tell us may answer all our questions."

"You're dead sure he *will* come? You don't think he may slide out, or that someone may polish him off to prevent his speaking?"

"I'm not a fool," Jimmy snapped. "McCarthy's had a man watching ever since Norah heard that maid of hers phoning him."

"How about the maid? Were you telling Singh the truth when you said she was in the hands of the police?"

"Yes; they had her down for questioning this afternoon, but they didn't get much out of her. I never expected that they would." He broke off as Friday entered the room; there was strong disapproval on the house-boy's face, a disapproval which had been growing steadily all the week.

"There's a man outside, Mist' Lane, a color'd man with a lady all veiled up. Ah tol' him to go 'round to the back doo' but he says as how he's got a 'pointment with you."

"He has. Show him in."

Friday left, suspicion showing in the very set of his shoulders; and a moment later Ruggles, who had been lying before the fire, suddenly pricked up his ears and growled. This, in itself, was unusual, for the pup was a friendly little chap, and I saw Jimmy glance down with an expression of worry. Ruggles was not yet himself from his experience of the night before and he had spent the day lying, quiet and listless, upon the hearth, but at sight of the couple who were entering, he sprang erect with an angry snarl.

To tell the truth, I didn't blame him. Singh, in a dark suit and turban, was weird enough, but the woman who leaned on his arm was even stranger. From head to foot she was in black, with a heavy crêpe-bordered veil which hung over her close hat to her waist in front, and almost to the hem of her gown behind. This suggestion of the *perdu,* concealing not only her features but her hands as well, gave a curious, inhuman effect. One felt that the lifting of the veil might disclose some dreadful thing.

The odd pair advanced to the center of the room, and Jimmy moved forward to meet them. All evening I had been wondering what his attitude would be toward Singh. The fellow was, without doubt, a blackmailer—and quite possibly a murderer. At the same time, there was something about him which vaguely commanded respect; and to-night he was not only accompanied by a woman, but was also, in a way, Jimmy's guest. Almost at once I saw that my friend had taken his tone from this last fact for his manner was that of a host. He held out his hand, and as the Hindu returned the civility it seemed to me a slight expression of relief crossed his dark face.

"This is my wife, sar."

"How do you do, Mrs. Singh," Jimmy spoke a trifle diffidently, and I guessed that he was wondering how to greet the veiled figure.

The woman bowed, and two slender hands lifted the filmy material and threw it back, disclosing the pale, lined face of a woman between forty and fifty. She was evidently weak and ill for her hands were shaking and her eyes were deep sunken and heavy-lidded. And yet, in spite of the ravages of time and some strong, recent emotion, I could see that she had once been beautiful. Her skin was infinitely lighter than Singh's, and her hair was brown rather than black; but her features were distinctly Oriental in cast, with that illusive loveliness of the East which is so difficult to put into words. As she turned her great dark eyes on me, I thought of the ladies of Hafiz and the "Thousand and One Nights".

Evidently Jimmy was equally struck by her appearance for he stood an appreciable time looking down into her face with a puzzled frown before he recovered and drew a chair up to the fire.

"I'm sorry to hear that you have been ill, Mrs. Singh, and I appreciate your coming to-night."

Lalah Singh accepted the chair and dropped into it with a pitiable air of weariness. "We have come because we need help," she said, and I noted that her English was perfect, without even the trace of accent which broadened her husband's vowels. "We are in need of a friend."

"Good." Jimmy picked up a cushion from the couch and placed it carefully under her feet. "You can count upon two of them. Mr. Carter and I always run in double harness." He drew up a second chair for Singh, offered him cigarettes, then stood, one arm on the mantel, looking down at the pair. "There's no use our trying to hide the fact, after the hint you gave us this afternoon, Mr. Carter and I are wild to hear your story."

Singh cleared his throat and began, a trifle uncertainly: "I have something to tell you, sar. But I do not know that you will believe me. It is hard for you Americans to believe many things which we of India accept without question."

"You might try us," Jimmy suggested cheerfully. "After all, I'm a writer, and believing things is part of my business."

"Yes; that is why I come to you instead of the police. They would only laugh at me."

"And probably worse," Jimmy agreed. "What you have to tell might cause you to be implicated in the murders, isn't that so?"

Singh looked startled. "You are psychic, sar."

"Not exactly. It's easy to see there must have been something pretty strong to hold you back from telling what you know since it's plainly scaring Mrs. Singh into nervous prostration. Was it because you were afraid to confess that you saw Grant again Monday night?"

"Yes," Singh nodded. "I lied when I told the police I had gone straight to bed after my walk. The truth is I returned at midnight and went into the lower house to see if Mr. Grant needed me."

"And you talked with him?"

"No; when I reached the top of the stairs the door was closed but there is a little square glass set in the panel—"

"We know it. You looked through and saw Grant?"

"Not Mr. Grant himself, I saw his reflection. He was at the far end of the room near the curtains, but the night outside was dark and the big window behind his desk reflected everything."

"Was he alone?"

"No; there was a lady with him."

"A lady!" Jimmy exclaimed. "Was it anyone you know?"

Singh's voice, coming from the shadowy depths of the chair, was low and grave. "Yes, sar. I knew the lady once, but she has been dead for many years."

"The doctor's wife!"

"Mrs. Waverly!" Both Jimmy and I spoke at once.

"Yes, sar. It was Mrs. Waverly."

"But . . ." Jimmy fairly stuttered in his astonishment, "but it couldn't have been . . . you must be mistaken!"

Singh shook his head. "I could not be mistaken. Mrs. Waverly was very beautiful. Once you had seen her you could not forget."

"But that was ten years ago," Jimmy objected. "Even if she were alive she would be changed."

"She was not alive," Singh was quietly certain, "and she was not changed. She was exactly as you see her in that portrait!"

"You mean she was in that gold dress?"

"Yes, sar, and her long hair was hanging down over her shoulders."

There was a moment of complete silence while a cold sort of horror seemed to envelop the room. My forehead was damp and I felt the sinking sensation which is associated with nightmares. Jimmy, too, seemed affected. For a moment he stared at the Hindu, then dropped back into his chair.

"Go on," he said, "tell us where she was standing."

"It was beyond the curtains, but there was a sort of light behind her and I could see her reflection in the window quite plainly."

"How was Grant acting? Did he seem frightened?"

"He was so frightened I thought he would go mad, sar. He was standing where the light fell on him and I—" he put his hand to his forehead and closed

his eyes with the same gesture I remembered the Colonel using, "I have not been able to forget his face. . . . ."

There was no doubt that the man believed his own words. Lalah, too, believed. She was glancing from her husband's face to ours with eyes that were dark with terror, and it was easy to comprehend the emotion that wracked her.

Jimmy came out of a temporary stupefaction to ask a question. "Have you seen anything of this . . . this apparition, Mrs. Singh?"

"No; I have not seen her, but I have been conscious she was there."

"Conscious? What do you mean?"

"I have smelled her fragrance. Mrs. Waverly was very fond of one particular perfume and she used it always. It was—"

"My God, don't tell me it was *jasmine!*"

"Yes; jasmine."

If anything was needed to complete our demoralization it was this. All the horror of an unseen and shadowy world seemed to reach out and enfold us. I don't know how long we were silent, battling with our several terrors, but in the end Jimmy spoke:

"You are absolutely sure there could be no mistake about Mrs. Waverly's death? I know her husband was away when it happened. Could she possibly be still alive?"

"No." Lalah Singh's voice was low but positive. "I was with her when she died."

"And was Grant . . . was he there, too?" The husband and wife exchanged quick glances and Jimmy spoke, almost harshly. "There's no use your trying to keep anything back. We know the relations between Grant and Mrs. Waverly."

Singh drew a quick breath of relief. "If you know already, we may speak. Mr. Grant was not there when she died."

"Afraid of cholera, eh?"

"No, sar. Mrs. Waverly did not die of cholera."

"But I thought the doctor—"

"We told her husband it was cholera because we did not wish him to know the truth. Mrs. Waverly killed herself."

This was news with a vengeance but both of us were beyond wonder. We permitted him to go on without interruption: "Mrs. Waverly was young, you understand, and she loved my master madly, but she did not wish to deceive the doctor. She insisted that when he returned she would tell him the truth."

"And Grant wouldn't have it?"

"No; he wanted things to go on as they were."

"It was he who killed her!" Lalah's voice broke in. She had been sitting quietly in her chair and the outburst was as startling as it was sudden. "He was growing tired, and he threw her aside. Even though my mistress killed herself, it was he who drove her to it. That is why she does not lie quiet in her grave."

In the silence that followed all of the Lady Elfrieda's words about "malign spirits" came back to me. They had seemed absurd and laughable at the time, but now . . . I was not so sure.

Jimmy evidently shared my thoughts. "You believe," he asked softly, "that Mrs. Waverly returned and killed Grant?"

"I believe that she returned and the shock killed him."

"But what about the Colonel? She had no quarrel with him."

Lalah shook her head. "Why she came I do not know, but I believe she was there again the night the Colonel died, and it was the sight of her that sent him out of the room and caused him to fall from the landing."

Jimmy started and sat erect. "You collapsed in the study," he suddenly remembered, "just after the Colonel fell. Was it because you saw your dead mistress?"

"No," Lalah spoke slowly. "I did not see her . . . I merely felt she was there., On the night the Colonel died I was in my bedroom, but, about eleven o'clock, when I started to go to bed, I discovered that Mowgli had disappeared. He adores Mrs. Steeb and is always trying to get to her so I knew he was probably upstairs. When I reached the landing I saw the little imp sitting beside the door of the Colonel's bedroom. Just as I started after him I heard a scream, somewhere far off . . . and then an awful jar, as though something heavy had dropped."

"The Colonel's body falling."

"Yes; I was so startled that I cried out, and an instant later Mrs. Steeb ran out of the bathroom and said the scream had come from next door. She told me to have my husband go over immediately and find out what had happened. A few minutes later the detectives came to tell us of the Colonel's death, and I went over to the next house with Mrs. Steeb."

"Just a minute," Jimmy interrupted, "while you were in the upper hall looking for Mowgli did you see anything of Mr. Steeb, or hear him call?"

"No; I went downstairs immediately."

"Very well, go on with what happened when you reached the other house. Mrs. Steeb has told us that you found everyone around the body in the upper hall. What did you do next?"

"I left them looking at the body and crept up to that room overhead. I don't know that I can make you understand what took me there, but I had loved Mrs. Waverly and I was not afraid of her; at least—not then. My husband told about seeing her the night Mr. Grant died and I thought perhaps if I went up into the study it might help her to . . . to return. . . ." Her voice trailed away uncertainly, and Jimmy nodded.

"You thought you might persuade her to go back to the . . . 'other plane'?"

"Yes," Lalah Singh was grateful, "that was it. I went into the room overhead. It was dark, and the curtains were half-drawn in front of the mirror so that I could not see, but I felt that someone . . . something . . . was there in the shadow. I went half across the floor, then—I do not know how to tell you—something seemed to grip me here." She put her hand to her heart. "Something so horrible that I could not go on. I knew if I looked behind those curtains I should die. My legs were failing, I felt faint, but I managed to get back to the door of the room, then . . . everything went black."

"She collapsed," Singh explained, "and they carried her next door."

Jimmy was leaning forward eagerly. "You say that you went half-way across the room toward the curtains. Are you sure you didn't see anything there?"

For a moment she hesitated, then: "Just before I began to feel faint, I remember, dimly, that I noticed something yellow."

Jimmy sprang to his feet. "Tell us what it was like!" he exclaimed, "Was it something tall . . . between the curtains?"

"No . . . it wasn't tall, and it wasn't between the curtains. It was just a strange sort of yellow light upon the floor."

CHAPTER 19
THE CAPTAIN'S THEORY

The next day was Sunday and I woke to the steady drumming of rain against the windowpane. For a long moment I lay, half-asleep, my subconscious mind fighting against the burden of thought.

Was it only the night before that the Hindu couple had sat in the room below and told their fantastic tale about the dead woman with her gold dress, her yellow hair? Was it possible that the whole thing was a fabrication? No; I was ready to swear that it was not. Nothing but sheer terror could have marked Lalah Singh's face in that fashion, and the whole demeanor of the man had shown sober belief. Mistaken he might have been, but lying he certainly was not.

He was even willing to be quite frank about the scheme to blackmail Norah; he had nothing against Miss Fallon, he explained, but she was rich—very rich—and would not miss the money. He and Lalah were desperate to go back to India. His reasons for this desperation were vague and, I thought, a trifle unconvincing. He could only repeat that Grant's death had frightened them so that they wanted to run away, and for that they needed money.

Jimmy asked, naturally enough, why they did not go to Chanda Steeb for the money. Surely she would let them have enough for a trip to India. It was here that Lalah

227

Singh answered for her husband. Mrs. Steeb would let them have it, and gladly, she informed us; Mrs. Steeb was so generous that she would give the clothing off her back to the poor, but she had no money of her own. All that her husband made went back into his researches. He was mad for money (Lalah had shown a depth of feeling here which was surprising), mad and cruel, wickedly cruel, and not half so sick as he pretended. He liked to have his wife wait on him hand and foot, liked to make a slave of her. . . .

It was at this point that some sort of warning seemed to pass from Singh to his wife, and her fierce denunciation of Steeb broke off. As though to modify her words, she added that Mr. Steeb was a clever man, very clever, and Mrs. Steeb was glad to slave for him because she believed that some day he would make a great discovery which would help the world.

Jimmy, who had been listening intently to her diatribe against Steeb, plainly lost interest when it changed to feeble praise, and switched to another subject. It was, to my surprise, the Lady Elfrieda. How often had she been in the habit of visiting Grant? How long did she stay after the séances were over? Was he in the habit of seeing her elsewhere?

It was here that Singh betrayed his first hint of reticence. He knew nothing about his master's relations with Mrs. Chapman, he protested, and still less about the séances. In order that he might not be accused of causing the manifestations, he was always sent out of the room when a "demonstration" was in progress. That had been the reason for the fixing of the bolt on the door, in order that people who were attending the séance could satisfy themselves that no one could possibly get in from the outside. He even professed entire ignorance of the spirits that were said to return at his master's bidding. He had never been present during a materialization.

His nervous distress, reflected by his wife, was so painful during this part of the inquisition that Jimmy took pity on them, cut his questions short, and permitted them to go home.

As I lay in bed, listening to the mournful sound of the rain, I was wondering what had caused their agitation when Jimmy asked about Grant's occult power. Was it possible that the Lady Elfrieda's vaporings were true and the man had actually broken through the veil which separated us from the dead?

I was fiercely rejecting the thought when the door of my bedroom opened and Jimmy appeared followed by Friday bearing a tray with two steaming cups of coffee. Jimmy was clad in a wooly blue bathrobe and his hair was still damp from a shower; combined with his round face and blue eyes, it gave him the look of a small boy who has just awakened from sleep, but there was nothing child-like about his expression which showed a preternatural gravity. He greeted me with a nod and indicated a table which Friday drew up by the hearth and set with coffee, cream and sugar. I was startled enough by this unusual attention to realize that there was something in the air, but Jimmy waited until Friday had kindled a fire in the grate and left the room before he spoke.

"Look here," he began, "I want to ask you something. Have you ever seen that Singh woman before?"

"Of course not. Have you?"

"Not that I know of, but I haven't slept all night for thinking of her. I swear there's something familiar about her face. It's as though I'd known her somewhere when she was much younger."

"But that's impossible," I protested. "You've never been in India."

"No; and yet there is something about the woman that haunts me."

"I think it's just her type. I felt as you did, at first, then I realized she was the prototype of a good many pictures I've seen. Persian prints . . . medieval saints, that sort of thing."

Jimmy was staring at me fixedly and I saw there was some idea forming in the back of his mind. "By Jove," he said softly, and again, "by Jove!" But when I questioned him he shook his head. "Just a mad idea. Not worth going into at present."

At that moment Friday appeared with a platter of ham and eggs, and, as we ate, Jimmy outlined the program for the morning.

"I'm looking for the Chief at any minute," he told me. "The District Attorney is back and they plan to take definite action to-morrow. The inquest on the Colonel will be held in the morning and after that the Chief expects to have the case against Stoddard in shape for the D.A. to give to the Grand Jury."

"The case against Stoddard?" My poor, overburdened mind struggled with the thought. So much had happened since yesterday that I had completely forgotten Dick Stoddard was still being held for the murders.

Jimmy saw my effort, and grinned. "Sounds quaint, doesn't it? Sort of back-in-the-dark-ages. It's hard to realize that the Chief doesn't know all we know."

"Of course, you'll tell him."

"And, of course, he won't believe me. Can you imagine hard-headed guys like the Chief and the District Attorney taking stock in a ghost story? Why, they'll laugh their heads off." He was watching me as he spoke and I knew he wanted an opinion.

"It *is* absurd," I agreed. "Worse than absurd; it's insane. And yet, somehow, all the time Singh was talking, I had a feeling—" I broke off helplessly, unable to express what was in my mind; but Jimmy nodded, quite satisfied.

"I had it, too. Still have, for that matter."

For a moment we stared at each other, then:

"You think there's something in it?" I asked.

"I *know* there's something in it. Look at this." He brought forth a typewritten page and spread it upon the table before me. "Here's a list I wish you'd look over."

I picked up the page and read the paragraphs, which were headed:

Things to be Remembered.

1. *The former owner of the house, Amos Harcastle, died in the same room as Grant.*
2. *Grant's mother died with the same expression of fear upon her face that was noticed in the case of Grant and the Colonel.*
3. *Norah Fallon, the Colonel and the doctor all speak of the phrase "fear of fear" used by Grant, and the doctor says that he lived in constant fear of some occult manifestation.*
4. *Norah Fallon, Mrs. Chapman and the Colonel all insist that Grant was nervous and apparently worried by something for at least two weeks before his death.*
5. *Mrs. Chapman says he spoke of giving a woman cause to hate him at some time in his life.*
6. *Singh and Lalah say that his treatment of Mrs. Waverly was responsible for her suicide.*
7. *Stoddard and the Colonel noticed a distinct odor of jasmine in the study on two different occasions.*
8. *Lalah testifies that jasmine was the perfume used constantly by Mrs. Waverly.*
9. *Upon the night of Grant's death, Singh looked into the séance room and saw what he believes to be Mrs. Waverly's spirit talking to Grant.*

10. *This spirit had long yellow hair, and in every other way resembled the portrait of Mrs. Waverly which was painted just before her death.*

11. *Upon the night of the Colonel's death, Stoddard heard him speaking to someone at the far end of the study.*

12. *A moment later he rushed out of the door with an expression of insane horror on his face and plunged headlong off the landing.*

13. *Wilson, a detective, glancing into the room immediately afterwards, testifies that he saw "something yellow", between the curtains. It was about the height of "a small man" and was "like a yellow veil".*

14. *Lalah Singh, upon going into the study a little later, had a feeling that there was something behind the curtains and saw a "yellow light upon the floor". This was accompanied by such a sense of horror that she fainted and was prostrated by shock.*

15. *Wilson, entering the study a few moments later, saw nothing, but experienced the same feeling of indescribable horror.*

16. *The doctor states that Grant often brought Mrs. Waverly back from the "spirit plane" so that he could talk to her, but that he never obtained a complete "materialization".*

17. *Grant's followers claim that he was frequently in communication with the other world and believe that he was killed by a "malignant spirit".*

The list came to an end and I laid it down, stunned by its completeness. "Good God," I said, "the thing's incredible! And yet, it's all true . . . every word of it."

"Yes." Jimmy nodded. "We have the testimony of at least eight witnesses, all crisscrossing in such a fashion that we'd be utter fools to deny it. And in addition, we have the testimony of our own senses. We were in that room, you remember, within an hour of the Colonel's death—and I felt that strange sensation, which Lalah and Wilson describe; that abominable sick horror."

"I felt it, too," I confessed. "And there was Ruggles. . . ."

"Yes," Jimmy shivered, although the room was warm. "I haven't put him down on the list because nobody would believe it who hadn't been there to see." He paused and stared at the paper with somber eyes. "By God, Phil, there's something unholy here, something abominable. Because of our ignorance we're helpless, and it may go on and on—"

Before he could finish he was interrupted by Friday who announced the arrival of Captain Hemming. Jimmy ordered him brought up, and a moment later the Chief was seated in an easy chair across the hearth. While Friday served him with breakfast, he recounted the latest developments of the case. The post-mortem report for the Colonel was complete, except for the toxicologist's findings on the contents of the stomach, and it showed nothing of interest. The technical equivalent of "Death from a broken neck" was the obvious conclusion. No poison showed in the blood, and the Captain was evidently not expecting any to appear in the stomach; and, as in the case of his brother, there were no important fingerprints in the séance room.

From his talk I saw that all doubts he had once entertained as to Stoddard's guilt had vanished; he was quite plainly ready, if not anxious, to turn the case against him over to the District Attorney. "Unless, of course, you've turned up something new," he ended, regarding Jimmy with his quizzical grey eyes. "I've an idea you wouldn't drag me out here on Sunday morning without a darn good reason."

"You've guessed it. Carter and I have got something for you . . . and it's going to upset your nice red apple-cart. It establishes a perfect alibi for Stoddard on the first murder."

"It does, eh?" Captain Hemming was plainly incredulous. "That ought to be interesting. Let's have it."

Quickly, and in as few words as possible, Jimmy repeated Singh's tale of his return to the house and his glimpse of Grant's reflection through the peephole in the door. When he started upon the subject of the doctor's wife and her death in India the Chief interrupted irritably.

"Good Lord, Lane, you're not expecting me to swallow all this ghostly hocus-pocus?"

"I don't care whether you swallow the ghost part or not," Jimmy told him. "But you must see where it puts you with Stoddard. Here's a witness who saw Grant alive after Stoddard left."

"Hold on!" the Chief exclaimed sharply. "I don't see that at all. Singh didn't see Stoddard leave the house, and he couldn't have taken in the entire room from that peephole in the door. Stoddard might easily have been at one side, out of range, or it's even possible that the figure he saw behind the curtains talking to Grant was Stoddard."

"With long hair and a gold dress?" Jimmy asked sarcastically.

"With anything you like," Hemming retorted. "You'll have to remember the Singhs are Orientals and something has evidently happened which has stirred them up and brought back the thought of Mrs. Waverly. If I were to make a guess, I'd say it's those trunks the doctor has been going through." He paused, then continued seriously: "There's a lot more in imagination than we realize, Lane. If you'd dealt with hysterical witnesses as long as I have you'd know that they're likely to see anything . . . with the mind's eye. In this case, I believe what that Hindu saw was some effect of light behind those curtains which created a sort of optical illusion. His mind immediately filled in the outlines of the portrait."

"I see what you mean," said Jimmy slowly. "You think that what he saw was a projected memory of the portrait, and that it was caused by a subconscious fixation on the subject of Mrs. Waverly which, in turn, was caused by memories brought back by the opening of the trunks."

"That's exactly what I mean. The whole business of her suicide in India, and their efforts to keep it from the doctor, must have been a terrific strain . . . and the fact that they were forced to continue serving Grant made it worse."

"You may be right," Jimmy admitted. "But, for all that, I don't envy the District Attorney when he goes to the Grand Jury with the sort of evidence you have against Stoddard."

"What's wrong with our evidence? In the case of both murders we have the motive, we know that Stoddard was there, and we know how he could have done the killing."

"How about that locked door?"

"Oh, we think we've got a solution for that, too. We can't be sure until we've checked up, but McCarthy and I believe there is some electrical connection concealed in the door which throws the bolt." As Jimmy stared at him without speaking, he continued: "Mac's up there now looking it over, and I'll bet he finds Grant had the door wired so that it could be opened and closed from the outside. That would explain the spook effects at Grant's séances . . . Singh sneaked in and helped him after the lights were out."

"Tell me," Jimmy spoke with apparent humility, "did you really think that brilliant theory out all by yourself?"

"Why, no . . . it was partly Mac's idea. He'd read of something of the sort."

"I wish Mac would let the cheap, wood pulp magazines alone," said Jimmy sadly. "They're beginning to have a deleterious effect upon his brain."

"Then I'm equally feeble-minded," snapped the Chief. "What's wrong with that theory?"

"Everything. The type of bolt, the lack of connections, and the fact that Stoddard had never been in Grant's house before and couldn't possibly have known how to work any such arrangement."

"He might have seen Singh work it when he went up."

"Hardly. In the first place, even granting there is such a contraption, Singh would never have tipped it off to a stranger; in the second, we know that the Lady Elfrieda was just coming out of the room and the door was wide open."

"Miss Fallon might have known about it and told him."

"Then lied to us afterwards, I suppose?" Jimmy shrugged his shoulders. "Oh, well, if you're going to start that sort of thing there's no use wasting our time in argument."

Before the Chief could answer Friday appeared at the door. "You're wanted on the telephone, Cap'n," he said, and led him to the extension in the hall.

It was a full three minutes before the Chief reappeared, and when he did, his expression of disappointment was almost ludicrous. "That was McCarthy," he told us, "calling from the Grant house—"

"To report that the secret spring is only another pipe dream," Jimmy finished for him, and the Chief nodded ruefully.

"He's taken the door down and gone over it thoroughly; there's not a sign of any mechanism for opening the bolt from the outside." For a moment he brooded, then: "I'm going up there now to have another look. Why don't you and Carter come along?"

Jimmy shook his head. "No thanks, Captain. We've seen all we want of that room. Personally, I hope I never have to enter it again. One thing I can tell you which may save time: there is no way of getting in or out except through the door, and there is no way of operating the bolt from the outside."

"If I could believe that, I'd be able to swallow your spook theory, Lane."

"The time will come when you'll be *glad* to swallow my spook theory, Captain."

The Chief looked fixedly at Jimmy, as though the seriousness of the words had affected him in spite of himself. "You're really in earnest?" he asked slowly.

"So much in earnest that I'm going to the Lady Elfrieda's tea this afternoon."

The Chief broke into a guffaw and picked up his hat. "I knew you must be kidding."

"I was never more serious in my life."

"But, good Lord, that Chapman woman—"

"Knows more about Grant's spirits than any other living person. As near as I can make out the Colonel thought the murderer was the doctor, the doctor thinks it is Singh, Singh thinks it is a Ghost, and what the Ghost thinks I mean to find out through the Lady Elfrieda."

CHAPTER 20
THE LADY ELFRIEDA'S TEA

To my annoyance I found that Jimmy was expecting me to accompany him to the Lady Elfrieda's tea. I had hoped for a quiet hour or so by the fire and a chance to recover some degree of tranquility but, as usual, my hopes were blighted. The Chief was scarcely out of the house when Norah Fallon arrived, very much upset and in need of reassurance. She had been playing, for the last week, the part of a carefree young hoyden in a picture (perhaps you saw the thing later; it was called *Bubbles,* I believe, and had to do with a beautiful little tomboy who simply couldn't behave) and the strain of laughing gaily before the camera and the "mike", while her thoughts were of the darkest, had left her exhausted. She was inclined to be critical of Jimmy's slowness in clearing up the case, and Jimmy, with his usual talent for sliding out of situations, shunted her on to me. I had to listen to her woes in the living-room while he went into a protracted session with Corrigan in the library. What happened there I do not know, but the reporter, who had gone into the room full of his usual slangy persiflage, came out as grave as a hanging judge.

"I'll get that stuff you want, J.L., and I'll have it in your hands to-night," he promised as he left, then added, with an ominous shake of the head, "provided *it* doesn't get one of us first!"

Norah was dismissed with a promise that we would pick her up for dinner, and four o'clock found us before the impressive door of Mrs. Elfrieda Jane Chapman.

The Lady Elfrieda lived in a high, narrow house on a hill near the Presidio; from the windows of her living-room it was possible to look down upon the bay, dull now, and leaden through the persistent drizzle.

Although it was not yet dusk the room was dark and a few emaciated candles scattered about did little to relieve the gloom. The furniture was modernistic, cut in triangles and squares, and the walls were stenciled with grotesque flowering vines that sprawled about with a sort of indecent abandon. Beside the low chairs and divans there were glass-topped tables of silver metal that looked like the furnishings of an operating room. Over the mantel, which was formed of cubes painted alternately black, silver and magenta, was, absurdly enough, an old-fashioned portrait of a heavy-set man with a square-cut beard and piercing black eyes. The deceased Mr. Chapman I decided, and, at the same moment, found myself hoping that we would not be forced to meet in the spirit.

A number of guests were already in the room; some sitting cross-legged upon pillows about the floor, others lost in the depths of the angular furniture. As I looked them over, I thought I had never seen such a fantastic crowd: cadaverous men, with Adam's apples that protruded above Byronic collars, talked to angular old maids in flowing garments and clanking jewelry; swarthy East Indians lurked in dark corners, and in the foreground a wild-eyed mulatto with long, black wool was instructing a group in the mysteries of voodoo.

I turned to catch Jimmy's eye but he was already making his way toward our hostess. The Lady Elfrieda was dispensing tea, sandwiches and cakes from a table in the corner. It was a long table, made, apparently, from a single block of wood, and was supported at the four corners by large silver balls. With a candle at either end, and heaped up food in the middle, it reminded me of a Chinese funeral where the food is laid out for the dead. It was with a distinct effort of will that I dragged my mind back from the gruesome thought and followed Jimmy to greet the Lady Elfrieda.

At sight of us she gave a little chirp of delight and ran round the table, both hands outstretched. "Mr. Lane! This *is* a surprise. I never *dreamed* that you would really come!" She signaled her satellites with little triumphant gestures. "Everybody listen! I've got a *beautiful* surprise for you! This is Mr. Lane, Mr. *James* Lane, with whose works I feel *sure* you are familiar." She looked around with her saccharine smile and cooed again, "Mr. Lane is very much interested in our spirit friends, and I *know* you will all be glad to tell him your experiences."

A delighted sound ran about the room and I gathered that they were more than willing, they were eager. To the last man they began to crowd forward, like hungry barnyard fowls. It was not until this moment that the Lady Elfrieda remembered my presence and her manners simultaneously. She waved an unenthusiastic flipper in my direction and murmured:

"This is Mr. Lane's friend, Dr. Carlson."

"The name is Carter," Jimmy corrected. "And he's not a doctor, he's a lawyer."

"Oh," she smiled vaguely, "I'm so sorry, but I'm frightful at remembering names. They seem so unimportant, somehow, when one is face to face with the *infinite.*"

What *was* important when one is face to face with the infinite I never learned, because she had taken Jimmy's arm and was leading him toward a couch in the corner. Before I could feel properly snubbed a stringy lady in Nile green descended upon me and insisted upon my taking

lukewarm tea and sandwiches which disclosed wilted lettuce between slices of stale brown bread.

There was a reason for the lettuce, she informed me.
Lettuce was food for the soul, partly because it grew out
of the earth, and partly because it was green . . . green
being a particularly psychic color, which was why the lady
herself *always* wore it.

By the time my instructress had worn herself out and
a long-haired youth, with a purple suit and a magenta tie,
had taken up the burden, I was reduced to a condition
bordering on madness. Someone had lighted punk sticks,
and the incense, combined with the smoke of innumera-
ble cigarettes, filled the room with an opalescent haze. It
became a place of somber mystery where dim and shadowy
figures drifted back and forth like disembodied spirits.

My head was reeling and, in desperation, I got to my
feet and crossed the room in search of Jimmy Lane. I
found him sitting between the Lady Elfrieda and a vast,
grey-haired woman with eyeglasses whom I remembered
having seen at Headquarters the day the Chief examined
Grant's followers. The two were showing him photographs
in a scrapbook.

"This will interest you, Phil," he said. "These are pictures taken at some of Grant's séances." He held one out
to me and I saw that it was of our hostess. There was nothing of interest about the portrait itself except that it was
extremely unflattering, but in the background, just over
her shoulder, a figure was dimly visible. The face was half-
turned away, indistinct in the shadows, but it was possible
to see that it possessed a dark square-cut beard.

"My husband," explained the Lady Elfrieda brightly.
"We were trying for a picture of my son, Ronald, but *poor*
dear Joseph simply *would* insist upon coming instead."

"Did you ever manage to get a picture of your son?"
Jimmy inquired, and she shook her head.

"No; every time we tried we got Mr. Chapman."

"This picture was taken in full light?" I asked.

"Yes; in front of that big window in the séance room."

"And you actually saw your husband beside you?"

"Oh, no," she seemed amused at my ignorance, "of *course* not! A spirit couldn't *possibly* stand the light. He only appeared after the plate was developed."

Jimmy seemed not to be listening. Instead he was going through the photographs in his hand while the grey-haired woman beside him gave a running commentary.

"That's Mr. Titcomb," she said. "And the spirit extra beside him is his son, Fred. He was killed in the War . . . an aviator. You can see he's wearing a helmet and goggles. There's one of me here . . ." She ran through the pile and produced it proudly. "That spirit extra is my sister, Kitty."

"Is it a good likeness?"

"Perfect," said the woman firmly. "Of course, you can't see much of her face because it's sort of turned away, but I'd recognize her curls anywhere."

Jimmy was bending over, looking at the picture, and his face was so serious that I began to grow alarmed. Was it possible that he was being taken in by this obvious chicanery? The thought infuriated me and when Mrs. Chapman stated blithely: "Of *course,* it's utterly impossible that there should be any sort of trickery," I turned on her.

"There's every chance for trickery!" I declared. "That particular fake has been exposed again and again. The medium gets hold of a photograph of a dead relative and then double exposes it."

"But I *haven't* any photograph of my husband," protested the Lady Elfrieda. "The *only* picture I have is that portrait over the mantel."

Jimmy held out the book and pointed to the photograph. "If you'll look closely, Phil, you'll see that this couldn't have been taken from that portrait. In the painting

Mr. Chapman is looking straight out, while in this his face is turned away, and the whole set of his head is altered."

I was forced to agree, but his opposition maddened me. "I don't care," I persisted doggedly. "Houdini and a lot of others have told just how these things are done. I still contend that Grant was a faker."

It was as though I had stood in the Vatican and denied the infallibility of the Pope. Instantly a hornet's nest was about my ears. Through the angry babble I caught the persistent tones of the Lady Elfrieda.

"He didn't only take *photographs,*" she declared. "His vibrations were continuously in harmony with the spirit plane, and the manifestations he produced were simply *wonderful.*"

A pimply-faced youth leaned over to confirm this. "I saw my grandmother twice," he said, "just as plain as I see you at this minute."

"Did you actually recognize her?"

"Well, of course, I couldn't exactly recognize her because she died before I was born, but she told me a lot of things—"

"And there was my great-uncle," a woman interrupted. "I recognized him, all right. He was one of those old-fashioned Southerners with a funny goatee and long white hair. He came and talked with me."

"Where did he appear?" Jimmy asked.

"Back of those curtains in Mr. Grant's séance room. Lots of the materializations appeared there."

"They did?" Jimmy looked interested. "Just how did they seem to come? All of a sudden?"

"No; not exactly. They formed under your eyes, sort of as if they were floating in the air."

The Lady Elfrieda leaned forward to contribute her bit. "That's one reason I *know* they were real spirits. All the time you could look *right* through them and see the mirror behind."

"You are sure of that?" Jimmy asked, and I saw that he was both astonished and puzzled.

"Absolutely sure," the Lady Elfrieda persisted, and half a dozen others added their affirmations to hers.

For a time he fired questions at the group, which were answered eagerly, then, suddenly, he seemed to lose interest. The scrapbook in his lap had dropped open at a page where there was a photograph and a newspaper clipping.

"That's a spirit picture of Amos Harcastle, Mr. Grant's control," the Lady Elfrieda explained. "And a clipping about his death. I happened to run across it in an old newspaper."

For a moment Jimmy studied the pictured face with its flowing beard and misty halo of white hair, then he turned to the clipping—which I read over his shoulder. A copy of it is now in my possession so it is possible to give it accurately:

PHILOLOGIST SUCCUMBS TO ATTACK
HARCASTLE DIES IN STUDY

Death claimed one of the country's leading philologists to-day when Amos Harcastle, 65, former professor at Browne University and author of numerous books, succumbed to a heart attack at his home on Russian Hill.

Harcastle had been ill for some time but was so much recovered yesterday that he rose and began work at his desk. His daughter, Mrs. Donald Wheeler, who resides in the next house, was in the nursery with her children when she heard her father fall. She hurried into the study, but he died before medical aid

could be summoned. The cause of his death
was given as angina pectoris.

In addition to Mrs. Wheeler, Prof. Harcastle is survived by a second daughter, Mrs.
Robert Silliman, and six grandchildren.

The Lady Elfrieda waited impatiently while Jimmy read
the clipping, then: "Don't you think you can persuade
Captain Hemming that Amos Harcastle returned from the
spirit plane and killed Mr. Grant and the Colonel?" she
entreated. "I can't bear to think of that *nice* Mr. Stoddard
being in a *nasty* jail."

Jimmy Lane's eyes went back to the clipping and I could
not tell whether he was studying it or was occupied with
some inner thought. Suddenly he rose and spoke abruptly.
"Will you pardon us if we run along, Mrs. Chapman? This
has all been very interesting, but Mr. Carter and I have a
number of things to attend to."

"Why, of *course,* Mr. Lane." The Lady Elfrieda rose in
her usual fluttery fashion. "I understand *perfectly.* I'm
only delighted that you came at all."

Jimmy had already covered the distance to the door but
he paused a moment to ask: "I wonder if you could let me
have a few more of your books on Spiritualism and psychic
phenomena? I was immensely interested in the ones you
loaned me last week."

Mrs. Chapman hurried over to a bookcase and returned
with several volumes. "Here," she said, "are Donivan's 'Evidence of Spiritualism', 'The Case for Spirit Photography',
by Sir Arthur Conan Doyle, and 'The Reality of Psychic
Phenomena'." She beamed on Jimmy as he took them under his arm. "Some day you will thank me for showing you
the *light.*"

For a moment he looked down at her gravely. "I rather
think I shall," he agreed, then, suddenly: "Oh, by the way,

I wonder if you'd mind being still a little more generous. Could you let me have a couple of those pellets of
incense?"

"Why, of *course!*" She fairly purred with delight and
brought forth a small box from the litter on the table. "I'm
flattered that you like my little fragrances."

Jimmy passed the books to me and slipped the box into
his pocket. "They are delicious," he said. "I shall burn
them while I read your books. It will give just the right
atmosphere."

"Oh, yes, atmosphere is so important, isn't it?" cooed
the Lady Elfrieda, and Jimmy glanced back toward the
room where the disembodied spirits still seemed to float
through murky gloom.

"Yes," he said gravely, "atmosphere is *everything.*"

A moment later we were out upon the street.

Chapter 21
The Gold Dress

Somehow I managed to hang on to my temper until we reached the car, then I flung the books on to the seat with unnecessary violence and turned on Jimmy Lane. "I'd like to know your idea . . . wasting a whole afternoon with a bunch of idiots like that after you promised Norah to work on the case."

"I was working on the case. I made some valuable discoveries."

"I hope you didn't make them from anything the Lady Elfrieda told you; that woman's as mad as a hatter."

"You think so?" He looked at me keenly.

"I do. All her fads and *isms* . . . 'Universal Peace', 'Love is Everything', 'The Spirit Plane' are so mixed up, you can't tell one from t'other. And look at that crazy house! Ugh! It made me think of The Cabinet of Dr. Caligari."

Jimmy smiled as though he were pleased. "You noticed that, did you? I wondered if you would."

"Of course I noticed it."

"Then perhaps you noticed something else . . . something which had direct reference to this case?" He was looking at me with a peculiar, teasing smile, and I stared back blankly.

"No; I can't say that I did."

"Too bad, Phil. You should have caught it, you really should." Instead of enlightening me, he lapsed into silence and I was too annoyed by the mad hour I'd been through to question him.

After a period of taciturnity, of which Jimmy seemed blissfully unconscious, I burst out irritably: "I'd like to know what you're going to tell Norah. We're picking her up for dinner, you know."

"*You're* picking her up. I've got several other things to attend to so I'm going to let you dine with her alone."

"But, hang it all, what shall I tell her?"

"Anything you like. Only don't forget that you're a married man and that Diana will be back next week." He saw my exasperation was increasing and reached over to pat my arm. "See here, Phil, I'm not trying to slip out of anything. You said you'd help in this case, and the greatest help you can give me just now is to keep Norah cheerful and off my neck. There are things I've got to think out and I can only do it alone."

What reply could I make to that except an apology for my gruffness? "You really think you're on the trail of the solution?" I asked, hoping for some hint of encouragement to take Norah.

"Yes," he said slowly, "I think I have some glimmering of the truth, but it's still so hazy . . . and so full of dark places that I want to sit down and work it out."

I won't linger over my dinner with Norah. She was trying to be cheerful, bless her heart, but her thoughts were with her lover and I could see that her self-control was near the breaking point. I tried desperately to put off her questions about Jimmy with a general statement that he was working on the case, but she insisted upon details and I was forced to tell her about our afternoon at the Lady Elfrieda's tea. Instantly she took fire.

"You mean to say that he wasted all that valuable time gabbling with a lot of old women?"

"Of both sexes," I agreed, trying to smooth her down by a lighter touch. But she would have none of my feeble wit.

"I don't believe he's doing a thing," she declared. "I think he's gone absolutely haywire on this spook stuff."

"You more than half-believe the spook stuff yourself," I challenged, and she turned on me a face so stricken that I was sorry I had spoken.

"That's the awful part of it. I *do*. But we'll never be able to make the police believe it, and they'll keep on holding Dick and, oh . . . I did so count on Jimmy Lane's keeping his head and getting him out of the mess. He promised he would! You know he did!"

She continued this wail through *Rex Sole en Papillote* at Solari's but the *Crêpes Supette,* served under the hospitable eye of Madame Solari herself, seemed to have a cheering effect, and by the time black coffee appeared the worst was over. She crinkled at me with her nice Irish smile and patted my arm across the table.

"I've no business to take it out on you," she said. "You've been a dear all through. But I certainly would like a chance to wring Jimmy Lane's neck."

I might have pointed out that it wasn't Jimmy's murder in the first place, and that he had been roped into the thing through good nature, but I knew better. "I'm afraid you can't get at him just now," I told her. "Failing that, what would you like to do next?"

Norah looked thoughtful. "It's a crazy idea, but I'd like to ride up to Russian Hill. If we prowled around it might suggest something to us."

I was delighted that she had given up the idea of pursuing Jimmy, and greeted her plan with enthusiasm accordingly.

Our ride up the hill in Jimmy's car was a silent one; both of us were trying, desperately, to keep our minds off

the thought of the District Attorney's action on the mor-
row. When the car stopped at the curb, I helped Norah
alight and offered her my arm for the steep ascent. I suppose she was thinking of the last time she had been there
for her hand trembled slightly and I could hear her breath
catch as she looked up at the row of houses which loomed
overhead.

The rain had ceased but menacing black clouds still
covered the sky and the wind from the bay was as keen
as a knife. There were no lights in Grant's study to-night
and the Colonel's house was dark on the lower floors, only
a glow in the third story showed that Steeb was working
there. There were lights in the doctor's house; one came
from the front room on the ground floor, the other from
some room at the back.

"Let's go see him," Norah said impulsively. "It can't do
any harm, and perhaps he might give us some idea to work
on."

I could think of no argument against it so we climbed
the steps to the doctor's house. The porch was slightly
indented and, as the Colonel had told us earlier, the
living-room was clearly visible from the space in front of
the door.

The doctor was not in sight but a woman was bending over an open trunk, replacing something in the upper
till. The light was behind her, but, as we rang the bell,
she swung about quickly and I saw her face. It was Lalah
Singh. Evidently she left through some rear door for, a
moment later, when the doctor came down the hall to
admit us, he was alone.

If we were unwelcome his perfect courtesy kept us from
feeling it. With exactly the right degree of cordiality he
invited us into the living-room and seated us before the
fire, He made no reference to the woman we had seen and
his first words were an apology for the state of the room.

"Although I believe it's a trifle more tidy than when you were here the other afternoon, Mr. Carter."

Looking about I saw that the place was now clear of the objects which had cluttered the furniture. The dresses and nick-nacks were gone, and only the letters and the diary remained on the desk. Norah's eyes lighted upon these and she spoke with a trace of compunction.

"I'm sorry if we've interrupted you, Doctor. We really shouldn't have come at this hour."

The doctor smiled sadly. "As a matter of fact, I'm glad you dropped in. I need someone to keep me from thinking." He seated himself at the desk as he spoke and laid his hand on the letters. "I've just come to an important decision. As Mr. Carter may have told you, I've been going through my dead wife's things, sorting them over and destroying what I do not care to give away. All this time I've been trying to get up courage to read her letters and her diary, but just a moment before you came in, I decided it would bring back so many heart-breaking memories that it would be wiser to burn them unread. I shall be glad to have your company while I do it."

As he spoke he picked up the letters from the desk and moved toward the fire. Norah turned to me with a look which plainly betrayed her agitation. I suppose Jimmy Lane would have known what to do under the circumstances, but, as for me, my mind had turned to jelly. I remembered, of course, what the Colonel had said about those letters. If the doctor was telling the truth and had not read them it was better they should be destroyed. If, on the other hand, he was lying and it was he who had killed Grant, the letters implicating his wife with her lover would be the most necessary sort of evidence and it might be that we were letting our last chance to save Stoddard slip through our fingers. And yet, what could I do to stop the doctor? He was already poking up the fire, making a nest of red coals upon which to deposit the bundle. Norah's breath was coming in quick gasps and her eyes were desperate. What she would have done to stop him I can only guess for, just as he reached toward the fire, a ring at the telephone forced him to put down the letters and pick up the receiver. A moment later he turned to us.

"I'm afraid you'll have to excuse me for a moment," he said. "Mrs. Steeb has called to say that her husband is worse. He still refuses to see a doctor but I'm going to slip up to the drug store and get her something to quiet him."

"Of course you must run along," Norah told him easily. "We were going to stay only a little while," and, as he turned toward the door, she put her hand on his arm. "Look here," she begged, "won't you let me burn those letters for you? It would be so much easier if you just came back and found them gone."

He hesitated a moment and looked down into her face, then seemed to brace himself and nodded. "Thank you," he said, "I think you are right. Will you take care of them for me?"

"I will," Norah promised, and, as the front door slammed, she turned to me with the letters. "I want you to slip out with these and take them down to the car." I must have looked a trifle doubtful for she went on quickly. "Oh, I know what you're thinking—that it isn't honorable. But I'm desperate! I won't read them nor let anyone else read them unless we find the doctor guilty. But I'm not going to have them burned when there's a chance they might save Dick."

Of course, she was right. I hurried down to the machine, and returned a few minutes later to find her looking into the fireplace with a worried frown. "It isn't very convincing," she said. "You can see for yourself there ought to be a lot of paper ash."

"There's a newspaper in that basket," I suggested, and together we tore the pages and thrust them into the blaze. But the amount of residue still did not content her.

"Look over by the desk," she commanded. "There may be some newspapers there. In the meantime, I'm going to take a peep into the trunk. I'm curious to know what Lalah was packing away."

I crossed the room to the desk but there were no news-papers, only a few sheets of notepaper, some envelopes, and the doctor's cheque-book. The latter was lying wide open upon the desk and it was evident that he had been writing in it recently. Idly, at first, I glanced at it, then looked more closely. A cheque had been torn out of the book and the stub, written in the doctor's neat, legible hand, showed that it had been for a thousand dollars and drawn to the order of Lalah Singh. Before I could speak there was a cry from the other end of the room where Norah was bending over the open trunk.

"Come here!" she gasped.

"What is it?" I was already by her side, looking at something which lay, half-concealed by tissue paper, in the top tray of the trunk.

"It's that dress," Norah told; me, "that costume Mrs. Waverly wore in the portrait up there." She bent farther over, and suddenly caught her breath in another little gasp. "Please," she begged, "see if it's my imagination. It seems, it honestly seems to me, that it still smells of jasmine!"

CHAPTER 22
BURMESE BLOOD

The clock was just striking ten as we reached Jimmy Lane's house. Norah had insisted that we leave the doctor's at once in order to report the new developments, but we might as well have remained for Jimmy was not at home.

"He done lef' right after dinner," Friday announced. "Said as how he was goin' t' do some shoppin'."

"On Sunday night?" Norah looked astonished. "What on earth could he buy?"

"Ah don' know, Miss Fallon," Friday was plainly aggrieved, "he didn't tell me a thing, but he lef' a paper on the desk fo' Mist' Cartah."

"It'll probably explain where he's gone," I said, and picked up the note which was scrawled upon a sheet of yellow paper:

If Corrigan comes, tell him to give you the message. I may not get back to-night. J.L.

Norah was reading this over my shoulder and she gave a little wail of disappointment. "I think it's wicked of him to go away without leaving word where he's gone. Here we've brought the most important sort of information and we can't get it to him."

She was right, of course, but there was no help for it. I was just about to lay down the yellow sheet when I happened to notice the reverse side. Jimmy had evidently been scrawling some notes on the case, and with growing mystification I read them over, once to myself, then a second time, aloud to Norah. Since the germ of the case was in those scattered sentences, I will give them here. The first was a series of questions:

Why was the Colonel walking up and down his room when we know his leg was bad?
Why were sounds heard in the next house when Amos Harcastle died, but not in the case of Grant?
Who does Lalah Singh look like?
Why was Mowgli outside the Colonel's door?

The next was a scribbled list. It was headed:

Spirits Materialized by Grant:
  Grandmother,
  Sister,
  Great Uncle,
  Harcastle,
  Aviator,
  Mr. Chapman.
  Why not Ronald Chapman or the doctor's wife?

And at the bottom of the page:

Have Corrigan look up:
  Newspapers on death of Harcastle.
  Cleveland Hospital fire, 1928 or 29.
    (Get names of surviving doctors.)
  Follow lead on Singh—Lalah—

Possibly you will be bright enough to see the meaning of these notes and where they fit into the story. I confess that Norah and I were not. They started us on a series of speculations so far from correct that I shan't give them here. In the middle of our discussion Corrigan appeared accompanied by Friday with a midnight lunch.

Corrigan fell upon the tray wolfishly. "First food that's passed these ruby lips since four o'clock," he announced. "When and if your young man gets out of the hoosegow, Miss Fallon, I claim a seven-course dinner at the St. Francis."

"I'll promise it to you now if you'll tell us where that wretch of a Jimmy Lane has gone," she said.

"I know no more than the dead," Corrigan declared solemnly. "We parted company at nine o'clock."

"Where was he then?"

"In the headquarters of the Telephone Company, putting in long distance calls to Cleveland."

"Have you any idea what he wanted with Cleveland?"

"Not a jit nor tittle. I only know that he ordered me to look up that Cleveland fire . . . the one where the X-ray film exploded. He wanted the names of the surviving doctors. When I left him he was running up a telephone bill as big as the National Debt."

As he talked he gathered up a cup of coffee, six sandwiches and a wedge of chocolate cake, then retired to the hearth settle with his loot. "Don't expect any more chatter out of me," he warned. "While I absorb nourishment you can spill your story."

Corrigan was in the confidence of Jimmy Lane so I saw no reason why I shouldn't tell him what we had learned on Russian Hill. When I told of the salvaging of the letters he paused and laid down his cup; at the description of the dress found in the trunk he abandoned his sandwiches; and the news about the cheque made out to Lalah Singh fairly sent him out of his chair.

"Say, this is immense!" he cried. "Perfectly immense!"

"I'm glad you think so," I remarked sarcastically. "So far as we're concerned it's all as clear as mud."

"It won't be after I've opened my little surprise package," Corrigan proclaimed blithely. "You see, I've got the other half of the story." He sat down and began on the chocolate cake, waving it to emphasize his remarks. "Jimmy Lane gave me three things to get for him: the hospital stuff, some clippings from old newspapers, and some dope on Singh and Lalah. You remember, I told you the other day that there was bad blood between Singh and Grant? Well, he wanted me to find out, if possible, what it was that Grant was holding over the Hindu. To-night I managed to get in touch with someone who gave us just what we need."

"What did you find out?"

"First, I found the rumor we heard about Singh was the goods, all right. He *was* an officer in an Indian regiment, but there was a mutiny, several white officers got bumped off, and Singh was implicated. They could never prove anything on him and he was let off, but Grant was gum-shoeing for the government at the time and he probably got something on Singh that he's been using as a club ever since. It must have been pretty bad because he's practically made a slave of the poor guy."

"Whew!" I stopped to consider the import of this. "That sounds interesting."

"If you like that, wait until you hear the rest! Singh was married to Lalah and, of course, she went with him to serve Grant. She had a younger sister, a regular little beaut, and Grant's brother, the fake Colonel, saw her and went goofy. He'd just been chucked out of the army for beating up that non-com. and I guess he didn't give much of a hoot what happened to him. Anyway, he ups and marries the sister. Grant had a mess of pups—they don't like black and white marriages over there—and kicked up a helluva row. The two didn't even speak for years. In the meantime, the Colonel's wife had a baby and died."

"And the baby was, or I mean is, Chanda Steeb."

"You're right."

"But, hang it all—" I was trying to make my mind accept the fact, "she isn't a native!"

"She is, technically. But they've kept so quiet about it I doubt whether even the doctor knows. Lalah and her sister were only half-native. Their father was Portuguese and their mother was from Burmah. That accounts for Lalah's fairness, and makes Chanda only one-quarter Burmese."

"That's why she was raised in a mission-school!" Norah exclaimed. "I thought it was queer. English girls are usually sent home to be educated."

"Jimmy twigged the same thing, and sent me scouting."

"Have you told him this . . . about Chanda Steeb, I mean?"

"No; I gave him the stuff about the Cleveland fire and the clipping on Harcastle's death but I only got this last dope an hour ago. I hot-footed it up here to give it to him, but if he's flown the coop there's nothing to do but wait."

"I don't think we ought to wait!" Norah exclaimed. "All of this stuff is terribly important. Don't you see what it shows . . . about Lalah and Singh?"

"Yes," Corrigan nodded, "I've been seeing for some time. The relationship gives them a reason for bumping off Grant and the Colonel. Grant's property came to the Colonel. The Colonel's went to Chanda, and if she hasn't made a will—"

"It would naturally go to the next of kin!" I exclaimed, appalled at the vista this suddenly opened. "But that means they'd have to kill the Steebs!"

Corrigan nodded slowly, and the three of us sat staring at each other for a moment, then Norah spoke in a low, tense voice. "It's horrible, simply horrible. We must do something . . . at once!"

"But Jimmy felt sure it wasn't the Singhs," I protested. "The night they were here he accepted their story as true."

"He may have accepted it that night," Corrigan agreed, "but I'll bet a cookie he's changed his mind since then. He particularly asked me to look up the question of Lalah and Singh."

"Don't you realize," Norah's voice was excited, "that they didn't tell that wild story about seeing spooks until after you and Jimmy Lane found Singh was blackmailing me? Jimmy was pretending to write those articles for the *Occult Review* and I bet Singh thought he was a spiritualist. He made up all that hocus-pocus about Mrs. Waverly's committing suicide in India and then haunting Grant just to put you off the trail."

"I'll admit that sounds like common sense," I said. "Just how do you figure Singh committed the murder?"

"I haven't figured it out yet . . . let's do it together." She dropped down on a cushion on the hearth-rug and began thinking aloud. "On the night Harlan Grant was murdered we know Singh was up there. He admits it himself. We also know he hated Grant, Jimmy figured out how he could have killed him, with that stone image, then escaped and faked the locking of the door."

"O.K. How about the murder of the Colonel?"

"That takes a bit of thinking." For a moment she mused, then: "Do you happen to know whether or not Singh was in his room on the night the Colonel was murdered?"

"No," I was suddenly alert, "I remember that Jimmy questioned that very point. Chanda Steeb said she'd sent Lalah back to her room with orders that Singh should go over to the lower house and find out who had screamed, but she also remarked that it was three or four minutes before she heard him go."

"He may have been dressing, of course," Norah said thoughtfully. "Then, again, he may have been just getting back from the lower house."

"But how could he?" I protested. "There were detectives at both the front and rear doors."

"That wouldn't have prevented his getting in," Corrigan pointed out. "Remember, the dicks weren't watching Singh, just the Colonel. Singh might have gone over to the house earlier and then hidden when he heard the Colonel coming."

"Where do you think he hid?"

"Behind those curtains in the séance room. But before he could do anything Stoddard arrived and had his talk with the Colonel. You remember Stoddard says when he left he was almost down to the front door before he decided to go back and look for those papers. No doubt Singh thought he was gone, came out from behind the curtains and went for the Colonel."

"And it was Singh that Stoddard heard the Colonel talking to."

"That's what I figure. He probably drew a gun on him, but before he could do any damage the Colonel beat it for the door."

"That's why he had such a look of terror on his face!" Norah exclaimed.

"Smart girl! You'd look nervous, too, if you had someone with a gun just two jumps behind."

"But he didn't shoot," I protested.

"He didn't have to. The Colonel was in such a hurry he pitched over the railing. Just as he fell, Stoddard came out into the hall on the second floor."

"But he didn't see Singh."

"Don't be silly!" Corrigan admonished. "If a two-hundred-pounder suddenly flopped out of the air and landed at your feet, do you think you'd be gazing around?

Not likely. You'd be down on your knees seeing if he was hurt."

"We're getting somewhere at last!" Norah cried. "What do you think happened next?"

"Let me see . . ." Corrigan ruminated. "If I remember rightly, Stoddard looked at the Colonel, found he was dead, then ran down the stairs. At the front door he met McCarthy and another detective. That must have taken at least two minutes, which would give Singh plenty of time to run down the upper flight of stairs and into the second-floor bedroom at the back."

"What did he do then?"

"That," Corrigan beamed, "is the most beautiful part of the whole business. There's a screen porch off the kitchen and the roof's only about four feet under the window of the rear bedroom. It'd be a cinch for Singh to have dropped from the porch to the ground, then slid into the Colonel's house the back way. The whole thing couldn't have taken more than three minutes at the most . . . which would give him plenty of time to be in his room when Lalah came down with Mrs. Steeb's order about going next door."

"What about the detective who was watching the back of the house?"

"McCarthy called him around in front immediately after the Colonel was killed. The idiot was so sure Stoddard did the murder that he didn't think it was necessary to watch."

"But the window," I interrupted. "If Singh had gone out that way there would have been a window left open. The doctor said they were all closed and locked."

"But he also said that Singh helped check the windows and doors. It would have been dead easy for him to have shot the lock when he was pretending to examine it."

"Of course," Norah agreed. "That makes it all clear."

"All but one thing," I said slowly. "You can say that Singh's account of a mysterious ghost was all fake if you like, but you've got to remember Wilson. He swore that he saw something tall and yellow behind the curtains."

Corrigan leaned back and laughed delightedly. "That, my brethren, is the sweetest thing of all. . . . He *did* see something tall and yellow."

"What was it?"

"I hate to tell you, I really do, it's such an anticlimax . . . but did you happen to notice the weather last night?"

"Yes; it was misting."

"Sure it was. And when Singh was sent over next door he was still in his white linen house suit, so he slipped on a yellow slicker."

"What?"

"A yellow slicker. The transparent kind. I saw him wearing one the other day. That would be 'tall as a short man' and 'sort of like a veil', which was the way Wilson described the yellow thing he saw between the curtains."

"But only if Singh were inside of it," I protested. "And he wasn't. He was back home by then."

"Sure he was . . . but he'd hung his slicker on one of those candelabra brackets by the side of the mirror while he was waiting for the Colonel and Stoddard to get through with their talk, and then in the excitement he forgot it."

Norah gave a little cry. "Of course! And that's why Lalah went up into that room!"

"Sure it was! Singh remembered he'd left the slicker there and told her to nab it if possible. By the time she'd sneaked up to the room it had probably dropped off the bracket . . . that's why she said the 'something yellow' she saw was on the floor. In case anyone had looked in before she got there, she wanted her story to match up with what they'd seen."

"I suppose she folded the slicker up—"

"Yes; and tucked it under her coat—"

"Then pretended to feel faint in order to get back to the other house and dispose of it!"

We were all talking at once, our words combining in a mad jumble as we rounded out the story. But suddenly we stopped and looked at each other in a sort of horror as we realized how perfectly it all fitted together.

"There's not a thing missing," Corrigan said softly; "not a single thing."

"No," I agreed, "it's all perfect. If only Jimmy Lane were here—"

"We can't wait for him," Norah said tensely. "We dare not. If we're right about the Singhs and they're after the money, then both Chanda and her husband are in frightful danger."

"But surely Lalah wouldn't kill her own niece," I protested.

"You don't know what she'd do," Corrigan interrupted quickly. "You'll have to remember she's the world's queerest mixture, Portuguese and Burmese. That's another thing Jimmy had me look up . . . the Burmese race. They've got a lot of Chinese blood, all mixed up with Siamese, Malay and East Indian. And, speaking of blood, here's the sweet little statement the encyclopedia makes about them." He stopped, took some notes from his pocket and read a few sentences: "'They are a conservative race, callous of life and jealous of their faith. Although usually of a kindly disposition, under provocation they are apt to become vindictive, and to resort to acts of revolting cruelty.'"

"Oh," Norah was almost wringing her hands with excitement, "please, *please* don't wait for Jimmy Lane! Call Captain Hemming at once."

Swayed by her emotion, I moved over to the telephone, and, with considerable difficulty, got the Chief at his house. I apologized as well as I could for calling him at that hour (it was after twelve) and offered my news as an excuse. Transmitted piecemeal over the wire into the ears of a man who was more than half-asleep, it must have sounded quite mad. The Chief listened with admirable patience until I started upon the matter of Singh and Lalah, then he exploded into words.

"See here," he rumbled, "I realize that you and Miss Fallon are bound to do all you can to save Stoddard, but when it comes to dragging me out of bed to listen to a lot of wild theories I draw the line!" He was evidently about to hang up when I stopped him.

"It isn't a wild theory. It's an air-tight case and you must, for your own sake, you *must* put someone to guard the Steebs."

More to quiet me than because he had any faith in our theory, he agreed to put a man on the job for the night. Although the whole thing sounded like moonshine . . . utter rubbish. He hung up on that and I relayed his promise to Norah who seemed vastly relieved.

"Knowing that Dick will get out in the morning," she said, "I can go home and sleep in peace."

"I'll take you home," Corrigan announced. "That is, if you aren't too proud to ride in a Ford that 'as seen better days, m'lady."

"I adore Fords!" Norah grinned. "I've got two of the little dears eating their heads off in the garage at home." She rose, picked up her hat, gloves and coat; as I helped her into them she turned and looked up at me. "You will get Jimmy started early in the morning, won't you?" she pleaded. "I feel so responsible, not only for Dick, but for the Steebs as well."

"I shan't wait until morning. I intend to sit right here and catch him when he comes in to-night."

We parted almost gaily, with the feeling that we had accomplished much, and it was not until Corrigan's car had snorted its way down the street and quiet had once more descended upon the house that I was visited by a sudden, disturbing thought: "Where did that yellow dress fit into our story . . . and why did the doctor give Lalah a cheque for a thousand dollars?"

Chapter 23
We Save Chanda Steeb

Dawn was breaking when I woke in Jimmy's study to find the room full of misty shadows and the fire burned down to a heap of grey ash. For a brief interval I lay, bewildered, trying to recollect why I was there, then hazily I remembered my promise to Norah. There was some word I must give Jimmy Lane . . .

It was while I was groping, half-awake, half-asleep, for the message that I became conscious of a prickling in my scalp and a vague but oppressive feeling of dread. As I forced my mind to its work I suddenly realized with a sick sense of horror what it was that distressed me. The room was full of the fragrance of jasmine!

In desperate haste I pulled myself to my feet and stood, dizzy with sleep, as Friday burst through the door. He was in a dressing-gown of purple and red blanketing, his feet thrust into enormous yellow slippers. His eyes were rolling wildly and the ebony of his face had a strange greenish tinge.

"Mist' Cartah! Mist' Cartah! You gotta come see Mist' Lane."

"You mean . . . something's happened to him?"

"Yes, suh," Friday gasped. "He's done gone crazy."

"Where is he?"

"He's been down cellar all night makin' conjur' tricks" (his voice followed me as I sprinted through the hall) ". . . with smoke and smells."

As I threw open the door and ran down the cellar steps, a blast of foul air greeted me and I saw that the basement room was dim and hazy with smoke. For an instant I thought there had been a fire, then I discovered Jimmy seated before a deal table upon which there was a row of burned incense sticks and a scattered heap of cigarettes. Three gutted candles were also in evidence and the bellows from the upstairs fireplace. At the front of the table was a small stack of books, some of them borrowed from the Lady Elfrieda, others obviously new. Among them I noticed Houdini's "A Magician Among the Spirits", Abbott's "Behind the Scenes with the Mediums", and two volumes of some work on chemistry.

Over and around the books, strewn across the chair and floor, there was the most amazing assortment of incongruous properties imaginable. When I was a child we used to play a game in which a large number of unrelated objects were piled upon a table and we were given sixty seconds in which to study the mass, then five to compile a list. Some little quirk in my brain made that sort of accurate observation easy, and I am, therefore, able to give a more or less complete account of the weird miscellany.

There was a black velvet couch cover which hung from a clothes-line overhead and formed a sort of curtained recess at one side; before this the wooden clothes-horse was draped with costumes from Jimmy's travel chest, a Chinese mask, an Arabian abba, a gauze veil from Stamboul and a yellow East Indian shawl. The mirror from the upper hall was leaning against the wall and a pane of clear glass stood beside it.

Upon the ironing-board was a fantastic collection including a corn-cob pipe, blackened at the edges with smoke, a tin pump gun of the type used for insecticide, four or five feet of rubber tubing, a length of gas pipe, a Santa Claus wig and whiskers (which Jimmy had worn in the Press Club Christmas frolic), an aviator's helmet, a perfume atomizer, and a theatrical make-up kit.

As I have said, the whole room was filled with smoke and thick with a fragrance which was compounded of equal parts tobacco, incense, and the heavy scent of jasmine. The combined fumes were so overpowering that they caught at my throat and sickened me. I was not astonished to see Jimmy looking pale around the gills.

"What in the name of thunder are you up to?" I demanded. "Have you lost your mind?"

"No," he shook his head wearily, "but I almost wish I had. It would relieve me of a lot of responsibility." He rose, leaned dizzily against the table and waved his hand about the fantastic *mise en scène*. "I've been doing a series of experiments, Phil, and it's told me a lot . . . but not quite everything."

"What do you mean?"

"I mean I've got the thing narrowed down to two people . . . but I'll be hanged if I can say which is the murderer. One has the temperament, but not the motive. The other has the motive, but not the temperament."

"Perhaps they're both guilty," I suggested. And, without waiting for an answer: "If it's a motive that's worrying you, we've got it. Norah, Corrigan and I made a lot of discoveries last night."

While he listened intently I recounted our experiences at the doctor's. The finding of the gold dress seemed to interest but not surprise him, and Norah's theft of the letters actually brought a smile to his lips; but the news Corrigan had gathered at the Indian colony proved inexplicably exciting.

"You say that Lalah is Chanda's *aunt?*" he demanded.

"Yes; which makes her next to inherit if anything happens to the Steebs."

"You're *sure* of that?"

"Corrigan was dead sure."

For an instant Jimmy looked at me, eyes burning, then he turned and made for the stairs. "Hurry!" he commanded. "We've got to get out there at once."

"Where?" I was only a step behind. "Where are we going?"

"To Russian Hill." He was already at the clothes-closet jerking out his hat and coat. Over his shoulder he addressed Friday: "Call Police Headquarters and get in touch with Sergeant McCarthy. Tell him it's absolutely essential that he and, if possible, Captain Hemming come to the Grant house immediately."

Friday gaped at him. "Me . . . me talk like that to the police? What if they won' pay no 'tention to me?"

"They will," Jimmy was already at the door, "if you tell them I said they might find another murder."

It was too early for Jimmy's chauffeur to be about so he took the roadster. Luckily the streets were fairly deserted but, even so, my heart was in my mouth as we roared up hills and round corners at forty miles an hour. Evidently, I reflected, Norah had come near the truth when she spoke of the danger to the Steebs for Jimmy's face expressed an anxiety beyond anything I had ever seen him display. He asked but one question on the way:

"Did the doctor return before you left last night?"

"No; he was still with Mrs. Steeb. We left a note explaining that we couldn't wait. Norah was determined to get the news to you as soon as possible."

"Smart girl. I wish to Heaven I'd had it last night. Oh, I admit it's my fault," he added quickly. "I should have wakened you when I came in. I've only myself to blame if . . ." He left the ominous sentence suspended in the air as he whirled the car about a corner and threw it into low gear for the steep ascent.

The winter sun was just appearing over the misty hills which lay beyond the bay; it was blood red, that sun, and the color was caught and reflected in the countless windows above us so that the heights seemed stained with crimson. Only the Grant house, shadowed by gloomy cypress, showed no life.

The Chief and McCarthy had arrived before us and were in conference with Wilson who had been assigned to watch the place. As we came up he was evidently giving his report.

"Everything quiet, Captain. Haven't heard a chirp all night."

The Chief, exasperated, turned to Jimmy. "Just what was the idea dragging me out of bed at this ungodly hour?"

Jimmy did not answer. He was already ten feet ahead, bounding up the stairs of the Colonel's house. Without stopping to ring, he tried the door which yielded to his hand. Crowding in behind him, we had an unimpeded view of the front hall with its carpeted floor and heavy velvet hangings. It was empty at the moment, but at one side, dimly discernible in the morning light, there was a little pile of luggage. Two suitcases, a hand-bag, a dark coat and a yellow slicker.

Before anyone could speak Jimmy raised his hand for silence. In the perfect quiet that ensued, we could hear footsteps descending the stairs. They were not honest, straightforward footsteps but muffled and stealthy, as though made on tiptoe.

I don't know what we expected to see at the dark turn of the staircase, I only know that we all stood tense and breathless, listening to the footsteps grow nearer and nearer, then stop, as though in sudden suspicion. It was at this moment that I realized a draught must be coming from the open door which would be plainly discernible half-way up the stairs. The same thought evidently occurred to McCarthy for he sprang forward, quickly followed by Wilson. There was a little gasping cry in a woman's voice, a low guttural exclamation, and the two reappeared with Lalah and Singh who were dressed for travelling. Singh was struggling fiercely but Lalah was on the verge of faint-ing and Wilson was obliged to support her.

Captain Hemming pushed forward to confront them. "So you thought you'd make a getaway, eh?" Singh looked desperately about the ring of faces until his eye lighted on Jimmy. "Mr. Lane . . . tell them I wasn't doing any wrong," he begged. "Make them understand I was just trying to get my wife out of this house."

"Where were you going?" the Chief demanded, and, still looking at Jimmy, Singh answered:

"We were going back to India. Dr. Waverly loaned us the money and we were going on the first boat."

"What were you doing upstairs?" the Chief asked. "Your room is on this floor."

"We were looking for Mowgli. He slipped away and we couldn't find him."

"Where are the Steebs?"

A strange look crossed Singh's face. "They are asleep," he answered. 'They have been sleeping in the laboratory. . . ."

"The *laboratory!*" Jimmy started toward the stair, and as the Chief barred his progress, "For God's sake don't stop me!" he snapped. "I may be too late." He dashed up the first flight, the Chief and I followed—leaving McCar-thy and Wilson to guard the Singhs.

By the time we reached the second floor Jimmy was already ten feet above us on the next flight, but at the lab-oratory door he stopped with a sharp exclamation. When we reached his side we found him bending over Mowgli.

The little animal was lying dead on the landing in front of the laboratory door. Its legs were twisted convulsively and the features of its tiny, half-human face were frozen into a grotesque expression of horror.

It is utterly impossible to give an accurate account of what followed. For a brief instant we three stood staring at the little furry body in Jimmy's hands. Not only was it a thing of horror but there was a strange, sickening nausea stealing over us, a dead weight which clutched first at the heart, then at the brain, bringing a black and hideous dread of what lay behind the door.

Suddenly, as though dragging himself out of a nightmare, Jimmy turned and threw his weight against the panels. The door burst open and we saw the room beyond. When I say we *saw,* I mean that the scene photographed itself with lightning-like rapidity upon our minds. At the moment I could not have been conscious of the details, but later, for weeks, I could close my eyes and remember the room; large and raftered, full of dim corners and strange distorted shadows from the apparatus Steeb used in his alchemy.

Through a single, uncurtained window the morning light was streaming. It fell upon Otto Steeb hanging, hideously contorted, over the arm of his chair, and upon Chanda, lying half-in, half-out of a window. The light fell across them, I say, and lent additional horror to their immobility, and yet that was not the thing which clutched at my heart and filled me with sheer, awful terror. It was the yellow mist which filled the place, waist high, and, in the draught between window and door, writhed snake-like toward the rafters.

There was a scream from Jimmy. "For God's sake, don't breathe!"

He hurried past me and sprang for the windows. Throwing up the shades, he beat against the panes with a chair and the glass fell about him in tinkling showers. The Chief and I dashed for Chanda Steeb. She had managed to get the window partly open before she collapsed and was lying where she had fallen, her head across the sill. We threw the window wide open and leaned out, drawing the sweet, sharp air into our bursting lungs.

Under the forced draught, the yellow mist was thinning; it was dropping down to the floor, where it lay like ghostly amber liquid about our feet and ankles. By the time we had drawn Chanda Steeb into our arms and were carrying her across the room, it had vanished as completely as steam in a warm room.

Quickly as possible, we brought the dead man and the unconscious girl downstairs and laid them in separate bedrooms. Chanda was breathing so lightly that, at first, we believed she was gone, but by the time Wilson arrived with Dr. Waverly her color was returning and she was drawing air into her lungs with labored gasps.

"Hot water! Ice!" the doctor ordered. "You've phoned for the pulmotor? Good! Have you any idea what chemical she breathed?"

"Some devilish gas," the Chief answered. "We don't know yet what it was but I mean to find out. McCarthy," he raised his voice, "bring in those Hindus."

McCarthy appeared at the door with the Singhs. They were shaking with terror, and Wilson was half-carrying Lalah.

The Chief strode across the room and faced them. "What was that poison you used?" he demanded. "Tell me!"

For an instant the husband and wife looked at each other as though exchanging a wordless signal, then Singh shook his head. "I do not know what you mean, sar."

The Chief glanced toward Chanda where she lay on the bed, fighting for every breath, and his fists clenched.

As he stood over Singh, I thought he would throttle the fellow. "Tell me what you used," he roared, "or by God—"

He was interrupted by a voice from the door. "Here is the formula, Captain."

We swung about and I realized, for the first time, that Jimmy Lane had not been in the room. He was standing on the threshold with a notebook which the Chief passed quickly to Dr. Waverly.

"Dicyanogen," the physician murmured, "hydrocyanic acid. Good. Now I know what to do." He issued hurried orders to McCarthy who left to fill them.

The Chief swung on Jimmy. "Where'd you find that notebook? In Singh's room?"

"No; in the laboratory. It was Steeb's."

"You mean that Steeb himself made the chemical?"

"Yes; he's been experimenting with a war gas."

"I see." The Chief's mind was working rapidly. "And Singh got hold of it somehow, eh? Why, that explains Grant's death . . . and the Colonel's. They were both killed by gas!"

"Yes," Jimmy's voice was very low, "that's how they died . . . but it wasn't Singh who killed them."

"Wasn't Singh?" The Chief stared from Jimmy to the notebook where the formula was entered in a square, precise hand. "If it wasn't Singh—" He gasped. "Then . . . then it must have been Steeb!"

CHAPTER 24
How It was Done

It was the mad climax of a mad hour, and I found my brain, already befuddled by what had gone before, utterly unable to cope with the Chief's pronouncement.

Steeb? Why Steeb was a cripple! We had it on the word of the doctor that it would have been impossible for him to have climbed the stairs of the house next door. How could he have committed the murders?

The same thought was troubling the Chief. "You must be wrong," he protested, "unless you're suggesting an accomplice."

"I'm not suggesting an accomplice. The murders were committed by one person . . . and one alone. But the murderer was never inside the house next door. Come with me, and I'll show you how it was done." Jimmy started toward the door and we followed him down the hall to the Colonel's room. "While you were working over Chanda I slipped in here," he said. "I knew pretty much what to look for . . . and I found it!" He crossed to the high wardrobe and threw open the heavy carved doors; the interior was full of the Colonel's clothing hanging from a central pole, but he moved it to one side and disclosed the back of the cabinet. Instead of being wood, it was a heavy velvet curtain.

"Good God," the Chief gasped, "it's an entrance to the room next door!"

"No," Jimmy shook his head, "as I told you before, there is no entrance to the séance room. This merely opens on to the back of the mirror."

As he spoke he drew aside the curtain and exposed a narrow alcove. "This is the depth of the walls between the houses. There's a button here, somewhere. . . ."

He groped, found it, and there was a metallic click. The dark surface of the wall swung like a door and we found ourselves looking down through a pane of the clearest glass into the séance room. "You see," Jimmy explained, "as we proved by the drops of gilt, this glass is absolutely solid in the frame. It is the mirror, back of the glass, which moves."

"But how . . . why—" The Chief was actually stuttering in astonishment.

"Grant used it in his séances," Jimmy went on. "I began to smell a rat yesterday when the Lady Elfrieda showed me the clipping about Harcastle's death. Phil didn't notice anything, but it struck me at once." He brought out his notebook and read aloud:

"'His' (that is Harcastle's) 'daughter, Mrs. Donald Wheeler, who resides in the next house, was in the nursery with her children when she heard her father fall. She hurried into the study, but he died before medical aid could be summoned.'

"The wording of that last sentence suggested to me that at that time there was a door from the study into the next house. I knew there wasn't any opening now, but we were told that Grant got that mirror from an old residence and that it 'came around the Horn'. We were told the same thing about the Colonel's furniture, so it was safe to assume that they were bought at the same time. Remembering the positions of the mirror and wardrobe, on opposite sides of the same wall, I judged that there was nothing accidental about the arrangement . . . they probably had been placed there to mask the old doorway. Another thing I heard at the tea carried me still farther. In describing Grant's 'spirit manifestations' the Lady Elfrieda said that they took place behind the curtains, that they were 'sort of misty', 'formed in the air', and that you could *see the mirror through them*. That stumped me at first, then I suddenly realized the truth. The reason they saw the mirror through the images was because they saw the images through the mirror. In other words, the spooks were *behind* the pane of glass and not in front of it."

"But they formed in the air—" the Chief began.

"If you'll notice, this room is on a three-foot higher level than the séance room next door; a figure behind this glass would seem floating in the air to anyone standing in the next room . . . especially if it was veiled by smoke."

A sudden light dawned on me. "That's how you spent the night! Experimenting with mirrors and lights in the basement!"

"Yes; and you'd be surprised at the effects you can produce with proper lighting, an electric fan, a little gauze, and some smoke. I actually scared myself."

"I suppose it was Lalah who played the lady spooks," the Chief mused. "And Singh played the men."

"It was Lalah who played the women, all right," Jimmy agreed, "but Singh couldn't have done the men. In the first place, he's much too dark; in the second, he was undoubtedly needed to catch signals from Grant through that peep-hole in the séance room door and transmit them over here."

"Then who was it?"

"The Colonel. One of the first things that made me suspicious of Grant's spooks was the fact that he seemed able to conjure up only elderly men with whiskers or women with their faces shadowed by long hair. The only

two exceptions were a young chap with a disguising aviator's helmet and goggles, and a grandmother who had died
before her grandson was born. All the people he brought
back were easy to fake, both in the mirror and in the
photographs."

"Those pictures were faked, too, of course?" I asked.

"Yes; as you said at the Lady Elfrieda's, they were double exposed on to the negative. The trick was too old to
worry me, but this," he indicated the mirror and glass,
"this is very good. I've read of its being done only once
before—and in that case it was by a stage magician and not
a medium."

"Hold on," the Chief had evidently struck a mental
snag. "All this explains Grant's spooks, but I'll be hanged
if I can see how it explains the murders. You said there was
no opening into the room next door."

"I didn't say that. I said there was no entrance large
enough for a person to pass through. That mirror frame in
Grant's study is very old. I think I once pointed out the
quaint, old-fashioned candle-holders and spoke of their
being wired for electricity. It suddenly struck me last night
that there was a medium of light between candles and electricity, and that those brackets had doubtlessly at one time
been piped for gas. Look there." He pointed to the back of
the mirror frame. "You can see the gaping ends of the pipe
from this side. With an ordinary tin pump gun, of the sort
that is sold in any drug store for insecticide, it would be
possible to send through enough of Steeb's devilish mixture to kill a man who was standing below."

"Below?" The Chief looked puzzled. "But gas is lighter
than air."

"Not all of it. I'll read you the properties toward which
Steeb was working in order to make his formula practical
for war purposes." He took the notebook from the Chief

and pointed to the first page where there were five or six lines in German. "As near as I can translate," he said, "it goes something like this:

> *"'It must be odorless.*
> *"'It must be instantly deadly.*
> *"'It must be heavier than air.*
> *"'It must be easily compressible into a small space.*
> *"'It must be capable of combining with air and becoming harmless quickly so that our own troops may follow and attack.'"*

Jimmy glanced up quickly. "You see how it worked? It was sent through the pipe into the candelabra where it dropped down on Grant and, later, the Colonel as they stood below."

"I see." The Chief was thoughtful. "I remember the doctor said that Steeb was able to get about from room to room on the same floor. And I also remember that the Colonel was out of his room—at the drug store—the night Grant was killed, while Mrs. Steeb was in her bedroom at the back of the house. That would have made it possible for him to slip in here. How about the night the Colonel was killed?"

"That night Steeb was supposed to be asleep in his room," I told him. "But nobody testified to the fact except his wife. She was in the bathroom heating milk when she heard the Colonel scream. She ran out into the hall, where she met Lalah, and sent her with a message to Singh. Then, according to her story, she ran across to her husband's room. I suppose what happened was that she found him gone, suspected the truth, and tried to shield him."

"O.K. so far," said the Chief. "Let's get back to the gas. As I see it, Steeb couldn't manufacture any great quantity of the stuff because he was short of money. He couldn't possibly fill the whole place with it so he signaled through the pane of glass and got Grant and the Colonel over to the part of the room which was farthest from the ventilators and cut off by heavy curtains."

"Probably," Jimmy agreed. "The bracket on the left of the mirror is arranged as a sort of loud speaker which, incidentally, explains Grant's 'spirit messages'."

"He called," the Chief went on, "and when they were directly in front of the mirror he sent the chemical through. In the case of Grant, the effect was instantaneous; with the Colonel, something went wrong. Before he got more than a whiff he started on a run for the door, but he was so groggy that he lost his balance and pitched over the landing, breaking his neck." He hesitated, frowning. "I see only one thing wrong with that line-up. There must be some way of detecting the effects of the gas, but the toxicologists—"

"Reported no poison in the stomach," Jimmy pointed out. "Steeb's gas was built upon a basis of hydrocyanic acid which shows only in the blood stream. In the case of Harlan Grant, the blood had been removed before the embalming took place. The Colonel's death was really caused by a broken neck; he didn't breathe in enough of the chemical to show up in the post-mortem."

The Chief had been listening, plainly testing Jimmy's theory at every point to see whether or not it would hold. Now he nodded. "Yes," he said slowly, "it all fits in perfectly. I suppose Steeb's motive was the money . . . he wanted it to finish his experiments. And he killed himself in the end because he lost his nerve."

"Or else," I suggested, "he thought his wife suspected something and intended to kill her, but, through some accident, the stuff got away from him."

"We can settle that when Mrs. Steeb is conscious," the Chief remarked. "But what beats me is how you happened to stumble on the answer, Lane."

"It was sheer stupidity on my part not to think of it earlier. In fact, Corrigan almost hit it—when he suggested that Steeb might have dropped a chemical into the room. Only he thought it came through the ventilator, and that threw me off because of Mowgli. He was in the room the night Grant was killed, and I was dead sure if Grant had been asphyxiated Mowgli would have gone, too. Things that happened later made me not quite so sure."

"What things?"

"In the first place, Lalah, who had been in the room shortly after the Colonel was killed, spoke of her heart pounding and of a feeling of horror so severe that it caused her to faint. Wilson, who had only glanced in the first time, went into the room and looked behind the curtains about ten minutes after Lalah, and he, too, was attacked by the same symptoms in a lesser degree. You and I, Phil, were there about half an hour later. We experienced a feeling of depression and a sort of mild horror, but the poor little pup, who was smelling around the bottom of those curtains, was almost overcome. When I got that all written down on paper you can see what it inevitably suggested: a chemical of some sort which was deadly at a low level (where it would hit the pup) but not at a height such as Mowgli could reach by climbing. I suspect, by the way, that he not only climbed to the rafters at the first sniff but actually stuck his nose out that open ventilator. The chemical must cease to be deadly very quickly as its effects were lighter upon each person who came in. I also figured that it must act upon the respiratory system and the heart because the so-called effect of 'horror' is produced largely by a heart spasm. The person who gave the best clue to that was Wilson, who spoke of his heart 'pounding as tho' it would burst'."

A thought suddenly struck me. "The yellow gas!" I exclaimed. "That's what Wilson saw!"

"Yes; when he glanced into the room immediately after the Colonel's death, the gas was still spraying down in a sort of waterfall from the candelabra. As he said, it was 'about the height of a man' and 'looked like a yellow veil'. Later, when Lalah arrived, it had sunk to the floor . . . the way you saw it upstairs a little while ago. Only, in that closed séance room, with no air currents, it was slower in combining with the atmosphere. There's a slight admixture of chloropicrine in with the cyanide. That accounts for the yellow color. The cyanide was responsible for the muscular spasm that left the ghastly expression of horror on their faces." He paused to add, a trifle apologetically:

"Don't take all this scientific stuff too literally. I got most of it over the telephone, long distance, from Cleveland last night and it's probably completely scrambled."

"The hospital fire!" I exclaimed.

"Yes; that's one of the things that suggested this solution. I remembered that the deaths in that fire were caused by fumes from burning X-ray films and it naturally suggested that Steeb might have stumbled on a deadly gas when he was experimenting for the film company. I got several of the doctors who were in the Cleveland fire on the phone last night and they gave me the dope I needed to fill in the gaps." He broke off as Dr. Waverly appeared.

"Mrs. Steeb is conscious," the doctor announced. "You may see her if you don't make her talk any more than is absolutely necessary."

Before the Chief could turn, Jimmy had crossed the room and disappeared through the door. When we followed we saw that he was bending over the bed, holding Chanda Steeb's hand, and speaking in a low, comforting voice.

"Don't try to talk," he commanded. "It isn't necessary because we understand everything. You husband murdered your father and your uncle by means of gas—that's true, isn't—"

For an instant she looked up at him with her wide grey eyes, then she nodded weakly. "Yes . . . it's true."

"He suspected you knew and tried to lock you in the room with the gas but accidentally dropped the retort and was killed himself. Am I right?" he continued, and again she nodded.

"Yes . . . you are right."

Jimmy turned to the Chief. "There, you have all you need. Suppose you let her alone until she's strong enough to make a statement. In the meantime, you can have the fun of letting Stoddard out of jail—with apologies."

"I'll do it," the Chief agreed. "And I never was better pleased in my life!" He turned and smiled toward the bed. "Sorry this should have happened to you, Mrs. Steeb. You must try to be a brave girl and get well." We followed him into the hall where he paused for a final word. "You have the laugh on me about Stoddard, Lane. I admit it. But, thank God, I've got one thing on you."

"That so?" Jimmy was standing, his back against the wall, smiling quizzically. "What is it you've got?"

"The faint elusive fragrance of jasmine," the Chief elucidated. "And the spook with yellow hair. Just as I said, they were all moonshine."

"Yes," Jimmy agreed, still smiling, "you're right. Captain, they were . . . moonshine."

With a wave of the hand that was almost gay, the Chief descended the stairs, and it wasn't until he had rounded the turn and was entirely out of sight that I realized Jimmy's nonchalant attitude was a pose. He was leaning against the wall, hands behind him, shoulders back, to conceal something which he was holding. It was a little newspaper bundle about twice the size of a man's hand. The corner was torn and from the tear something was protruding. With a gasp of astonishment I saw that it was a lock of yellow hair.

Jimmy glanced up suddenly, caught my eye, and, with the rapidity of a prestidigitator, shoved the bundle inside his coat. "Mum's the word," he said, warningly, and motioned me to follow down the stairs.

As we made our way toward the roadster, I grabbed his arm and shook it impatiently. "For God's sake, tell me where you found that thing you've got in your pocket."

"I found it in the wardrobe behind the Colonel's clothes."

"Then the spook with yellow hair wasn't moonshine?"

"No; the only moonshine is the stuff I let you and the Chief work out."

"You mean that Steeb didn't do those murders?"

"Of course I mean it. They were done by our saintly little friend, Chanda."

CHAPTER 25
AND WHO DID IT

You can picture the effect of that cool pronouncement, coming from Jimmy Lane as he slipped under the wheel of his car. You can also, I think, picture my reaction as I stepped in beside him and protested, over the roar of the engine:

"You must be mad! It couldn't have been Chanda Steeb!"

For a moment he was too busy to answer, but as the car swung down the hill, he nodded slowly. "That's the way I felt at the beginning, when it first began to come over me that she was guilty. I fought with myself for hours."

"But whatever gave you the idea—"

"A number of things. As soon as I decided the murder was done through the wall I knew that it must have been committed by someone who knew the trick of the séances. That eliminated the doctor and Lady Elfrieda . . . they obviously believed in Grant and his spooks, and were always in the séance room when the materializations took."

"You mean that you suspected them?"

"I suspected everyone. You can't name a person in the outfit that I haven't had my eagle eye on at one time or another. As I say, it couldn't have been the doctor or Lady Elfrieda, neither could it have been the Colonel because he was one of the victims. That left only the Steebs and the Singhs. But Singh was out on the street at the time

Grant was murdered, and we know, from Chanda herself, that Lalah was on the stairs when the Colonel died."

"Why couldn't it have been Steeb?"

"Because of the doctor's wife."

"*What?*"

"Because of what Singh told us about seeing the ghost of the doctor's wife the night Grant died. If ever I saw a man speaking the truth it was Singh. He *did* see something . . . I was convinced of that, and it meant he saw either Lalah or Chanda playing the part behind the mirror. Since I'd eliminated Lalah from the murder of the Colonel, it narrowed the thing down to Chanda Steeb."

"I still can't believe it!"

"You will. Just picture the life that girl led. She was taken out of a highly religious atmosphere in a mission-school and forced to stand by, helpless, and witness her father and uncle's hold-up schemes. She undoubtedly married Steeb with the hope of getting away from them. Instead, he settled down to live off her family while he worked out that precious formula of his. I fancy that Chanda helped him for a time—under a misapprehension. Knowing that she would never be willing to assist if she knew the truth, Steeb probably led her to believe that they were working for a new fumigant or insecticide. Can't you see the horrible shock it must have been to a woman, who was heart and soul in the work for peace, when she discovered she was partly responsible for a new and peculiarly horrible form of war gas?"

"You think she killed him because of the gas?"

"I think she killed all of them because of the gas. They were all in it together, you see. That's the reason the Colonel was raising money on their securities . . . so that Steeb would have funds to complete his experiments. With a gas such as he describes in his notes they would be able to dicker with shady governments and make a fortune."

"But why did she have to kill all of them?"

"Because all three knew the formula. They didn't trust each other . . . not so far as you could throw a live bull! Both the Grants insisted that Steeb keep them informed of every change he made in the mixture."

"How do you know—"

"Mainly by intuition. Also, there's the rough notes for a contract between the three of them, in the back of Steeb's notebook."

"But," I protested, "it still seems impossible! Everyone has told us that Chanda Steeb is abnormally kind-hearted."

"You've used exactly the right word, Phil . . . *abnormally*. She picks up sick dogs and cats, she fights against the sufferings of war. That's why the thought of turning a devilish gas loose on the world, a gas for which she was in a large measure responsible, drove her temporarily insane."

As we talked the car had been speeding through early morning traffic, past the residence district, to the Presidio. Now it swung on to a road which ran along a sheer cliff overhanging the bay. Jimmy stopped his engine and threw on the brake. Beyond us the Golden Gate was visible, the white fangs of the surf gnawing cruelly at its base. Below, the water lay deeply and darkly blue. For an interval Jimmy Lane sat with his face toward the sea, then he shook his head. "Don't ask me to judge Chanda Steeb. My brother was gassed in the War, you know, and if you'd seen the torment he went through . . ." He paused, then added somberly: "If I told her that I guessed the truth, it would be only to thank her for what she'd done."

"But her way of doing it . . ."

"Was clever, diabolically clever. And with a certain grim humor about it. They all died, mark you, by means of their own hellish brew. There's a touch of the Oriental about it, Phil. That's what first made me suspect Lalah Singh. It wasn't until you brought me word about Chanda's mother that I settled finally upon her. The whole thing—with its perfumes and ghosts and dead loves—was too picturesque to be the work of a Western mind."

"But I still don't see—"

"Neither do I . . . but I can guess. You remember, the doctor had warned Harlan Grant about his blood pressure? Told him that any strain or shock might be fatal? Undoubtedly, that gave Chanda her first idea. She knew about the doctor's wife from Lalah, and of her uncle's part in her death. She also knew of Mrs. Waverly's fondness for jasmine. At some time she had probably noticed the opening of the gas pipe from her father's bedroom into the séance room and she started her campaign by sending just a little essence of jasmine into his study from time to time. We know that it worried Grant because of his nervousness, and his remark about the fear of fear."

"I meant to ask about that. Just what did he mean?"

"Exactly what he said. Put yourself in the man's place, Phil. He had been raised in a spook-haunted house by a mother who professed to bring back the dead. Her death gave him a horrible shock at an age when it would be most lasting. For years he dug around in India, studying metaphysics and various kinds of magic without ever finding out anything which he couldn't explain. When he came to America, he started cashing in on the tricks he'd learned in the East. But all this time, while he was faking spirits, he must have had a deep, subconscious feeling that there might be something in it after all. He lived in perpetual terror that some fine day he would come up against something that he *couldn't* explain . . . something that would frighten him horribly. You can easily see why he called this feeling the 'fear of fear' and why that mysterious perfume preyed upon his mind."

"But it didn't kill him!"

"No; so Chanda, as I figure it, went one step further. The doctor happened to be unpacking those old trunks and the gold costume turned up among his wife's things. Chanda was in and out of his house constantly, and it was probably easy to abstract the dress. With that and a yellow wig, she must have been enough to startle Grant pretty severely. But he was tougher than the doctor thought. The shock didn't kill him, as she'd hoped. Perhaps he suspected it was a hoax and went over to the mirror to get a closer look at the 'vision'. It was then that Chanda played her trump card. She sent some of Steeb's gas through the pipe into the next room and, at the first lungful, Grant went into a convulsion which threw him against the table and dislodged that little stone image. Then he fell to the floor—"

"Striking his head against the standing lamp," I interpolated.

"Yes: if it hadn't been for that accident, the coroner's office would never have mixed in, and Dr. Waverly's perfectly honest diagnosis of death by apoplexy would have been accepted. Chanda played to hard luck all the way through . . . not only then but also in the case of her father's death. She'd hoped to make that look like suicide. You remember the elaborate tale she told us about his having something on his mind ever since her uncle's death, and of how he walked up and down his room all night?"

"Yes." My mind sped to the notes Jimmy had made on the back of the yellow paper. "And you questioned it because of the condition of his knee?"

"Sure I questioned it. If you'd ever had a touch of arthritis you'd know that you don't go tramping up and down when it's settled in your knee-cap. It looked fishy at the time, only I didn't suspect Chanda of lying. I thought there might have been someone else in the Colonel's room. It wasn't until that clipping about Harcastle's death made me suspect an opening in the wall that I put two and two together. If you remember, nothing was heard at the time of Harlan Grant's death, but in the case of the Colonel, both his cry and the sound of his fall was heard by two people. When we sent the doctor over to duplicate the sound, the cry was completely lost and we got only a faint vibration from the fall. The explanation, of course, is that when the wardrobe is open and the mirror swung back there is only a thin plate of glass between the two rooms and sound carries through. Undoubtedly, the sound of Harlan Grant's death was heard by Chanda, but there was no one else about to catch it so she pretended to have heard nothing. In the case of the Colonel's death, she had to admit hearing the scream and fall because Lalah was on the stairs and heard it as well. At first I thought Steeb was guilty and Chanda was trying to shield him. But later I remembered Mowgli. Lalah found him just outside the bedroom door the night the Colonel was killed, you remember, and she'd previously told us he always tried to get to Chanda when he was loose—"

"Which made you suspect she was in the bedroom, not the bath," I interrupted.

"Yes." Jimmy stopped, characteristically, to mourn. "Poor little Mowgli, his death is the only one that gets me. He was caught by the gas creeping under the door of the lab. when he went up the stairs to find his beloved Chanda. There ought to be some sort of a sermon in that."

"Give me the rest of the story," I demanded. "Do you think Lalah suspected what was going on?"

"Not at first. I'm dead sure she and Singh were absolutely sincere that night they came to the house and told us about Mrs. Waverly's ghost. But later Lalah began to suspect. It must have been almost impossible for her to believe her niece was guilty, but in the end she must have been convinced."

"How?"

"By finding the gold dress among Chanda's things. The girl probably hadn't been able to slip in to replace the dress in the trunk because Dr. Waverly was working steadily in his living-room. The way I see it, Lalah found the costume, guessed the whole thing, and tried, loyally, to put it back for her; but she and Singh were terrified lest they be drawn into the affair, so she went to the doctor and begged for money for the passage to India. The doctor is a kindly old cuss, and she'd been good to his dead wife, so he gave her, or loaned her, the money for the trip."

Jimmy paused a moment, took off his hat and allowed the fresh breeze to play across his forehead. Then he continued with his story:

"As I told you before, things didn't go exactly as Chanda intended. The fracture at the base of the skull made the police suspect murder; and the Colonel's death involved poor Stoddard. Of course, when she tried to kill her father, she had no idea of Dick's being in the house. She's not the sort who would willingly involve an innocent man. When she saw things were going hard with him she worked out a plan which would not only remove the last one who knew the formula but would also give a fall guy to the police in place of Stoddard."

"You mean her husband?"

"Yes; Steeb. He was in an awful mental state by then, of course. You remember the way he acted Saturday afternoon when we went up to the lab.? He must have realized that his gas had been used in both deaths, but he had no way of knowing who was responsible. As near as I can make out, he suspected both the doctor and Singh. So he shut himself away from them both. There's a horrible irony in the fact that the only one he trusted was his wife!"

I shuddered. "It must have been awful when he realized the truth."

"He never did realize it. You remember she phoned over to the doctor for 'something to quiet him' while you and Norah were there last night?"

"Of course I remember."

"Well, that was the beginning of the end. As soon as you told me of that call, I knew she must be planning something desperate . . . and I was right. She gave him a sleeping draught in a cup of cocoa."

"How do you know?"

"Because I found some scattered particles of powdered chocolate on the table beside the Bunsen burner in the lab. I think she fed it to him in cocoa, then washed the cup and, as soon as he'd fallen asleep in his chair, prepared her little scene."

"Her scene?"

"Yes; we walked in on it a little while ago with the Captain, and it wasn't bad, was it? The glass retort that held the gas smashed on the floor, Steeb dead in his chair, and the whole thing so beautifully obvious that a child could guess he'd killed Grant and the Colonel; then planned to kill his wife, but had accidentally broken the retort and perished himself."

"You mean she staged the whole thing?"

"Of course I mean it. She got everything ready, smashed the retort, then stuck her head out the window so that she'd get only enough of the stuff to make her a trifle sick. Only, our busting in rather upset her plans. I fancy she'd expected to be discovered by Singh and Lalah. You perceive that she didn't put on her act until she heard them moving around on the floor below."

His voice died away and I sat trying to adjust my mind to a picture of Chanda Steeb, with her lovely, serene face, in the role of a murderess. Jimmy evidently sensed my thoughts for he turned and spoke softly.

"You'll have to consider her heredity, Phil. You remember what Corrigan found out about the Burmese . . . that they are 'callous of life' and 'apt to resort to acts of revolting cruelty'. Combine that blood with Portuguese, Welsh and American, and you've got a mixture which is capable of anything." He smiled a little twisted smile. "Funny thing, I suspect it was that strain of New England she got through her American seafaring grandfather that accounts for her fanaticism, just as it was the Oriental blood of her Burmese grandmother that gave her an instinct for murder."

"And it all goes for nothing!" I exclaimed suddenly.

"What do you mean?"

"I mean that the formula's still in existence. That wretched notebook is in the hands of the police."

Jimmy actually grinned as he reached behind him. "It is *not* in the hands of the police," he said. "I saw fit to abstract it from the Chief's pocket before he left. The old dear is probably having a conniption at this moment." He regarded the thing thoughtfully, then shook his head. "I doubt if this is the actual formula. Chanda Steeb would never have permitted it to remain. It's probably an earlier and unsuccessful one that she left for evidence. But just in case that it might give someone an idea—"

He reached into the heart of the book, tore out a handful of pages, shredded them into tatters, and let them float out into the breeze. As they fluttered down the cliff toward the water they slowly turned before our eyes to harmless white butterflies. As the last one left his hands, Jimmy reached into his pocket and drew forth the newspaper package I had seen earlier.

"I shall just heave this after them," he said.

"But if it's that wig it will float," I objected.

"I doubt it. It's weighted down with a six-ounce bottle of essence of jasmine." As he spoke he raised his arm and the package shot out in a long curve, then dropped down, down, until it broke the surface of the deep water below.

For a moment Jimmy bent over, watching. Then he turned back to me, a little smile lighting the gravity of his face. "That," he said, "is most decidedly *that*. Now we can go home and get some breakfast."

"But Chanda Steeb—" I began.

"Will be a pathetic invalid for a week or so, and, after that, a broken-hearted widow."

"You intend to go on with your lie to the Chief—about Steeb?"

"I did *not* lie to the Chief," Jimmy protested. "If you'll recall our talk you'll see that I merely gave him various bits of evidence that I had turned up with the help of you and Corrigan. If he pounced upon Steeb as the guilty party, it's no affair of mine. And, hang it all, Steeb was guilty, Phil! Can you see it was his murderous brew that started the whole thing? So far as I'm concerned, Chanda Steeb is just as much a heroine as though she'd gone out and killed a mad dog—three mad dogs, if you like—which was threatening a lot of children. That's all we are where war is concerned, just helpless children."

He was starting the car now, and his final words came over the roar of the motor. "It isn't as though Chanda Steeb is likely to have acquired a taste for murder. I fancy she'll go back to India and work among her own people. Probably she'll save ten lives for every one she has taken."

As usual, Jimmy Lane was right; but in a way he could scarcely have foreseen. If you read the accounts of that mission-school fire in India you are bound to remember how Chanda Steeb died marshaling the last of her forty charges from the burning building. The International Peace League held a service in her memory, and Jimmy and I attended with the Stoddards (Mr. and Mrs.). Only the Lady Elfrieda was absent . . . unavoidably detained at a "rest cure" up the bay, which is, I suspect, a polite name for quite a different type of establishment.

As Jimmy pointed out on our way home, his concealment of the truth had done no harm. The Chief was satisfied; Norah and Dick were more than satisfied; they were ecstatic; and only Corrigan, reduced to re-hashing a story which had already broken in the P.M. sheets, was inclined to be captious about the Grant case. I'm afraid when he reads this and learns what Jimmy Lane held out on him, there will be another murder. . . .

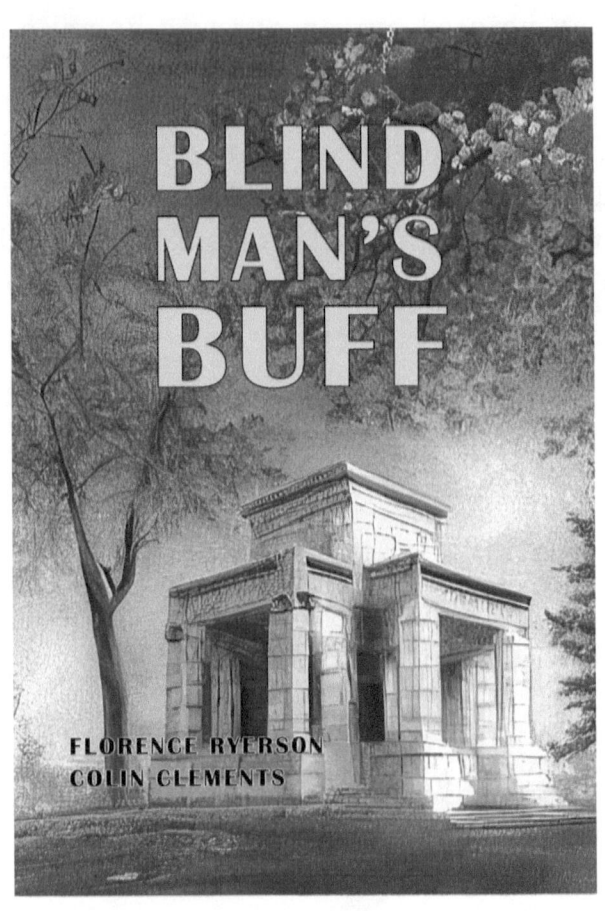

Also Available

Coachwhip Publications

CoachwhipBooks.com

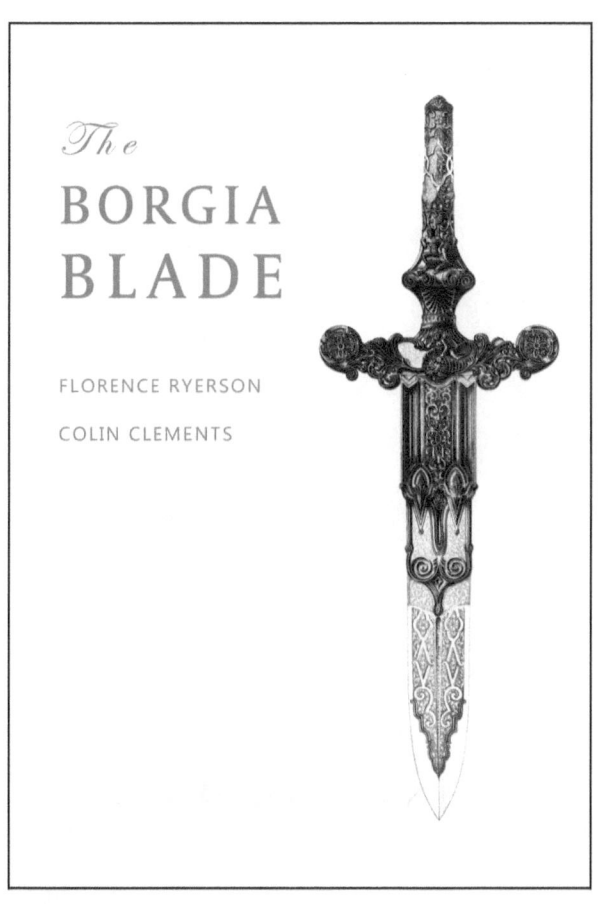

The

BORGIA
BLADE

FLORENCE RYERSON

COLIN CLEMENTS

Also Available

Coachwhip Publications

CoachwhipBooks.com

THE CASE OF THE
ADVERTISED
MURDER

MINNA BARDON

Also Available

Coachwhip Publications

CoachwhipBooks.com

BLOOD-RED DEATH

MINNA BARDON

Also Available

Coachwhip Publications

CoachwhipBooks.com

MURDER AT THE KENTUCKY DERBY

CHARLES PARMER

Also Available

Coachwhip Publications

CoachwhipBooks.com

Also Available

Coachwhip Publications

CoachwhipBooks.com

Also Available

Coachwhip Publications

CoachwhipBooks.com

DESIGN
for MURDER

Frederic Arnold Kummer

Also Available

Coachwhip Publications

CoachwhipBooks.com

SAMUEL ROGERS

YOU'LL BE SORRY!

YOU LEAVE ME COLD!

Also Available

Coachwhip Publications
CoachwhipBooks.com

Also Available

Coachwhip Publications

CoachwhipBooks.com

www.ingramcontent.com/pod-product-compliance
Lightning Source LLC
Chambersburg PA
CBHW021952010726
47494CB00003B/708